NO PAST FORGIVEN

VALERIE KEOGH

Copyright © 2020 Valerie Keogh
The right of Valerie Keogh to be identified as the Author of the Work has been asserted by her in
accordance to the Copyright, Designs and Patents Act 1988.
First published in 2020 by Bloodhound Books
Apart from any use permitted under UK copyright law, this publication may only be
reproduced, stored, or transmitted, in any form, or by any means, with prior permission in
writing of the publisher or, in the case of reprographic production, in accordance with the
terms of licences issued by the Copyright Licensing Agency.
All characters in this publication are fictitious and any resemblance to real persons, living
or dead, is purely coincidental.
www.bloodhoundbooks.com

Print ISBN 978-1-913419-40-0

ALSO BY VALERIE KEOGH

The Dublin Murder Mysteries

No Simple Death

No Obvious Cause

No Memory Lost (coming April 2020)

∼

The Three Women

∼

The Housewife

Secrets Between Us

Exit Five from Charing Cross

∼

The Hudson & Connolly series

Deadly Sleep

The Devil has Power

Such Bitter Business

Wicked Secret

*For my brother-in-law.
Detective Garda Gerry Doyle (retd.)
With thanks for all your help*

My grateful thanks to the owners of the Clare Island Lighthouse for permission to use their boutique guest house in this novel. I have tried to be true to the description of it but have made some changes for the sake of the storyline. Anyone wishing to stay there should check out the website for details where they can also see some fabulous photographs.

http://www.clareislandlighthouse.com/en/

My characters, Daisy and Tadgh, who manage the guest house in this novel, are not based in any way on the owners whom I have not yet had the good fortune to meet. I hope I have managed to do both this wonderful place, and Clare Island, justice.

An Garda Síochána: the police service of the Republic of Ireland.

Garda, or gardaí in the plural.

Commonly referred to as *the guards* or *the gardaí*.

Direct translation: "The Guardian of the Peace."

1

Detective Garda Sergeant Mike West was having a rare morning off. He'd got up at the usual time, dressed and readied for the day and then thought, what the hell, made coffee and sat reading the newspaper. Starting with last week's, he worked his way through the days until by nine he had only yesterday's paper to read. At nine, on the dot, he stopped and rang Foxrock Garda Station, leaving a message with the duty sergeant, saying he'd be in later.

Andrews, he knew, would be flummoxed. Grinning at the thought of his partner's face when he heard the news, he went back to his newspaper, turning a page with a sigh of contentment.

His Greystones house was, despite many improvements and additions over the years, an old house. Doors opened and closed noisily and almost every floorboard squeaked so he knew when Edel was up and about. He moved to fill and switch on the kettle, anticipating her arrival, humming under his breath. When she didn't appear, he assumed she'd gone back to bed. Maybe he'd bring her up some coffee. She liked a strong cup of it to start her day. He was getting used to her ways already.

Freshly-made coffee in hand, he headed out into the hallway and looked up the stairs in time to see a vision in lace-trimmed camisole and French knickers coming down. He had just enough time to admire an outfit that exposed as much flesh as it covered before with a cry, Edel tripped and tumbled down the stairs. A half-empty mug she'd been holding went flying, clattering from step to step in her wake, emptying itself on the way.

Tyler, the chihuahua, frightened by the noise, ran out, yapping and adding to the confusion. West shushed the dog, put the coffee he was holding down on the hall table and stooped to help her, pulling the camisole down over an exposed breast. 'Are you okay? Have you hurt yourself?' He saw colour flood her face and guessed her dignity, pride and self-respect all hurt. But, as she moved her limbs, trying to adjust into a more dignified position, he noticed that she wasn't wincing in pain.

'I'm okay,' she mumbled. 'I thought you'd be gone to work; it's after nine. I was coming down to see if my jeans were dry.' She wiped her hand on the edge of her camisole and looked back up the stairs in horror. 'Oh no, what a mess I've made.'

She had indeed. West took a look at the brown stains on the off-white walls, the splashes of coffee that spattered the cream carpet on almost every stair. He was about to say it's not that bad, when he caught Edel's eye. He couldn't lie. There'd been enough of those. Looking back up the stairway, he smiled. 'I'm sure it will wash off the walls. And, to be honest, I've never liked that carpet. It was there when I bought the place, I've just been too lazy to change it.'

Standing, he reached down for her hand and pulled her to her feet. 'Now, how about I go and get you a dressing gown and you come and have some breakfast.'

They sat around the walnut table that dominated the dining end of the extended kitchen. West kept the conversation deliberately light, speaking of the garden, the plans he had for planting and then, laughing, they talked about what colour carpet would be suitable for the stairway. He didn't mention her plans for Wilton Road, her ex-husband or the recent disastrous foray into volunteer work that had almost killed her.

He made more coffee and opened a packet of biscuits, emptying them onto a plate and bringing them to the table with a flourish. 'Morning coffee,' he said with a smile.

When there was a lull in the conversation, Edel mentioned a removal van she'd seen outside the house. 'I saw boxes and furniture being offloaded and carried into the house next door.'

'It's rented,' West explained. 'There was a young family in it for about a year, they bought a house in Kilternan and moved out about six weeks ago.' With that, he glanced at his watch, surprised to see it was nearly midday. 'We've talked the morning away, I'd better get moving,' he said, 'will you be okay?'

Edel smiled at him. 'It's such a nice day; I thought I might go for a walk.'

It was the first time she'd mentioned leaving the house since he'd brought her home from the hospital a week before. It was probably a good sign; he shouldn't worry about her, but he loved her and she had a tendency to get herself into scrapes of all sorts – life-threatening ones at that. So why wouldn't he worry? He settled for saying, 'Don't overdo it.' And with that restrained comment, and a smile, he left.

2

Edel sat a while longer after the front door shut. She'd seen the worry on Mike's face; it was understandable she supposed. He'd rescued her and saved her life, but she wasn't a child, she didn't need watching. It was mid-afternoon before she was finally ready to venture out. She didn't walk far, just to the local shops about ten minutes away. She bought a couple of bottles of wine, some biscuits and a packet of doggie-shaped treats for Tyler.

The removal van was gone by the time she returned, the usual peace and quiet of the street restored. Wondering who'd moved in, she stopped outside the house. The curtains were open, but she couldn't see anyone inside. She was about to move on when the front door opened, and a man appeared. Tall and broad, he stood and stared at her, his face dour and unwelcoming. 'Sorry,' she said, rushing to explain her nosiness. 'I live next door, well actually I don't, but I'm staying there. I saw the removal van earlier; I was just curious who our new neighbours were.'

There was no change in the man's expression. With a brief look behind, as though someone had called him, he said, 'Me and my wife.' Without another word, he stepped back and shut the door.

The tears that came instantly to Edel's eyes told her more than anything that she wasn't quite recovered from her recent ordeal. Shoulders slumped, she walked on to West's house, pushed open the gate and trudged up the path. Curiosity wasn't a crime and she hadn't been doing any harm. She threw a look of dislike at the house next door, surprised to see a face looking out at her – not the man but a rather attractive woman. As soon as Edel saw her, the face vanished.

'Strange pair,' she muttered, opening the door and heading inside. For a first outing, it hadn't been too successful. Except for the wine. She took out the two bottles, admired the labels, hoped they were halfway decent, and put them on the table.

After days of eating little, her appetite had returned. For the last few nights, West had brought home a takeaway. Perhaps she should cook dinner to show her appreciation for all he'd done for her. After a search in the fridge and cupboards, she decided on lasagne, one of her favourites and, humming, started to prepare it.

She had no idea if he would be home for dinner or not. Theirs wasn't what you would call a normal relationship. In fact, it wasn't a relationship by any definition. He'd kissed her in the hospital, but since then, nothing.

She knew he had feelings for her. But her feelings for him were more complicated. She owed him a lot. For goodness' sake, the man had saved her life. But gratitude wasn't any basis for a relationship. He was kind, trustworthy, handsome. Was that enough?

She was skinning tomatoes when a thought struck her. When he brought her here the first day, she'd said she owed him so much, how could she ever repay him. A curious expression had crossed his face that she didn't understand or question at the time. She understood it now. 'Idiot,' she said, squashing the tomato with a wooden spoon. He was kind, trustworthy, handsome and extremely intelligent. He wouldn't kiss her again until he was sure she wasn't responding because she owed him. 'Aargh!' She squashed the second tomato just as West opened the kitchen door.

'Are you trying to frighten that tomato into submission,' he said calmly, picking up one of the bottles of wine she'd bought, an eyebrow raising, so Edel guessed it must be good. Or maybe very bad?

'I'm making lasagne,' she said, hitting the tomato with less force. 'You didn't have any tinned, so I'm using fresh.'

'I love lasagne,' he replied, opening a drawer and taking out a bottle opener. 'I also like Châteauneuf-du-Pape. I'll open it, let it breathe a bit.' He checked his watch. 'I'm not usually home this early, actually. But Andrews has everything under control so I thought I'd take an early afternoon.'

Edel shook her head. 'Late mornings, early afternoons, do you ever work?' She grinned at him, knowing exactly why he was home: he was worried about her. 'You could have rung, you know,' she said.

West smiled but said nothing. 'I'll fill up Tyler's feeding stations while you're beating up those tomatoes.'

There was a cosy domesticity about it all. Edel cooking dinner, West feeding the dog before sitting at the table and taking out that day's newspaper to read out snippets he thought would interest her. When the aroma of lasagne began to waft into the room, he poured them both a glass of wine. 'That smells delicious,' he said.

Edel checked her watch. 'Five minutes,' she said.

To her delight, it turned out perfectly, and tasted even better. 'Okay,' West said, accepting a second helping, 'you are now the official cook.'

The silence that followed quickly became uncomfortable as each considered the temporary nature of the current situation. Finally, Edel, unwilling to upset the mood of the evening, smiled and said, 'I'll settle for that title.' The future, she decided, was just that. It could wait. She switched the conversation to the strange couple next door and told him what she'd seen. 'He seemed very unfriendly,' she finished.

'Moving house is very stressful; you probably just caught him off guard.'

'I suppose, but there was something a bit strange about the way he stared at me, and as I came up the garden path, I saw a woman peering at me from behind the curtain. And, later, I heard some banging and shouting.'

'They're unpacking,' he said. 'It's not a quiet or enjoyable process from what I remember. I think you're reading too much into it.'

Edel was about to pursue the matter when she saw a worried expression flit across his face. He'd been with her in the hospital when the doctor had told her that being kept prisoner might have delayed psychological impact, as might the morphine she had been injected with. Did he think she was becoming paranoid?

Almost frantically, she searched for a safer topic. 'I was thinking about your stair carpet,' she said, remembering that she had indeed looked at the ruined carpet and wondered about its replacement. 'The wooden floor in the hallway is so lovely, I wondered if you'd consider staining the stairs to match and having one of those runner type carpets, with stair rods. You know the ones I mean?'

It was the perfect topic of conversation and they chatted amicably for the rest of the meal, the only contentious issue being when Edel said she'd pay for the carpet and the work involved. 'After all, I'm the one who ruined your carpet.'

'You keep making delicious dinners like this,' West said, pushing away his empty plate, 'and we'll be quits.'

It didn't seem like a fair exchange to her. Perhaps, when the work was being done she'd have an opportunity to be more insistent.

It was dark when she returned to her bedroom. Leaving the light off, she moved to the window and looked at the house next door. There wasn't a light to be seen in any window; it was just as it had been the night before when nobody lived there. It was odd. Or was it just that recent experiences had left her suspicious of everyone and everything, except West.

Switching on the light, she put the people next door firmly out of her head. It was all perfectly normal. Then she shivered. Hadn't that been what she'd thought of Liz Goodbody? And look how that had turned out.

3

West sat in his office reading the latest crime statistics. Finishing, he picked up the first of that month's persons-of-interest list, scanning the names, checking out the available photographs and committing them to memory. Some of them were nasty characters, their list of crimes including assault, rape, robbery, and drug dealing.

'There's always drug dealing,' West muttered, putting the first page down. They'd taken Adam Fletcher out of the equation and it hadn't made a dent. 'May as well throw a stone in a pond,' he added, picking up the next list.

'Talking to yourself?' his partner Detective Garda Peter Andrews said, coming into the office.

'Stones, ripples, and how quickly they settle,' West replied. With a smile, he shook his head and threw the list across the desk to Andrews. 'More pictures to add to your collection.'

'I thought they were going to stop sending paper copies,' Andrews said, flicking through the pages.

'Have you ever seen Clark sitting at his computer?'

Andrews gave a half-smile to this sally, and dropped the

reports back on the desk. 'I'm not sure if Sergeant Clark knows how to switch it on, to be honest.'

The two men had taken an immediate liking to one another when West was transferred to the Foxrock station after a disastrous and very short-lived posting to Glasnevin. The story of what happened was common knowledge, causing more than one colleague to look at West with narrowed eyes. Andrews had taken the new Garda Sergeant under his wing, initially from profound pity, followed quickly by genuine regard. They were cut from the same cloth; honest, straightforward, solidly-decent men. West, having spent several years working as a solicitor, brought skills to the job that Andrews admired. West, on the other hand, admired Peter Andrews' street savvy and his ability to winkle information from the most unlikely source. They made a good team.

But even good teams had their differences.

Andrews had been aware from the very beginning of his partner's unsuitable attraction to a suspect in a case they were working on. Aware, and openly critical. When the case had been solved, and Edel Johnson no longer a suspect, he'd shrugged at West's reluctance to contact her. But apart from telling his wife, Joyce, how infuriating he was, he didn't interfere.

And then Gerard Roberts was murdered, and once again, Edel was mixed up in it. Andrews watched West and Edel and their romantic fencing, wondering if they'd ever get together. It hadn't looked likely, but when they thought she was dead, he'd seen the desperate look of grief on West's face. The depth of sorrow in his eyes said, like nothing else did, that he loved her.

'How's Edel?' he asked now, noticing the slightly distracted look that West wore.

'Does nothing ever get past you? It's nothing. Well, nothing really.' West tapped his fingers on the desk. 'It's just... the house next door... it's been empty for a few weeks. A couple moved in this morning and Edel thinks there's something strange about them.'

'And is there?' Andrews asked. Nothing surprised him these days; there were a lot of odd folk out there.

West shrugged. 'No idea. They've just moved in; I haven't met them.'

'No harm in checking them out, is there?'

'You know the rules against using Garda databases for personal reasons as well as I do, Pete.' West's voice was firm.

Honesty never prevented Andrews bending the rules when necessary. He easily justified it, never doing it for personal gain, always in the interest of a good outcome or to speed up processes that he felt were sent specifically to try his patience. He knew West didn't approve and saw it as the thin edge of the wedge. 'There are other ways of finding out about people,' he said mildly. 'There's little privacy these days with everyone shouting their lives out on social media.' Knowing West would be reluctant to pry, he added, 'Leave it to me.'

West met Andrews' gaze. Butter wouldn't melt, he thought, shaking his head. 'I suppose it would put her mind at ease,' he admitted. 'But strictly under the radar,' he said, his only admission that he knew Andrews would use Garda resources if he found anything out of the ordinary. Or if he didn't.

4

The following days passed quietly. When Saturday came, chilly but blue-sky bright, West considered whether to ask Edel to come for the walk along Dún Laoghaire pier. It was two weeks to the day since they'd originally planned to walk it, plans that had been scuppered by events.

He gazed at her over his coffee cup. She was looking better every day; her face was still too pale and shadows lurked under her eyes, but her auburn hair glowed, and her cheeks had filled out, just a little. She was getting there. He wasn't sure about himself.

He was just about to suggest the walk when she put her cup down. 'After breakfast,' she said, 'would you be able to drive me to Wilton Road. I'd like to pick up any post and gather a few bits and pieces including' – she plucked at the shirt she was wearing – 'some more clothes.'

'Of course, no problem. I'd nothing else planned.' After all, there was tomorrow and other weekends for that walk along the pier.

'Maybe I'll pick up my car at the same time.'

'The doctor said you shouldn't drive until you've been back

for your check-up,' West reminded her. 'That's not until next week.'

'But I'm fine, Mike,' she said.

He shook his head. 'Your insurance would be invalid.' He could see a mulish expression cross her face and knew she wanted to argue the point. 'Trust me,' he said, 'it's not worth it. I'm happy to drive you.'

'Fine,' she said, throwing her hands up. Finishing her coffee, she stood and put the mug and plate into the dishwasher. 'About ten minutes?'

She didn't wait for an answer and he watched her leave, a frown on his face.

A little over ten minutes later, they walked side by side down the short path to the front gate which he shut religiously every day. Most of the houses on the road had paved their front gardens to provide off-road parking but he had resisted the temptation, liking the idea of the front gate, the ritual of opening and closing. He supposed he was a little old-fashioned. He caught Edel's smile as he opened it and allowed her to go through first, wondering if she found him to be a bit of a fuddy-duddy.

He was closing the gate behind them when he heard the neighbour's front door opening. Automatically, Edel and West looked round. A woman stood in the doorway, her eyes sweeping the sky as if admiring the day. West instinctively took note of her average height, average build and rather plain features.

He felt a tug on his arm. 'We should say hello,' Edel said, and without waiting for his answer, walked a few steps down the footpath until she was directly in front of the neighbour's house. 'Hi,' she called, 'Edel and Mike. We live next door.' Getting no reaction, she added, 'Welcome to the neighbourhood.'

West grinned as Edel turned and caught his eye with a

beseeching expression. He joined her, standing close enough to feel her tense body relax. 'We're just heading out,' he said to the woman, 'it's a lovely day. Nice to meet you.'

Maybe his tone was more relaxed and friendlier. For whatever reason, the woman responded, leaving her doorstep and taking a few steps down the garden path towards them. Close up, West decided she was prettier than he'd first thought. 'My name is Denise,' she said, stopping a few feet from her gate, near enough to them to be able to answer without raising her voice. 'Ken's still unpacking. I suppose I'd better go and help him or I'll be in the doghouse.' She looked back to the house before giving them a smile and heading back inside.

In the car, West started the engine. 'See,' he said, 'quite normal.' Denise and Ken. He'd tell Andrews. Even first names would make it easier to do a search.

Edel glanced at him. 'You didn't think she looked a bit nervous?'

'No, I didn't. She looked like a perfectly normal woman dealing with the horrendous job of unpacking. The sun is shining, she'd probably much prefer to go for a walk.' He tried to keep his voice even, but he guessed a hint of exasperation had leaked out when he saw her slightly subdued face.

It was an unfortunate start to the day and there was silence on the drive to Foxrock. West indicated and turned into Wilton Road and parked in the driveway of Edel's house. It had been over six months since he'd arrived to investigate the dead body she had found in the graveyard behind her house. Over six months since she had discovered the terrible truth about her husband. A lot had happened since that first meeting.

They didn't spend long there, neither wanting to linger. Edel found a suitcase and packed all the clothes she thought she might need for a few weeks, collecting her laptop and bringing everything down to the hallway. She threw a smile to West who sat in the kitchen watching her through the open door. 'All set?' he asked.

'Almost,' she replied. 'Just one more thing to do.'

Heading back upstairs, she stood in the bedroom she had shared with her husband for such a short time. *Her husband*. She sat on the bed and smiled sadly, thinking of the man she'd loved, a man she never really knew, a marriage built on lies.

What a poor judge of character she was. Taken in by Simon, and by Liz Goodbody. She shivered when she remembered being locked away in that deranged woman's house. Being that close to death had been terrifying. But it was time to stop being a victim. Taking a final look around and straightening her shoulders, she decided it was time to take control.

She'd sell the house and buy something smaller, maybe an apartment. If there was any hope of a relationship with West, she needed to move out and show him she could stand on her own two feet. She also needed to decide if she wanted to be with him for the right reason, not because she was too afraid to be on her own, or too grateful to turn him down.

With that decision firmly in her head she headed downstairs, and with a nod to West they headed back to the car.

'I'm going to put it on the market,' she said. When he didn't comment, she turned to him. 'I'm also going to start looking for somewhere to buy; an apartment, probably.' His face was unreadable. She reached a hand out and laid it on his arm. 'You're a good man, Mike. Kind and considerate but–'

West held up a hand, stopping her mid-sentence. 'But you're not interested in a relationship with me. You don't have to spell it out, I understand.'

She tightened her grip on his arm. 'No, I don't think you do,' she said. 'I was going to say... but I don't want you to feel that I want to be with you because I'm grateful, or because I have nowhere else to go. I am grateful to you, of course I am, but it's not why I want you to kiss me.'

West looked at her and blinked. 'I hope I'm not hearing things,' he said softly, 'because I'd swear that the beautiful woman I've been dreaming about for months has just asked me to kiss her.'

She reached a hand out and laid it on his cheek, keeping it there as he moved closer, and kissed her, very gently, as if she might break.

Edel smiled when he lifted his head, her hand still caressing his cheek. 'You do understand why I have to move out, don't you?'

'Yes,' he replied. 'I understand, but it doesn't mean I have to like it.'

'Good,' she said, and smiling again, she moved her hand to the back of his head and pulled him toward her. When their mouths were within kissing distance, she stopped, their breaths intermingling. 'I'm not fragile,' she said, and caught his lower lip between her teeth, pulling it slightly.

'You may not be, but what about me,' West said.

She was still laughing when their lips met and this time he didn't make her feel breakable.

5

On Monday, Edel rang the estate agent who'd sold them Wilton Road only a year before and asked to have the house put on the market.

'Certainly,' he said, his lack of surprise indicating he knew the full story behind her decision. 'We have all the details still on file, if nothing has changed, we can just go with them.' Relieved not to have to enter into protracted conversation, Edel said there'd been no change at all. She was pleasantly surprised at the price he suggested, a considerable amount more than she'd paid.

'The housing market has stabilised,' he explained. 'Houses in that area are selling quickly; I don't think it will be on the market long. If you drop me in a set of keys, I won't have to bother you when I have somebody who wants to look around.'

The details settled, Edel hung up.

Buying was equally easy. Thanks to internet searches, she soon had three properties that caught her fancy. One in particular appealed because it mentioned sea views. Edel dialled the number, and within minutes had a viewing lined up for the next day.

Feeling happier than she had for a long time, she shut her computer and stood to look out the window. A sea view would be wonderful; she wondered how extensive it was. It didn't matter; it would give that sense of space she craved at the moment. It was more expensive than she had planned and it would use up all her current capital, but if she got even near to what the agent had suggested for Wilton Road, she'd be okay. She was mulling over this when a car pulled up and the next-door neighbour climbed out.

Edel watched him, not bothering to be discreet. She'd thought him tall when she saw him in the doorway, but now she saw he was bulky too. 'Ken,' she mumbled, remembering his name. Denise, who was shorter than Edel's five feet six by a couple of inches, must look tiny in comparison. She remembered the nervous look Denise had given the house. 'I bet you're a bit of a bully,' she said.

She watched as he walked up the garden path. Even from where she stood, she could see he had a mean look on his face, his brow deeply furrowed, his mouth a thin line between mottled cheeks. Not a pleasant-looking man. She wondered what Denise saw in him. And then, with a sigh, she remembered Simon; he'd been so handsome, so charming and what a shit he'd turned out to be. She moved away from the window and went back to thinking about sea views and beautiful apartments.

Next morning, she walked to Greystones DART station and caught the train to Blackrock, arriving early enough to look around the shops and have a coffee. The apartment block, set down a quiet road within neatly-manicured grounds, was a smaller development than she'd expected. Checking the front door, she counted the doorbells and then stood back to view the building. There were only eight apartments, four to a floor. She felt a shiver of excitement before thinking of practicalities. With only eight, the service charge was sure to be high, she must remember to ask.

She was waiting only minutes before a car pulled up. A smartly dressed, middle-aged man climbed out and gave her an assessing look, his face brightening when she lifted her hand in acknowledgement. They shook hands and introduced themselves.

'Here's a copy of the sales particulars,' Doug McElroy said, handing her over a neat folder. Pulling a bunch of keys from his pocket, he unlocked the front door and stood back to allow her to enter.

'These apartments don't come on the market very often,' he said, leading the way up carpeted stairs. 'We've already had a lot of interest.'

Edel thought this was just typical estate agent speak until he opened the door to the apartment. It led directly into the lounge, a large high-ceilinged room with a fireplace and shelved alcoves. The decor was neutral and in good shape. The agent pointed out the obvious advantages, but she wasn't listening, her eyes were fixed on the one thing that had immediately sold it to her. The stunning view over the sea from the wall to wall window at the far end of the lounge. It was perfect, she decided, before she'd even seen the two generous bedrooms and the small kitchen or heard the cost of the rather exorbitant service charge. 'Have they had any offers?' she asked, walking to the window.

'Not as such,' the agent said.

'Fine,' Edel said, and without drawing breath, continued, 'I'll make a full asking-price offer.' She turned to him with a smile.

'Deal.'

'It was that easy?' West asked her later over dinner.

Edel didn't miss the flicker of annoyance that crossed his face that she hadn't asked his advice, or at least taken him to see it before she made an offer. 'It's easy when you know what you're doing,' she replied, her voice rather cool. 'It isn't the first property I've bought. It was what I wanted – and I had the money... or at least most of it. I'll need to get a loan until the house is sold but I've been told it will sell quickly, so there shouldn't be a problem.'

West put his fork down and pushed his barely touched meal away. 'It's just–'

She held a hand up to stop him. 'It's just that I made the decision all on my own without my big white knight helping me. Is that it?'

When he said nothing, she reached for his hand. 'I'm so grateful to you, Mike, you know that. But I'm not the helpless woman you think I am.' Seeing he was going to interrupt her, she squeezed his hand. 'Let me finish. If we are to have any chance of a relationship together, you have to understand that I am not just a victim. Not Simon Johnson's, Adam Fletcher's, or Liz Goodbody's. I'm not just a woman who became involved in a horrendous series of events. I am much more than that.'

West laid a hand over hers. 'Don't you think I know that,' he said. 'I've watched you be knocked down and get up fighting each time. I know what you're capable of, but I also worry about you. You have been through a lot, and I don't think you've recovered from your last ordeal yet.'

She pushed her hair behind her ears, a gesture part frustration, part irritation. 'Getting on with my life is how I'll recover. Not staying here, in this cotton-wool-lined nest you've made for me. Just because it's comfortable, doesn't make it any less of a...' She stopped, biting her lip as he pulled his hand away.

'Prison? I'm sorry if you feel you've exchanged one prison for another,' he said, standing up. Scraping his dinner into the bin, he put the plate in the dishwasher and left the room, ignoring her as she called his name.

Edel sat for a moment before following him into the lounge where he sat with the television switched on to some programme she knew he wasn't watching. Tyler, curled up beside him, raised his head and looked at her before closing his big eyes and resting back onto West's thigh.

'I didn't mean to offend you,' she said, sitting down on the other side. 'It would be so easy to stay here and be looked after. You do it so well,' she added, hoping to raise a smile, disappointed when his face stayed stony. 'You'd get tired after a while, Mike. Tired of being a carer when what you really want to be is a lover.'

This got his attention. He turned to look at her, grey eyes assessing, turning from flint to the velvet she was used to. 'Can't I be both?' Reaching out a hand, he touched her cheek.

She smiled and held her hand over his. 'Yes, when you stop thinking of me as a victim and start looking at me as a woman. And moving out, getting a place of my own, taking control of my life. That'll help. I promise.'

Maybe she was right. West watched as she walked away. He heard her tidying up in the kitchen and stopped himself going to help. She probably was, he decided, mulling over what she'd said. Truth was, since he'd met her, she *had* been a victim, time and time again. And then she'd nearly died. Was it any surprise that he'd taken to treating her like a baby needing twenty-four-hour care? Maybe that's why they had never progressed beyond a kiss. He had no choice now but to sit back and see what happened after she moved out. He put a hand down to pet the gently snoring chihuahua. 'It will be back to you and me then, Tyler,' he muttered.

6

Peter Andrews used his home computer to start his investigation into West's neighbours. All he knew was their first name, and where they lived. It wasn't much to go on, but it was enough. He wasn't particularly skilled when it came to internet searches but what he lacked in expertise he made up for in persistence.

'What are you looking for?' Joyce asked, coming to find him when she'd not seen him for a while. He quickly filled her in. Joyce, who like Andrews hoped to see Mike and Edel happy together, came to sit beside him. 'Are you hoping to find something or hoping not to?' she asked.

'She's seeing bogey men behind every face,' Andrews explained. 'If Mike can assure her the neighbours are run-of-the-mill, ordinary people, maybe she will relax. And if she relaxes, he won't be so worried about her.'

'And you won't have to worry about him,' Joyce said, standing and dropping a kiss on her husband's head. 'I'd best go down and see what Petey's up to, he's a bit quiet.'

Their five-year-old was a bit like Edel that way, Andrews thought, watching her go. If there was trouble about, both were sure to find it. He'd rung around local estate agents earlier, and by telling a mixture of half-truths and lies he found out the neighbours' surname – Blundell. When he had that, he rang someone he knew in the department of the Inland Revenue who owed him a favour and found out what they did for a living. Denise Blundell, it turned out, was a consultant paediatrician, currently working in Crumlin. Ken Blundell, the manager of a gym in Cabinteely.

With this information he was able to access both their workplaces and find some photographs. Denise's looks were bland, forgettable, the kind of face people never remember, the forensic artist's nightmare. Ken on the other hand, in a gym kit that showed off bulked-up muscles, looked like a poster boy for steroid use. Andrews, seeing his narrow lips and mean eyes, knew he was going to break the rules and check him out on the Garda database. Maybe Edel had good instincts. But being dodgy looking didn't necessarily indicate anything wrong.

As Andrews was having this thought, Edel returned from a longer than usual walk. Every day, she pushed herself and was beginning to feel good. Everything was falling together nicely; her offer on the apartment had been accepted without delay. It was a vacant purchase, the owners having moved to France a number of weeks before, so it was a matter of waiting for the paperwork to get sorted. Four weeks max, she'd been told, and she couldn't wait.

She was reaching to open the garden gate when a car pulled up outside the neighbours' house. It had been a few days since she'd seen either, she turned automatically, determined to say hello.

It was Denise who stepped out, she was relieved to see, less sure about confronting the rather large Ken. 'Hello,' she said, moving to intercept the woman who was reaching into the back seat for her bag, pulling it with her as she straightened.

'Hi,' the woman replied in a tone that didn't invite further conversation.

'Are you settling in okay?' Edel persevered.

'Fine, thank you,' Denise replied, turning away, but she'd closed the car door on the end of her scarf and was forced to turn around to release it. When she did, Edel noticed the bruise on her cheek. It had been fairly well camouflaged, and probably wasn't noticeable earlier in the day, but at this late stage whatever make-up she had used to cover it had rubbed away.

'You've hurt your cheek,' Edel said.

Denise gave a small, self-deprecatory smile. 'I walked into an open door,' she said, and with that, turned and walked into her house.

'I knew it,' Edel said under her breath. 'I just knew it.'

When West came home shortly afterwards, she explained to him what she'd seen. 'I told you she looked the nervous type. He's hitting her. The bruise proves it.'

West, tired after a day where everything seemed to go wrong, just wanted a nice meal and a glass of wine. He was just about to say so, when he saw Edel's concerned face. 'She might just have walked into a door.'

'Do you really think so?' she said, shooting him a look that told him there was no getting out of this discussion.

Opening a bottle of wine, he poured a glass for her and one for him. 'Accidents do happen,' he said calmly. Then because he knew she was genuinely worried about the woman, he decided to confess what he'd done. 'Because you thought there was something funny about these people,' he told her, 'I asked Andrews to have a look at them. He's doing some digging.' It was just a little white lie, he thought, she didn't need to know it was Andrews' idea.

Edel's beaming smile and look of gratitude almost gave him a twinge of guilt but the ache of hunger was stronger. He'd missed lunch and saw no sign of dinner being ready any time soon. 'How about we go out for dinner?' he said. 'Indian?' he suggested, relieved when she agreed. There was an Indian restaurant a short walk from the house, the food was good, and he was starving.

Over dinner, to his dismay, Edel brought up the couple next door again. 'Can't you talk to him? Warn him he'll be in trouble if he hits her again.'

West took a swallow of the cold beer he'd ordered. 'Let's just wait and see what Andrews finds out, before we go in heavy-footed.' When she looked about to argue, he put his fork down. 'Enough,' he warned, 'I can do nothing. Give it a rest.' He saw her jaw drop open in surprise; he'd never spoken so sharply to her before. But she couldn't have it both ways, could she? Either she wanted to be treated like an equal, or like a victim. Being treated like an equal meant accepting the good, and the bad.

'Fair enough,' she said, to his surprise. He thought he was in for a protracted argument. Relieved, he tucked into his chicken vindaloo with renewed pleasure.

'When do you expect the sale to be completed?' he asked, knowing it was something she liked to talk about, even if it was something he didn't particularly want to hear. It was going to happen; he should deal with it with good grace.

Happy to talk about her plans, Edel chatted on while West finished his meal and sat back with his beer watching her. She'd been very thin when he'd first met her; she'd put some weight on and looked much healthier now and had curves where curves should be. He finished his beer, raised a hand to a passing waiter and ordered another. Something cold was definitely in order, between the vindaloo and Edel's curves, things were definitely too hot for him.

By mutual, if unspoken agreement, they hadn't pushed their relationship on to the next step, both waiting to see how things panned out when she moved out, when they were for the first time since they'd met just a man and a woman who were attracted to each other. Maybe then they'd stop dancing around one another, West thought, watching her animated face.

He wasn't really listening, he realised, coming back into the conversation when he heard her say *three weeks*.

'Three weeks?' he repeated, surprised. Surely, she didn't mean moving out so soon?

Edel nodded, smiling. 'Yes, I know, it's quick, isn't it? Everything is going so smoothly.'

'What about Wilton Road?' Mike asked, preferring to talk about anything, rather than her moving out.

'The agent has had a few viewings,' she said, 'he seems pretty positive about it.' A silence followed, each of them lost in very different thoughts. Edel was the first to speak. 'I thought I'd go over there tomorrow and pick up all my personal stuff. When the house is sold, I thought I'd get a house clearance company to come in and take everything else.'

West remembered some nice pieces of furniture and said as much.

Edel shook her head. 'I want to start afresh. I'll offer the new purchasers first dibs, but then I want it all gone. It's the easiest way.'

Starting afresh. Where did that leave him?

7

A poor night's sleep didn't help West's mood the next day.
'I shouldn't have had chicken vindaloo so late last night,' he told Andrews when he commented on his red-eyed, pale-faced look.

'Oh, was that it?' Andrews said, in the tone of voice which said loudly he didn't believe him for a minute. However, he knew when not to push so instead he tossed a folder onto the desk.

'The Blundells,' he said, sitting down and nodding toward the folder. 'They moved from their last rented house because the gardaí had been called following a domestic. No charges were brought, but shortly afterwards they gave their landlord notice to quit. Funny thing,' he commented, 'they move quite frequently.' When West looked at him in disbelief, Andrews nodded. 'Yes, I checked back with various stations. A domestic dispute was reported at each of their previous dwellings, sometimes more than once.'

'And no charges were ever brought?' West asked, with a shake of his head at the predictability of it all. Why didn't the woman just leave? If she didn't have family or friends to go to, there were lots of shelters. Pride, fear, disbelief, all of the above, West had heard the same story before. He reached for the folder. 'So, if they follow that cycle, it's only a matter of time before someone, and it will probably be Edel, has to ring the gardaí.'

He scanned the first couple of pages quickly, and raised his eyes, meeting Andrews' in disbelief. 'Her?' he said. 'She's beating him up; you have to be kidding me. He's my height, she's tiny, five four, at a guess.'

'I thought it was a misprint when I read the first report, but I spoke to the garda who wrote it up. They'd been called by neighbours, arrived a short time later and knocked on their door. They had to knock a few times before it was answered by Denise. She tried to convince them it was the television, some programme they were watching too loudly, she promised to keep the noise down and tried to push them away. But they insisted that they needed to see her husband. They were going to give him a ticking off; sure that it must have been him. When they insisted, she got angry and flounced into the house. They found Ken Blundell in the kitchen, washing blood from a nasty gash on his arm. He'd taken off his shirt, so they could see other injuries, older bruises, small scars.

'When they questioned him, he refused to talk. Said it had all been a misunderstanding. He refused to press charges. Shortly afterwards, they moved.'

Tutting, West flicked through the reports. Six in all, the same sad tale in each. 'I've heard about it, but never come across it before, have you?' He looked across the desk at Andrews.

'Once,' he said, 'a couple of years ago. There was a young couple living in the village. She beat the shit out of him on a regular basis. He ended up in hospital a couple of times, but like Ken he never pressed charges.' Andrews drew a deep breath. 'I spoke to him and asked him why. He said he didn't want to be known as the man whose wife beat him up. He'd never live it down, he said. They moved a year or so later, and I've no idea what happened to them.'

'Denise Blundell is a paediatrician,' West said, as if that should prevent her being abusive toward her husband, as if he weren't all too aware that domestic abuse crossed all social barriers.

'It takes all sorts,' said Andrews with a dismissive shrug. 'More importantly, what are you going to tell Edel?'

Flicking through the reports, West noticed it was generally after a few months that troubles began. 'Nothing,' he said. 'She'll be moving out in three weeks and once she's in her fancy, seaview apartment, the Blundells will be of no concern to her.'

He ignored Andrews' look of surprise. 'But thanks for this,' he said, dropping the file into a desk drawer.

A meeting with Inspector Morrison took up the remainder of the morning, and paperwork most of the afternoon. Just after five, weary from being desk-bound all day, he picked up his car keys and slid his arms into his jacket. He'd shut his office door when he heard the phone ring and with a frustrated grunt, returned to answer it.

'Mike!' Edel cried in a tone of voice he knew only too well. She was in trouble.

He gripped the phone. 'What's wrong?' he said, trying to keep his voice calm, feeling arteries tightening.

'I can hear screaming. From next door. I think he's killing her.'

West closed his eyes. Damn and blast. Why couldn't people behave? 'Okay,' he said, 'I'm leaving here now; I'll be there in twenty minutes. Stay put. Okay?'

'Twenty minutes! That's too long. I have to go and help her now.'

'Edel,' he said, 'you don't understand...' But he was talking into a dead phone. Hanging up, he swore loudly and went out into the general office. Andrews was gone, home to his wife and son. He wasn't a man to hang around unnecessarily, a sentiment West usually heartily endorsed. But not today, when he could have done with his solid, calm presence.

But his luck was in. If it was solid and dependable he wanted, he couldn't do better than the young garda sitting at a desk, brow furrowed in concentration. Garda Declan Foley was definitely the type he needed. He was assigned to Sergeant Clark and had little to do with West on a day-to-day basis, but he'd always found him willing to oblige and, more importantly, he never asked too many questions.

'Declan,' he called, attracting the young garda's attention. 'You in a hurry away?'

Garda Foley shook his head, his ready smile appearing. 'No, you want me to do something for you?'

'Yes, come with me,' West said, and filled him in as they walked. Seeing the desk sergeant was Tom Blunt, he stopped. 'I've had a call from Edel,' he explained, 'there's some disturbance in the house next door. I thought I'd take Garda Foley here, and go and investigate. The call hasn't been logged in. Will you do that for me?'

Blunt, a man who never used two words when one would suffice, simply said, 'Okay.'

West nodded. The call would be logged in and nobody would know it came through a slightly irregular route. And Edel would be kept out of it.

He explained the truth of the situation to Foley before they reached his car. 'We came by the information through less-than-regular channels,' he said. 'If you'd prefer not to get involved, I completely understand.'

'I'm working with Sergeant Clark,' Foley said with a grin, 'most of our information comes through irregular channels. Some of it comes from very dodgy places.'

West, who didn't regard Clark too highly, realised he wasn't exactly in a position to criticise. This is what came from irregular practice, he thought, laying the blame for his niggling guilt unfairly at Andrews' door.

Slightly less than twenty minutes later, they pulled up outside the neighbours' house. Getting out of the car, both men listened for a moment. If anyone was still screaming, it couldn't be heard out on the road. West didn't bother trying his house; he knew Edel would have been unable to stop herself. He wasn't sure if he admired or despaired of her reckless disregard for her own safety.

They approached the neighbours' house slowly, listening for sounds of violence, checking windows for signs of breakage. Everything seemed okay.

The front door was shut. West used the heavy metal knocker, banging firmly, waiting only a minute before banging again, harder and for longer.

Finally, they heard the latch being turned, and the door was opened. West felt tension ease a little to see Edel standing there, whole and unhurt. 'Mike,' she cried, reaching for him, 'thank God, he's bleeding badly and they won't let me call an ambulance.'

West held her in a brief hug to reassure himself that she was safe, nodding over her head to Garda Foley who didn't hesitate, took out his phone and made the call.

'Where are they?' West asked. She pointed into the back room. 'Okay,' he said, 'now I need you to go home and stay there. We'll handle it from here.'

Relief left Edel feeling shaken. She'd run to help when she heard the shouts because she knew what it was like to be a victim, to be at the mercy of someone else. But when she'd knocked and Denise had answered, staring at her in a very strange way and not at all like a woman who'd been shrieking only moments before, Edel was taken aback. She stood there, not knowing what to say. She'd have gone away, feeling like a fool, if she hadn't heard cries of despair from inside the house.

Denise had tried to close the door, but Edel pushed by and ran to the sound, stopping in disbelief and horror when she saw the big burly man, lying on the floor with a pair of scissors embedded in his belly.

'Call an ambulance,' she'd shouted at the woman who followed her into the kitchen. Ken, perspiration rolling down his cheeks, shook his head. 'No, we can't do that. Denise,' he begged her, 'you have to pull it out, put some stitches in it. It'll be fine.'

Edel looked from one to the other, aghast. Some stitches? From the size of the scissor handle, the blades had to be at least six inches long. They must have perforated something. There was sure to be some internal injury. Already, his clothes and the floor around him were red with blood. It was going to take more than a few stitches to sort this out.

She watched as Denise approached him. Was she really going to pull it out? A vague memory came to her, from some film or novel, something about not pulling knives or sharp objects out in case the removal caused worse bleeding. 'Don't,' she cried, startling the woman, who turned to her, a puzzled frown between wide staring eyes.

'We have to call an ambulance,' Edel repeated, looking around for any sign of a phone. Why hadn't she thought to bring her mobile?

Ken held a hand toward his wife. 'No, please, you can't do that. I'll be fine.'

Edel looked at him, and at the silent, staring woman. 'You

stabbed him,' she said, deciding bluntness might be the only way to get through to her. She seemed almost catatonic.

Denise blinked, and looked at Ken before shaking her head. 'It was an accident,' she whispered.

Good, Edel thought. 'Okay,' she said, 'I'll tell the ambulance crew that it was an accident. Where's your phone?'

'No,' Ken shouted, trying to reach the handle, the movement causing him to groan and fall back. The puddle of blood increased. His face took on a waxy paleness, his head dropping to one side; his eyes flickered once and closed.

'If we don't get an ambulance soon, he's going to die,' Edel said to the woman who stood unmoving, 'now tell me, where's the phone?' Afraid to leave in case Denise pulled out the scissors, terrified Ken would die in front of them, she shouted, 'Where's the damn phone?'

She heard a banging on the front door. Mike, she hoped, galloping to the rescue once again. 'You'd better answer that,' she said, but when Denise didn't move, she ran herself, opening the door and falling into West's arms.

West waited until he saw Edel reach his front door before heading into the kitchen. Denise Blundell stood against one wall, her expression a mixture of shock and horror. Deciding she wasn't going to be a danger to them, he concentrated on the wounded man on the floor.

'How the mighty are fallen,' he muttered, swiftly assessing the injury, noticing the blood loss. He laid a finger over the man's carotid pulse; it was thready and rapid. He guessed the blood he was seeing on the outside had its match on the inside. If they didn't get him to hospital soon, he wasn't going to make it.

Garda Foley entered the kitchen as West stood. 'They're on their way,' he said, glancing at the grey-faced man on the floor.

West approached the woman. 'Denise?'

'It was an accident,' she whispered.

He glanced back at the man on the floor and the handle of the scissors that stuck out of his abdomen at right angles. She'd jabbed it straight in, the scissors pointed and probably sharp, going easily through the flesh and expanding the hole as it went. It would have stopped only when the handle got in the way. What a rage she must have been in.

'We'll have to take you in for questioning,' he said quietly, seeing her blink as the information sank in. 'Is there anyone you'd like us to call. A friend?'

Denise shook her head.

'Do you know a solicitor?' West asked, knowing the woman was going to need a good one.

She shook her head again.

The distant and distinct sound of an ambulance came to them through the open front door, the sound getting louder as it came closer. Without being asked, Garda Foley headed out to the road to direct it.

Within minutes, the two-man ambulance crew entered and dropped a gurney down beside the injured man. They listened to West's brief synopsis of events before concentrating on their task.

West and Foley stood back, admiring the speed and skill of the two men, neither getting in the other's way as they tried to stabilise the man prior to moving him. One inserted a cannula and started an intravenous drip, while the other carefully cut Ken's shirt away and attached electrodes to his chest. Within seconds a monitor beeped reassuringly, the ECG bouncing across the small screen. They used a copious amount of tape to fix the scissors in place; only when they were satisfied with this, did they slide Ken smoothly onto the waiting gurney. Raising it on its wheels, they moved to the ambulance.

Leaving Foley with Denise, West walked alongside. 'What do you think his chances are?' he asked, knowing men of this calibre usually had a fairly good idea.

'His blood pressure is seventy over thirty, and his pulse a hundred and twenty,' the paramedic answered, as if this said it all. When he noticed West's blank look, he explained, 'Indicates internal bleeding. If we can get him into theatre fast enough, maybe. If not...'

West stood back and watched as the ambulance, siren blaring, headed off. Some neighbours, disturbed by the noise, had come out to see what the problem was. He spent a few seconds reassuring them that all was okay before he went back towards the house. Glancing at his own home, he saw Edel peering out her bedroom window, and gave her a wave.

Back inside, Denise Blundell was still standing by the wall, looking blank. Garda Foley, with initiative West wished more of his team possessed, was taking photographs of the bloodstained floor. He looked slightly embarrassed when West came in, and blushed when commended for his actions.

'Do you want me to fetch a coat, or jacket?' West said to Denise. 'I don't know how long you're going to be.'

When she nodded, he went upstairs, opening doors until he found what he wanted. Taking a warm jacket, he brought it down and handed it to her.

There were two interview rooms in Foxrock Garda Station, each identical to the other, but for some unknown reason, although they had numbers one and two on the doors, they were always called the Big One and the Other One.

'Take her into the Big One,' he said to Foley when they arrived, stopping to fill the desk sergeant in on the situation.

'Is she under arrest?' Blunt asked.

'Not just for the moment, Tom,' he said. 'We need to go carefully.'

In his office, he gave the situation some thought before picking up the phone. 'Drew,' he said, when the call was answered. 'I need a favour.'

Thirty minutes later, Drew Masters, an old friend from university, walked in without knocking. 'This better be a good one,' he said, opening his suit jacket and sitting down.

West smiled. 'Well, maybe an interesting one.' In a few sentences, he filled him in on the situation.

Masters frowned. 'There's no doubt she did it, I suppose?'

'Absolutely none. She said it was an accident, but there's no way, Drew, that a pair of scissors is going to accidentally embed itself in your stomach.' He opened his drawer and took out the file Andrews had prepared for him. 'Have a look.'

The solicitor flicked through the reports and looked across the desk at West, with a startled expression. 'You hadn't told me who it was, Mike. This is Denise Blundell. *The* Denise Blundell.' Seeing West's blank face, he explained. '*Professor* Denise Blundell, the paediatric surgeon.' He ran a hand over his face, his legal mind assessing the damage something like this could cause someone like her. 'She is highly regarded, internationally renowned, and has revolutionised paediatric surgery in Ireland.' He flicked through the reports again. 'Jesus, Mike, if this gets out, she'll be destroyed.'

West groaned. 'He may die, Drew.'

Masters was one of the city's top criminal lawyers. 'He may not,' he argued, 'and, anyway, maybe it *was* an accident.'

Having seen his friend argue that black was white, West decided he had done the best he could for Denise Blundell. Why he had, he wasn't too sure, but it may have been something to do with the absolute horror he saw in her eyes when she'd looked down on her husband, even as she was saying it was an accident.

Masters spoke to Denise in the interview room and returned to West's office. Waiting for news from the hospital, they spoke about old times and gossiped about mutual friends. 'I hear you're seeing an auburn-haired beauty,' Masters said, when they'd talked about everyone else.

West laughed. 'Seeing is the right word, Drew. It's a complicated situation.'

To his relief, the phone rang with the news about Ken Blundell. He was going to make it. The scissors had nicked an artery; there had been a lot of blood loss but no lasting damage. He'd be out of hospital within a few days.

He murmured his thanks and hung up. 'Okay,' he said, back in police mode, 'she didn't kill him.'

'And going on previous history,' Masters said, 'he's unlikely to press charges.' Seeing that West was going to argue, he held up his hand. 'I spoke to my client,' he said, 'if you're willing to drop any charges, and keep this quiet, she's willing to sign up for anger management training. I've recommended one in San Francisco; it's more discreet than the one in London, and, I believe, more effective. It's a two-week-minimum course, followed by one week every year, and she has to commit to a five-year plan.'

'And you can guarantee she'll attend?' West asked, slightly dubious about his friend's ability to monitor this.

Masters crossed one beautifully creased trouser leg over the other. He met West's questioning grey eyes and inclined his head. 'I can give you a one hundred per cent guarantee. She will attend.'

It was unorthodox, to say the least, and it was bending the law to suit the financially able. But, in any case, Masters was right. Ken Blundell probably wouldn't want to press charges.

West could proceed without him, drag Edel in as witness, and Denise might get a custodial sentence. She might. But she was more likely to get a slap on the wrist and be sent home. Catching Masters' raised eyebrow, he knew his friend knew the score as well as he did. Pressing charges would achieve nothing except to destroy Denise professionally. And the country would have lost a much needed, and obviously excellent, paediatric surgeon. 'Okay,' he said. 'If you can guarantee it.'

Masters nodded. 'And you can guarantee this won't get out?'

It would require a bit of manipulating, but luckily, nothing illegal. Well, not really, anyway. 'Yes,' he said.

Masters stood and returned to his client, leaving West sitting at his desk, wondering if he'd done the right thing. He should have gone through the appropriate channels. The end result would have been the same, but on the way, no matter how much he stressed the need for discretion, details would have leaked, and Denise Blundell's career would have been destroyed. '*In a minute there is time for decisions and revisions which a minute will reverse,*' he muttered, before picking up the phone and getting to work.

He was tired by the time he got home that night. It took longer than he'd thought to ensure Denise Blundell's presence in the station would be kept quiet. Luckily for him, Sergeant Blunt was still on shift. A quiet word in his ear guaranteed nothing would get out from his desk. Masters agreed to take Denise home, both men agreeing that going to the hospital to visit her husband at that time of the night wasn't a good idea. There might be some talk, but if there were it would soon fade away.

It was nearly midnight, and there was no light showing from Edel's room, just a soft glow from a lamp in the hallway.

It had been a long day; he was tired but he was also hungry and headed to the kitchen for something to eat. Tyler, asleep in his bed, raised his head and dropped it again. 'Lazy mutt,' West said, and went to the fridge. There was a note stuck on the front. *Lasagne in the microwave.* Smiling, West switched it on, reached for an open bottle of red wine and poured a glass while he waited for the ping.

Of course, he'd put it in for too long, so he sat with it, the aroma tantalising while he waited for it to cool. He sipped his wine, refilling the glass when it was empty.

He'd just started to eat when the door opened and Edel padded in on bare feet, her body swathed in a heavy dressing gown, causing him to remember the camisole and French knickers with a twinge of regret. 'Hey,' he said, around a mouthful of lasagne.

'Hey yourself,' Edel replied, reaching for the wine and pouring herself a glass. 'I'm sure you're exhausted, and probably don't want to talk about it but can you tell me what happened.'

She was right, he really didn't want to talk about it, but she'd gone to the trouble of making sure he was fed on his return. Deciding he owed her equal consideration, he gave her an edited version of the evening's events.

'So, Ken's okay?'

He forked another piece of lasagne into his mouth. 'Yes, they say he'll be out in a few days.'

'And she's not going to be charged? But he could have died.'

'But he didn't. She's promised to do an anger management course. That's the best outcome.'

'I scream when I'm angry,' she replied. 'It wouldn't enter my head to hit or stab someone.'

'I remember,' he said, grinning. She'd certainly screamed enough times at him.

Lifting her glass, Edel looked at him with a smile. 'What do you do when you're angry or upset?'

'I don't really get angry about things,' he replied. 'Annoyed and irritated, but not angry. There doesn't seem to be much point.'

'Upset then?' she pushed, genuinely interested in knowing how this big, gentle man ticked.

West, remembering Brian Dunphy, and the sight of Edel lying unconscious in Liz Goodbody's house, said quietly, 'I cry.' He smiled at her surprised look. 'Don't worry,' he reassured her, 'it doesn't happen often. Mostly, I surround myself with people who care about me.'

There seemed to be a question included in that last sentence. Edel reached out for his hand. 'I care about you, Mike.'

His eyes met hers without a word.

They both knew that wasn't enough.

8

As it happened it was five weeks before Edel moved into her apartment in Blackrock. And in those weeks, West saw little of her.

It wasn't deliberate, he told himself. The morning after the Blundell business, he had a call from a colleague in the Drug Squad to alert him to a new designer drug on the streets and his days suddenly became busy.

'It didn't take long to replace Nirvana, did it?' West said without surprise.

Inspector Bob Phelan chuckled down the line. 'Nirvana, that's so last season, Mike. I think we've had three or four since that. The current craze is called, believe it or not, Zombie Z, as in the letter but pronounced Zee not Zed. It's generally called ZeeZee by the idiots who take it. It's basically Nirvana under a different name. Gaps in the market don't last for long.'

'I'll tell the lads,' West said, making a note on the pad in front of him. 'We might do a swoop on the usual haunts, see if we can get an idea of how pervasive it is.'

'That'd be good,' Phelan said. 'I'd appreciate an update.'

No Past Forgiven

Hanging up, West checked his watch. He reckoned most of the team would be in the general office, easing themselves into a new day with copious amounts of coffee.

He was right. 'Listen up,' he said, raising his voice only slightly, catching their attention, waiting until they'd taken their mugs of coffee and moved to stand closer, faces showing various stages of interest and alertness.

Andrews crossed with two mugs of coffee; he quickly sipped one before handing the other to West. His notorious mix-up of sugared and unsugared coffee elicited small smiles from the group.

'Okay, listen up,' West said. 'I've had a call from Inspector Phelan. Some of you know him from the Bareton Industries case.' He saw heads nod and continued. 'Well, the gap left by taking Nirvana out of play has been filled with something new. Zombie Zee, it's called, or ZeeZee. It's Nirvana by another name, according to the inspector, so some other crafty beggar has discovered how to manufacture it.' He looked around the faces he had come to know over the last couple of years. They made a good team. 'I want to know how much of it is out there. So that means we visit every pub, nightclub, and gathering place in our area.'

'Garda Andrews, will you do a rota,' he asked, getting the nod he expected in return. 'We want to show a strong presence, so I'm going to ask uniforms to help. Hopefully, it hasn't hit our patch yet, but if it has, I want to know about it. If it hasn't, a strong Garda presence might help keep it at bay.' Seeing sceptical looks on some of the older faces, he grinned. 'Okay, I know I'm being naively optimistic, but let's do our best, eh?' He turned to go back to his office, and remembering something, turned back. 'I probably don't have to remind you, but speak to your contacts, see if anyone knows where the stuff is coming from.'

Leaving Andrews to organise the rota, West headed back to his office where he sat and wrote a report for Inspector Morrison, setting out his plan to address the issue, and requesting permission to use uniformed gardaí to increase visibility. 'Blah, blah, blah,' he said aloud as he penned the politically correct letter and emailed it to the inspector.

He sat for a moment and then went back to the general office. Andrews was sitting at his desk, a list of names in one hand, a pen in the other, and a half-filled A4 pad in front of him.

'Put me on the rota too,' West asked. It was on the tip of his tongue to ask why Andrews wasn't using the computer to do it but he saved his breath. His way might be slower; but nobody ever complained when the rota went out. He had fairness down to a fine art.

Andrews looked up at the request. 'You serious?'

'Absolutely. I'll go out with each of the men in turn. It will be good for me, good for them.'

Andrews, who was sure the lads wouldn't think so, shrugged, said nothing and waited until West went back to his office before tearing the sheet off the pad he was writing on, rolling it into a ball and dumping it into the bin. He wished, not for the first time, that West and Edel would get their act together and give them all a bit of peace.

'Cherchez la femme,' he muttered under his breath.

The news, as he predicted, didn't go down too well with the team.

'Ah Jesus,' Seamus Baxter muttered when he heard.

Mark Edwards and Sam Jarvis said, 'What?' in simultaneous horror while Mick Allen gulped noisily.

West was well regarded by the men, they admired him,

thought he was a good copper but they were also slightly in awe of him. Plus, as Edwards politely put it, he was keen on dotting every bloody i and crossing every bloody t. There would be no slacking, taking shortcuts or accepting the odd half pint from generous-minded landlords.

∼

Over a dinner of shepherd's pie that evening, conversation between West and Edel was stilted and strained. He told her that he'd be busy over the forthcoming weeks. 'Something's come up at the station,' he said, without elaborating, 'so you needn't do dinner for me for the moment.'

'Fine,' Edel replied, and minutes later got up, put her plate in the dishwasher and left the room.

West put his fork down, his dinner half-eaten. He used to be good with women, he thought, rubbing a hand over his face. He scraped the remainder of his meal into the bin and took a beer from the fridge.

In the lounge he switched on the television and watched the news with little interest. Footsteps overhead, frequent at first, stopped after a while. He pictured her lying in bed, probably wearing that damned camisole and knicker outfit. 'Maybe, I've gone about this all wrong, Tyler,' he said, one hand caressing the little dog curled beside him.

But he knew, for the moment, he couldn't change anything.

∼

He saw little of her over the next few weeks; he was serious about going out with the team, seeing for himself what was going on. It was good to see his patch closer up, and no harm getting his hands dirty with real work instead of being chained to his desk by the never-ending reams of paperwork.

It turned out to be more enjoyable than he'd expected. He knew most of the pubs in the area, had been for a drink in them all at one time or another, and was greeted with a friendly nod in one or two. Most of the landlords, he knew, had no problem with his presence, listening intently as they were informed about the potential threat of a new drug.

'Another new one,' the landlord at the Fox's Tail said with a shake of his head. 'I'll keep my eyes open, but you know how it is, Sergeant, these pushers have it down to a fine art.'

'I appreciate that,' West said. 'If you do see anything out of the ordinary, let us know. We're going to be more conspicuous over the next few months. See if we can keep it from getting out of hand.' There was no point in saying they'd prevent it, neither West nor the landlord had any illusions.

Garda Baxter, standing behind him, made frantic movements with his hands when they were offered a drink on the house. West chose to ignore him and thanked the landlord. 'Perhaps, we'll come back when we're off duty and have a pint.' With a smile to denote the silliness of the rule, but in a tone of voice that said he took it seriously, he added, 'but not on the house, thanks. Rules, you know.'

The landlord, who frequently offered the detectives from Foxrock station a free pint, darted a look at a foot-shuffling Baxter, and smiled to show he hadn't taken offence. 'You'll be welcome,' he said, and with that headed off to serve a customer who was drumming impatiently on the bar.

West knew that accepting the odd free pint didn't do any harm. But he also knew it was the start for some, for the ones who thought that if taking a pint was okay, why not a free meal. Next step was a small bribe for a minor service, leading to a bigger one for something major, until one day they woke up and realised they'd sold their soul to the devil.

It was a very easy slippery slope to fall down. And if for a microsecond, he thought of Denise Blundell, he quickly brushed it aside. That was a different situation altogether.

It was no harm that he was out and about with the men, but he was happy to see, at the end of a month that, bar the odd free pint being offered, he saw no more serious infractions. Nor was there any sign of Zombie Zee; he breathed a sigh of relief, maybe they'd be lucky.

'Keep up a garda presence,' he told Andrews, 'have the uniforms call in to each venue on a rolling rota. It might help. Meanwhile, I want our lot to start on the schools. Arrange a meeting with the head teacher in each, get the information out there. Have the uniforms patrol outside when schools are out.'

The men groaned when told; pubs, clubs and downmarket venues were one thing, schools were something else altogether. Suddenly, they were all tied up with ongoing cases, except Sam Jarvis, last in, and sacrificed by all for the greater good. 'He'll be better with them anyway,' Baxter said, but couldn't support this statement when questioned except by a 'he just would' that had Andrews shaking his head.

As it happened, Jarvis was quite happy to spend his next few days traipsing around the local schools. It made a change from the seedier element of their patch that he'd been unlucky enough to have been lumbered with.

West, content that as much as they could do was being done, to the team's relief, took himself off the rota.

'Are you sure?' Andrews said, taking a noisy slurp of his coffee. 'You know if you want to spend more time away from your house, you could come and babysit Petey, let me and Joyce have a few nights off.

West eyed him balefully and refused to rise to the bait. 'I'm sure,' he said, 'now get out, and let me get on with this damn paperwork Mother Morrison keeps sending me.'

Andrews left and once the door was shut behind him, West threw his pen on the desk and sat back in his chair. He wasn't fooling Andrews; he certainly wasn't fooling himself. It was time he stopped pussyfooting around and made a stand for what he wanted.

9

West volunteered to help Edel move when the time came, shifting the few items she'd decided to keep from Wilton Road, and the belongings that had accumulated since she'd moved in with him.

They'd finished packing and were standing outside her house when she turned to him and said, 'I've accepted an offer.'

He was in the process of manoeuvring a small bookcase into the back of his car and stopped to look at her. She hadn't told him one had been made.

'It's a bit lower than I expected, but I've given it a lot of thought and decided I just want it over with.' She met his gaze. 'You do understand, don't you?'

He wasn't sure he did, and ignored the question, returning to the piece of furniture that seemed to be much bigger than it looked in the house. He pushed, grunted and finally managed to get it in. Piling the rest of the items on top, he closed the boot and turned to her. 'Is that it?'

Edel was staring at the house. 'I'd hoped to live here forever,' she said softly. 'Raise a family. So many dreams. All an illusion.'

She turned to him. 'Yes, that's it. I've arranged for a house clearance company to call tomorrow. They'll take everything else.'

It wasn't a long drive, but the traffic was heavy so it was nearly thirty minutes before they pulled up outside the apartment block in Blackrock. It was the first time West had seen it. He got out of the car and looked around, taking in the well-kept small garden, the allocated parking and security lights. It would do nicely.

He met Edel's gaze. 'I like it,' he said with a smile.

Unloading the car, they shoved everything inside the front door and took it up in the lift to the first-floor apartment.

Edel opened the front door and stood back to allow West to enter first and see what had captivated her. She smiled as he did just what she had done – walked to the window and stared out at the view.

'Wow,' he said, turning to her as she joined him, 'this is stunning.'

'It's what sold it to me,' Edel admitted, and looked up at him. 'I'm still not great with enclosed spaces, and no,' she said, putting a hand on his arm, 'that wasn't a plea for sympathy. It's just the way it is. For the moment. But it's getting better.'

'What are you going to do?'

'First,' she said, moving away from him and waving at the boxes and bags, 'I'm going to move this into the spare bedroom. All the furniture I ordered is coming today, including, I hope, my bed. When it arrives, I'll unpack everything, and turn it into a home.' She looked around, imagining it the way she hoped it would be. 'And then, I'm getting back to work. I have that novel almost finished; it just needs some tweaking. The publisher who handled my children's books is interested in looking at it.' Running her hands through her hair, she lifted it up and held it in a knot on the top of her head, using her other hand to rub the back of her neck. 'I've had an idea for another novel. I'm going to start on that as soon as I can.'

'Not autobiographical, I hope,' West said, half-jokingly.

'God, no,' Edel said, closing her eyes and dropping her hair. 'I escape into my writing, Mike. No reality allowed.'

They moved all the bits and pieces from the hallway into the apartment, piling it into the spare room.

'I'll stay and give you a hand with the bed,' West offered.

Edel shook her head. 'No need, thanks, they're going to assemble it for me. It cost a little extra, but it'll be worth it.'

Just then the doorbell rang, announcing the arrival of the first of the furniture. West, knowing he would be in the way, decided to beat a hasty retreat. 'I'll come back and take you to dinner,' he said, 'you'll be exhausted after this.'

Edel threw him a grateful glance, before giving her attention to the delivery men, directing a bed there, a desk somewhere else and various other items to the four corners of the apartment. The second delivery company arrived before the first had left, and for a few minutes it was chaos. Luckily, they took the vast amount of packaging with them, leaving Edel with an apartment that bore a marked resemblance to a furniture showroom.

It didn't look a lot better when she'd moved things around. It looked cold, show-houselike. Everything that made a home was missing, the knick-knacks, the worn but much-loved pieces, the curios picked up here and there. Disappointed, Edel wondered if she should go back and pick up some more things from Wilton Road. Would that work?

With tears close to the surface, she tried again, rearranging furniture and moving things about. It didn't make any difference. It was awful.

By the time West arrived, two hours later, she had moved

everything several times, getting more and more depressed with each arrangement.

'Come in,' she said, answering the door and waving him in, her voice despondent.

'Didn't it all come?' West asked, 'you're not looking too happy.

She waved a hand around the room. 'It's terrible.'

With the closed-in face of a man who knew he needed to tread carefully, West looked around. 'It looks okay.'

'No, it doesn't,' Edel wailed, the tears coming now. 'Look at it, everything is awful.' She expected comfort, a hug at least, and felt quite aggrieved when instead, he looked around again and said, 'Give me an hour. I'll be back. Just wait.'

Without waiting for a reply, he vanished.

∽

It was slightly less than an hour later when he returned. When she opened the door, he shoved a couple of overfilled black bags at her and left again, coming back moments later with two more. 'Now,' he said, 'go, wash your face, change into something pretty and leave this to me.'

Unable to think of one word in reply, she did as she was told. Thirty minutes later, feeling refreshed by a hot shower and change of clothes, she opened the door into the large sitting room and gasped.

'My mother always said I should have been an interior designer,' West said softly. 'I just added a few things and sorted out the lighting.'

A colourful throw covered the back of the cream sofa, lamps were positioned on a small table at each end, throwing soft light over it and making the colours sing. Another lamp, on the floor in the corner, threw light upward through the leaves of a plant, making strange shapes on the ceiling.

The shelving unit built into each side of the fireplace, empty thirty minutes before, now held an assortment of strange objects. Picking one up, Edel admired the rich carving.

'That's Ganesh,' West said, moving to stand behind her. 'In India he is revered as the remover of obstacles. Amongst other things. It's a house-warming present.'

'The remover of obstacles,' Edel said with a smile, putting it back. She looked at the other things he had brought; three polished wooden balls, sitting side by side, a piece of driftwood, and two empty photograph frames. He'd taken books from the bookshelf she'd put in the spare bedroom, had obviously chosen them for the colour of their covers and sat them one on top of the other. Altogether, it looked perfect.

Remembering his beautiful home in Greystones, Edel shouldn't have been surprised, but she'd assumed others were responsible. Charmed, both by his kindness and his talent, she walked around the room again. It was just as she had wanted it to be. Warm, homely, stylish.

'Thank you,' she said, turning and wrapping her arms around his neck, 'this is probably the nicest thing anyone has ever done for me.' She kissed him softly before pulling back to look around the room again. 'I was beginning to think I'd made a terrible mistake. But now...'

'It's a start,' West said. 'A couple of photographs in those two frames will look better.'

'What do you suggest?' Edel said, laughing. 'One of you, and one of me?'

'Actually,' he said, 'I was thinking more of both of us together in each, on a holiday somewhere.'

'A holiday?' Edel said, taken aback and then seeing his smile, considered it, her head tilting slightly. 'Yes,' she said, surprising them both.

There were a number of different restaurants in Blackrock, but they opted for the nearest, an Italian restaurant, the decor traditional, the food superb.

'Where do you suggest we go?' Edel asked, picking up a slice of pizza with her hand and taking a generous bite. 'This is divine,' she said, removing a string of mozzarella from her chin.

'I have somewhere in mind,' West said, 'will you trust me? I think it's somewhere you might like, but I'll have to check availability.'

Her mouth full of pizza, Edel just nodded. A magical mystery tour. Why not? And anyway, she did trust him. Plus, having seen what he'd managed to do with the apartment, he had far better taste and style than she had. Which was galling, in a way.

Back at the apartment, she invited him in for a coffee. 'Before you go,' she added hastily, in case he thought she was offering more. She wasn't ready, not yet.

He smiled. 'No,' he said, 'before I go, I'd just like this.' He lowered his mouth to hers, gently at first, slowly increasing pressure, moving his lips on hers.

Edel felt a heat she hadn't known in such a long time. Since Simon. She pulled away. 'I'd better go in; I don't want the neighbours to think I'm a hussy.'

'Goodnight, Edel,' he said, and kissed her again, lightly this time, smiling as he did so. 'Sweet dreams in your new home.'

He waited until she'd opened the door and gone in before walking to his car, his step lighter than it had been in days.

Now all he had to do was find that place he wanted to take her. He'd heard of it, years before. A hotel in a lighthouse, how magical would that be?

10

Up at his usual time, he switched on his laptop and did a search while he ate breakfast. It didn't take long to find what he wanted, a simple search for lighthouse and hotels bringing it up immediately. Not a hotel, in fact it was a boutique guest house, but it was more than perfect. He peered at the stunning photographs; it would be a magical place to spend their first night together. Checking the time, seeing it was only seven thirty, he didn't think they'd appreciate a call to check availability. He'd do it later from his office.

Thinking of it kept his mind from lingering on Edel or the silence that seemed to fill the house. It used to be a peaceful, relaxing quiet but now… now it felt sad… lonely. Even the damn dog was quiet. He dropped his empty bowl in the sink and decided against having coffee. He'd stop on the way to work and get a takeaway.

In the station, sipping a double macchiato, he switched on his computer and looked at the website again. The Clare Island Lighthouse was a small place, only seven rooms and each totally different. The tower room, with its winding staircase to the bedroom sounded romantic. He considered the sauna room but wasn't sure what her thoughts were on getting hot and steamy in that particular way.

When he clicked on the Achill View room his eyes widened. It was accessed by a curved oak stairway and had huge picture windows looking out over Achill Island and the sea. A super king-sized bed, underfloor heating, and a fire – that was the one, no contest.

He knew Edel would love it. Checking his diary, he figured he could take a week off soon. Andrews wasn't taking time until later in the year, and Inspector Morrison would be happy as long as one of them was there.

At nine, he rang to ask about availability, crossing his fingers as he did, knowing how much depended on getting this right.

Five minutes later, he hung up with a grin on his face. The Achill View room was theirs, the week after next. A whole week in a fabulous, isolated place. Just the two of them. Picking up the phone again, he rang his mother. 'Can you have Tyler,' he asked, 'I have to go away for a week.' He gave the impression it was work-related, and she quickly agreed without asking prying questions. Hanging up, he sat back.

Hearing Andrews' voice in the general office, he went to the door and called him in. 'I'm taking a week's leave,' he said, sitting down again, waving Andrews into the chair opposite. 'I'm taking Edel away for a holiday.'

Andrews looked pleased. 'Somewhere sunny, I hope?'

West shook his head. 'Actually, probably not. I've booked a guest house in Clare. Well, on Clare Island, to be precise. A room in an old lighthouse, overlooking the sea.'

'It'll rain, but I suppose that won't bother you too much,' Andrews said, with a knowing chuckle.

West ignored him. 'I've a few cases to tidy up before then,' he said, opening a folder in front of him, dismissing Andrews, who went back to the general office.

Putting thoughts of Clare Island and Edel to the back of his mind, West concentrated on policework. But the day, after its good start went quickly downhill.

Early afternoon, they were called to investigate a hit and run. Two teenagers had been knocked down by a car speeding down Westminster Road; one escaped with minor injuries, the other was in intensive care.

'It doesn't look good,' Edwards said to West on return from the hospital. 'I spoke to the doctor. One lad, Milo Bennet, fifteen, is on a ventilator, the doctor indicated it was simply to allow time for the family to get in.'

West frowned. 'And the other?'

'Barry McDermott, also fifteen, a broken arm. That's all. He was on the inside; the other lad took the brunt of it. Barry said the car was definitely a blue Ford Focus but couldn't tell us anything more. Jarvis and Allen are canvassing the area, see if anyone saw anything. Baxter's gone to the local garages, we reckon there must have been some damage to the car, these were big lads, Mike.'

'The car was coming from the Deansgrange direction?' West stood, and went to a map of the area on the wall of his office.

'Yes, the two lads were walking towards Foxrock, the car came behind them.'

'Okay,' West said, narrowed eyes finding Westminster Road. The car could have come from any of the smaller roads that joined it, or if they were in luck it came from the Stillorgan Road. This was a busy junction and had traffic cameras monitored by Transport Infrastructure Ireland. West tapped the map at the intersection of the two roads. 'Check with the TII, see if they can pinpoint a blue Focus here. I know it's a common model, but it's a short time frame, we might get lucky.'

Edwards nodded and left and a short while later he was on the phone pleading the serious nature of his request. Less than five minutes later, he was standing in West's office doorway, a satisfied look in his eyes. 'We are in luck, only two Focus passed that intersection in that period and only one turned down Westminster Road.' He handed a slip of paper to West. 'I gave the reg to the National Driver Licence Service, the liaison officer there was most accommodating – it's surprising how fast red tape can be bypassed when you mention two injured young boys.'

West took the paper and read the name and address. 'Good work. Get back onto the TII and ask them to follow the car back as far as they can. It would be nice to see where she'd been to give us more context when we arrive at her door.'

A flash of annoyance crossed Edwards' face. 'I should have thought of asking that,' he muttered. 'I'll go do it now.'

Fifteen minutes later, West was listening to Andrews talking about the work rota and trying not to yawn, when the door opened.

'Sorry,' Edwards said, when both men looked at him, 'but this is important.'

'You got more info from TII?' West guessed.

'Yes, they got back to me very quickly.' He crossed to the wall map and pointed. 'They followed the car back to the intersection with the Bray Road and then they did one better, they looked back and found it going through the same junction thirty minutes before.' He smiled in satisfaction and moved his finger down the road. 'Cornelscourt Shopping Centre. Since it was a pretty safe bet that our driver had gone there to do some shopping, I gave the security team a buzz and asked if they could help.' He looked from one to the other. 'The centre has a very sophisticated CCTV system and they've just phoned to say they've found something we might find of interest.'

'Good work, Mark,' West said. He looked at the rota they'd been discussing. Paperwork and administration. It wasn't why he'd joined the gardaí. 'I'll finish looking at this later, Peter,' he said to a resigned Andrews before putting on his jacket. 'Let's get over there and see what our helpful security team have found.'

It didn't need all three of them, but West hadn't the heart to tell Edwards to stay behind and he knew there was no point in telling Andrews. So it was that fifteen minutes later, three of them were peering over the shoulders of a security man who had introduced himself simply as Charlie, their eyes flicking between the six screens he was monitoring.

'In just a minute,' Charlie said, 'watch the left-hand corner of this screen.' He pointed to the top middle screen that showed the section of car park directly in front of the supermarket exit.

It seemed longer than a minute. They watched people leaving with heavily laden trolleys, some with the bewildered classic *where did I park my car look* that vanished to be replaced with a look of relief as they remembered. There were the frequent beeps of car horns to be heard, and annoyed faces to be seen. Cars stopped and changed direction without warning in their search for parking. It was pretty chaotic. West was surprised they didn't have accidents. No wonder they'd splashed out on a state-of-the-art CCTV system.

'Watch,' Charlie said, with the self-satisfied tone of voice that said he knew they'd be impressed.

All three detectives tensed and as they saw what the security man had spotted, they made muttered sounds of agreement, West releasing an audible 'yes'. The woman was obviously agitated as she rushed from the front door pushing a full trolley. She hurried straight across the car park without looking right or left, forcing cars to break, one reversing car blowing its horn as it almost hit her. At her blue Focus, they saw her check her watch, close her eyes and shake her head before opening her boot and all but throwing her shopping inside. When her trolley was empty, she pushed it out of the way and jumped into the car.

'She was in too much of a hurry even to return the damn trolley,' Andrews muttered.

'Yes, 'cos that's the biggest crime she's committed today,' Edwards said, drawing a glare from Andrews and a quelling look from West.

Seconds later, she reversed from the parking space at speed and turned the car to exit the car park.

'I captured this image as a still,' Charlie said, reaching for an A4 printout. 'Here you go, clear as a bell.'

It certainly was. A clear shot of the licence plate; the driver's frowning face, her two hands gripping the wheel, proving beyond doubt she was the driver.

'Now,' Charlie said, 'switch to this screen.' He pointed to a screen on the lower bank where a camera was set to cover the entrance from the car park. The same blue Focus exited without stopping and crossed the southbound lane of the Bray Road, forcing cars to brake hard to avoid collision before driving down the northbound lane at speed.

'The most direct route home for her is down Westminster Road,' Edwards said. 'It looks as if she was in a tearing hurry to get home.'

West picked up the printout Charlie had made for them. 'Thanks for this and for your help,' he said. 'Is it possible to get a copy of the CCTV recordings too?'

'No problem,' Charlie said and with that assurance the three detectives headed back to West's car.

There was no conversation on the short drive to Torquay Road, a tree-lined street with upmarket homes, the occupants generally well-to-do. They were heading to destroy someone's cosy little world. It wasn't something West ever took pleasure in but then he thought of the young man in the hospital bed, who'd never see tomorrow. His family's cosy little world had already been destroyed.

'It's down near the intersection with The Birches,' Andrews said, directing West as they got closer.

Edwards, leaning forward, muttered, 'It's well for some, isn't it?' as he peered through the trees to catch a glimpse of the beautiful houses on either side.

'This one,' Andrews said, pointing to the left.

West turned into a cobbled driveway and followed it to the front of a surprisingly modern house. 'I expected something older,' he said, pulling to a stop.

'Some of the older houses sold plots of land for development,' Andrews explained, getting out of the car and looking around. 'No car,' he commented.

Edwards, out of the car as soon as it had stopped, was looking around the side of the house. 'There's a double garage over here,' he called out.

'Let's see what the story is,' West said, and they approached the doorway en masse, Andrews and Edwards dropping back slightly as he pressed the doorbell. It was a situation West had been in so many times, but since Glasnevin he never faced it without thinking of Brian Dunphy. He allowed the memory, treating it as a kind of homage to the big, cheerful garda who had died so needlessly.

He was just about to ring again when the door was opened to the length of a safety chain, forcing West to peer sideways at the woman within. 'Mrs Parsons?' he asked, holding up identification. 'We'd like a word, please.'

The door closed and stayed shut for several minutes. West imagined he could hear her heartbeat through it, a flight of fancy he didn't share with the two men behind. Andrews might have appreciated it, but Edwards would wonder if he'd lost his marbles.

Rather than ringing the doorbell again, West knocked gently on the door. 'Mrs Parsons, we need to speak to you. Please.'

It was another minute before the door opened. The woman had put on a confused but friendly smile. 'So sorry, I had to run to see to the baby.' The lie was obvious, her eyes flitting restlessly, lower lip trembling. 'Now, how can I help you?'

West held up the printout of the car the security man had downloaded from the CCTV. 'You were in a great hurry to leave, Mrs Parsons,' he said.

She laughed nervously. 'Goodness, it must be a quiet day in the world of crime. Hurrying is hardly an offence. Was I driving too fast? Is that it? Was I caught on a mobile speed camera or something?'

Before West could answer, the sound of a baby's cry came from inside. The woman ignored it for a moment, but as the cry escalated, she looked toward the sound and back to West. 'I'll have to go and see to him,' she said, 'he's not been well.' She went to close the door, but West quickly put a hand out.

'We'll follow you in, if we may?' he said, but it wasn't a question and they all knew it.

The hallway led into a room that spanned the back of the house; to one side a huge kitchen glistened with stainless steel and granite worktops, on the other, comfortable-looking sofas were grouped around an enormous television. The dining table and chairs were set in front of a wall of folding glass doors, the deck beyond hinting at how the area was used in the summer. On one side of the table, a small child sat in a highchair, open mouth emitting high-pitched screams.

'Hush, hush darling,' the mother said, picking the infant up and rocking him. It didn't quieten the noise and made conversation impossible.

As the only one of the three who'd experience with children, both Edwards and West looked to Andrews for guidance. But his blank look said as clearly as words, he'd no idea what to do, so the three just stood and waited.

No Past Forgiven

'I'll go and change him,' the woman said loudly, and left the room, the sound fading as she mounted the staircase to the bedrooms.

It was ten minutes before she returned, and when she did it was without her child. 'He's gone to sleep at last,' she said, looking weary. 'He's had a chest infection for the last week. The antibiotic, I think, gives him bellyache.' She lifted and dropped her hands in a what-can-you-do manner and moving to the kitchen, took down some mugs and a cafetière. 'Would you like some coffee?' she asked, turning back to them.

West nodded, and the other two followed suit.

It was only when they were sitting around the table with mugs in their hands that the subject of their visit came up. She'd had time to plan what to say, West saw, observing a new composure when he placed the printout on the table in front of her. 'Before you say anything, Mrs Parsons, I need to read you your rights.' Her expression didn't change while this essential formality was done. 'Your car, Mrs Parsons, where is it?'

She drank some coffee before answering. 'Parked in the garage,' she said. 'My husband, Nick, he likes to park out front, so I always put mine away.'

'We'd like to have a look at it. Is that okay?' West asked.

She held her mug in front of her mouth. 'Do you have a warrant?' she asked.

Rather than answering her question, West said, 'You were seen driving at speed from Cornelscourt.' He tapped the printout. 'The time indicated here, Mrs Parsons. That's when the image was recorded. Ten minutes later, on Westminster Road, which we know to be the fastest route home for you, two teenagers were knocked down by a speeding blue Focus. So, do you think I'll have a problem getting a warrant?'

Meeting his gaze, she put the mug down. 'They were messing about,' she said, her voice low. 'I saw them as I approached, they were on the path pushing one another and suddenly they were there, in front of me.' Her eyes grew large and she blinked. 'I saw one getting up.' She looked around the faces that stared at her. 'In the rear-view mirror,' she clarified. 'I saw them getting up.'

'Both of them?' West asked.

'Well, no,' she admitted, 'but I'd turned the corner, you know, so they were out of sight.' When the men stayed silent, she laughed uncomfortably. 'They're okay, aren't they? They didn't break anything, did they?'

'Why were you in such a hurry?' West asked, putting off the inevitable.

She ran a shaking hand over her hair, tucking strands behind her ears. 'I'd run out of medication for Max,' she said. 'I went to our local pharmacy, in the village, but it was closed. Someone's funeral or something.' A frustrated sigh escaped her. 'Cornelscourt was the next choice. When I got there, I remembered we were almost out of milk and a few other things, so I decided to go into Dunnes and do some shopping. Before I knew it, it was half an hour later.'

'You'd left the baby here. Alone,' Andrews said, his tone condemnatory.

'It was only supposed to be a few minutes,' she said defensively, 'he was asleep when I left and still asleep when I got back, so no harm was done, was there?'

It was time to disabuse her of that notion, West decided, taking a deep breath. 'Unfortunately, there was,' he said, 'the teenagers you knocked down–'

'I saw them get up,' she interrupted.

'One,' West said. 'You may have seen one get up, but you certainly didn't see the second. He hasn't regained consciousness. They're waiting until his family arrive to say goodbye, and then they will most likely switch the life support off. He is fifteen, Mrs Parsons.'

Ella Parson's face froze, her eyes dilating in shock.

'Ring your husband,' West said gently. 'Tell him to come home. I'm afraid you're going to have to come with us.'

By the time Nick Parsons arrived home, his wife had stopped trying to justify what she'd done. Instead, she'd picked up her baby and cuddled him, kissing the child as if she would never let him go.

West met the husband at the front door.

'What the hell is going on?' he said, seeing West. 'Is Ella okay? Has something happened? My God, Max? Has something happened to my son?'

'No,' West reassured him, 'not your son. And your wife is safe. She is, however, under arrest.'

Nick Parsons looked blank. He blinked and tried a laugh that came out wrong, more a squeal than laugh. This was all so outside his experience. Dentistry was a fairly humdrum, if lucrative, occupation. 'I'm sorry,' he said, 'maybe I'm being very stupid, but did you really say that Ella was under arrest?' At West's nod, he spat out, 'Why? For goodness' sake, what on earth could she have done?'

West told him.

Ten minutes later, they led the tearful woman to the car, her husband promising her that everything would be all right, that their solicitor would meet her at the station. 'Just say nothing until he gets there,' he reminded her again as she climbed into the car.

The solicitor was, to their surprise, waiting when they arrived and he insisted on speaking to Ella Parsons in private before any interview by the police.

When West and Andrews entered the Big One, the solicitor was still speaking quietly, his hand on Mrs Parsons' arm. He looked up as they entered, and keeping his hand where it was, he addressed them. 'I'm afraid there will be no interview, gentlemen,' he said firmly. 'My client is suffering post-natal depression and is under the care of a psychiatrist. I've arranged a room for her in St John's Clinic and he is going to assess her mental state tomorrow morning. Until then, my client has nothing to say. Now' – he turned and put his hand around his client's shoulder – 'I'm taking Mrs Parsons to that clinic. I'll be in touch when I have the psychiatric report.'

West and Andrews watched as they left. 'That's the last we'll see of her,' Andrews muttered.

West nodded tiredly. Andrews was probably right. They'd spend valuable man-hours ensuring the case was watertight because they had to, and it probably wouldn't go to court. Remembering the solicitor, and knowing something of the man's expertise – the legal profession was too small in Dublin not to have heard of him – West knew there was no *probably* about it. It would never go to court.

~

At home, in the quiet that he was struggling to get used to again, he opened the fridge, eyed the selection of ready-made meals he'd bought to replace Edel's cooking and closed it again. Instead, he poured a healthy measure of Jameson and sat, Tyler curled beside him snoring gently. It took a few minutes for the whiskey to chill the stress of the day and put everything into perspective. After all, Ella Parsons wasn't a career criminal. Would anything be gained by sending her to prison? It wouldn't bring the boy back, and any satisfaction the family would gain at her arrest would be short-lived. Even if she went to prison, it wouldn't be for long, and their boy would still be dead.

He finished the whiskey. Such is the way these things are

justified. Sighing, he poured another, slightly smaller, and reached for the phone. He needed something cheerful to do and he knew just what that was.

'Edel,' he said, 'we're going to have fantastic photos to put in those frames.'

11

West didn't tell Edel where they were going, just told her to pack warm clothes, a rainproof jacket, a hat, and something nice for the evenings.

'We're not going camping, I assume,' she said, looking out at the rain as he drove from her apartment car park.

'Maybe,' he said and shot her a smile that made her heart race. He hadn't said so, but she assumed they'd be sharing a room, a bed. She sighed deeply and smiled as West sent her a quizzical look. 'You'll like it, I promise.'

Reaching a hand to rest it gently on his thigh, she said, 'I know I will. To be honest, it doesn't really matter where we go, because probably for the first time since we met, you're not a guard and I, thankfully, am not a victim.'

It was a relaxed journey; they chatted about this and that and stopped in Athlone for coffee in a little place West knew that served, he promised her, the best scones in the country.

'You're right,' she said, licking jam from her fingers. 'Would it be piggish to have another? I might never be back this way again.'

'The justification of the weak,' West commented, watching her tuck into the second scone with obvious pleasure.

'Oh yes,' she agreed, and because everything was going so well, she added, 'I thought I might need the extra calories.'

West reached over and kissed her jammy mouth. 'Maybe we should just check into a hotel here in Athlone.'

Her laugh caused heads to turn. 'No way,' she said. 'I'm looking forward to the surprise. Anyway, didn't your mother ever tell you about delayed gratification being good for the soul?'

Smiling, West kissed her again. 'It will be very delayed,' he said, 'if we don't get going. It's a long way yet.'

'Not Galway, then?' she said, as they headed back to the car.

'Not Galway,' he agreed. Passing through Oughterard, almost two hours later, he asked if she was hungry. 'There are some nice places to eat here.'

'I don't think I'll ever be hungry again,' she said. 'But I don't mind if you want to stop. I'll just have a coffee or something.'

'I'd prefer to keep going,' West said, 'it's a bit of a way yet.'

'Clifden?' Edel guessed, trying to think of any place she knew this side of Galway.

West smiled and said nothing.

It was grey when they left Dublin, but the sky had cleared by the time they'd reached Galway. It stayed that way as they drove along the Clifden road.

Edel, still convinced this was their destination, was taken by surprise when he indicated to turn right off the road. 'So not Clifden?'

'Nope,' he said.

She peered at the signpost as he slowed for the turning. 'Leenane? Is that where we're going? It's supposed to be very pretty.'

'Not Leenane,' West said, slowing as the road became

narrow and windy. Seeing a parking area up ahead, he pulled over. 'Let's admire the scenery,' he said, getting out.

As far as they could see, they were surrounded by purples, greens and browns, every tone and shade blending into hills and mountains. The road they were on vanished around a bend, but they could see it, appearing and disappearing in the distance, a grey ribbon through the landscape. West reached into the car and switched off the engine. The silence was sudden and complete.

Almost afraid to speak, Edel whispered, 'You forget, living in Dublin, how incredibly beautiful it is on this side of the country and how quiet it can be.'

'It's beautiful,' West agreed, turning to look at her. 'I'd be tempted to say *just like you* but it's a shame to spoil all this...' – he waved a hand at the rugged landscape – 'by descending into cliché.'

'Cliché away,' she said with a grin.

He shook his head. 'I'll try and come up with something more original. We'd better keep going, it's a long way yet.'

'We're going to run out of country soon,' Edel said as they continued to drive, mile after mile, turning off the Leenane Road, towards a town she'd never heard of. 'Louisburgh? Is that where we're going?'

She watched West shake his head, gave up and went back to admiring the scenery. When he pulled into a car park overlooking the sea and turned off the engine, she looked around, puzzled.

'We're almost there,' he said. 'We've to change transport here.' He pointed to the harbour where a large boat nudged the pier. 'We're catching the ferry.'

'We're going to Achill Island,' Edel said, sure this time she was right, shaking her head in disbelief when West shook his.

'Wrong again.'

'I give up,' she said, laughing. 'Where on earth are we, and where are we going?'

'This is Roonagh Pier,' he told her, taking her suitcase and his holdall from the boot. Lifting a hand, he pointed out to sea. 'That's where we're going,' he said. 'Clare Island.'

Edel didn't quite know what to say. Her knowledge of the island was limited to knowing it existed, that was all. She tried to look excited. 'Great,' she managed, 'I've never been there.' She must have been a better actress than she'd thought because West looked pleased. He locked the car and strode off with their luggage to where people were starting to board the ferry.

She swallowed the faint feeling of disappointment and followed him. So much time spent fussing over which of her dresses to bring, finally deciding on the most elegant and now, it looked as though they'd be staying in the suitcase.

With a smile she hoped didn't look as forced as it felt, she followed West aboard and stood beside him at the rail, catching her hair in her hand as it blew around her face. 'How long does it take?' she asked, leaning into him, her mouth so close to his ear she could have nibbled his lobe.

Smiling, he put an arm around her shoulder and drew her closer still, dropping a casual, almost possessive kiss on the top of her head. 'Twenty-five minutes, they said. We can go below if you like or stay here. We're so lucky with the weather.'

And they were. Early November was late to be travelling in Ireland when the weather could be cold, wet and grey as it had been when they left Dublin. But here, the skies were blue and it was definitely a little warmer. If they were lucky it might last for a few days. Certainly, it had been a risk, West thought, his arm still holding Edel close, but one that seemed to be paying off.

He took in the other occupants, mentally arranging them

into three categories; locals, islanders and tourists. It was a game he played when he went anywhere. He told himself it kept his perceptive skills sharpened, never wanting to admit the truth. People made him curious.

'Do you want to go inside?' he asked Edel, feeling her shiver a little. 'Are you cold?'

She shook her head. 'No, well,' she laughed, 'a little, but the scenery is stunning.'

'That's Croagh Patrick,' he said, pointing toward a snow-topped peak, 'and that's Achill Island over there. Haven't you been to these parts before?'

'I'm almost embarrassed to say I haven't been further west than Clifden. I had a friend who used to visit Achill every year; she would tell us great tales about the place. I don't know why I never got there, or to Clare Island. It was always *one day*. You know how it is.'

The harbour came into view and within minutes they were disembarking. There was a great deal of hustle and bustle, friendly chat, loud and cheery greeting. West looking around, wondered how he would know who his driver was, but he needn't have worried, seconds later a hand clapped him on the shoulder.

'Mike West?'

West quickly gave the man a once-over, immediately liking what he saw; the cheerful, open face, bright intelligent eyes, casual, well-worn but expensive clothes. He smiled and nodded. 'That's me. You're from the lighthouse?'

'That's right,' the man said, extending his hand. 'Tadgh's my name.'

West dropped his holdall and shook his hand. 'Pleased to meet you, Tadgh, and this is Edel Johnson.'

'Well,' the man said, shaking her hand, 'introductions over, let's get going. I'm sure you'd like a drink after your long journey.'

Not a tent at least, Edel thought, shaking her head when West offered her the front seat, climbing into the back, and buckling her seatbelt. *A lighthouse. Oh God, please let there be a proper shower and toilet.*

Tadgh drove like a man well used to the vagaries of the road, taking the bends on the narrow road with practised ease. 'D'you have a good trip across?' he asked, looking first at West and swivelling to look at Edel. She gasped in fright as another car came barrelling along in the opposite direction, gaining a smile from the man who simply pulled over onto the hard shoulder to allow the car to continue on its way without slowing down.

'He always drives like a maniac,' he told them, 'lives over in Toormore House. I think he thinks this is his private road.' Pulling back onto the road, he continued, 'we're turning off here.'

It was a straight road then to Clare Island Lighthouse and they arrived without any more drama, pulling up in front of a series of whitewashed buildings that extended from the fat round lighthouses. 'Two,' Edel said, getting out and staring. 'There are two lighthouses.'

West, who had seen the photographs and knew what to expect, smiled at her excitement. Even he had to admit, the photographs didn't do it justice. The place was amazing.

Tadgh, opening the boot to take out the luggage, turned to explain. 'The first one was badly damaged in a fire in 1813, but rather than repairing it, they simply built another and didn't bother to knock the first one down. I suppose they assumed, if left to its own devices, it'd take itself back to the sea quick enough. It gets a bit wild here in the winter.'

Picking up the luggage, he led them through a small wrought-iron gate. 'The entrance to the guest house is just here,' he said, pushing the door open with his shoulder.

A guest house. Edel, reassured by a word that promised at least a certain level of comfort, found herself catching her breath as Tadgh led them from the entrance hall into what he referred to as the *drawing room*.

'Take a seat,' he said. 'I'll go and tell Daisy you're here.' He closed the door behind him.

'Wow,' Edel said, moving to the fire, holding her hands out to feel the heat and then turning to look around the room. 'This is gorgeous, Mike,' she said, taking in the comfortable sofas, beautiful wooden floor, old period furniture. She walked to the window, peered outside and reached a hand up to feel the curtains. 'Linen,' she said, turning to him again. 'Where did you find this place? It's fabulous!'

'I'd heard about it years ago,' he said. 'I wanted to take you somewhere special and it seemed to fit the bill. Somewhere away from everything we know, somewhere...' He stopped. Seeing her smile, he knew he didn't have to explain any further. 'I chose well?'

'I was a bit anxious at first,' she admitted. 'I did think for one horrible moment you were going to take me camping.'

He laughed. 'No, I definitely don't do camping, Edel. This,' he added, looking around the luxurious room, 'this, I do.'

The door opened, and a slight, attractive woman came through, hands extended to both. 'Welcome to Clare Island Lighthouse,' she said, 'I'm Daisy, the manager.' And it didn't seem the slightest bit awkward for West and Edel to each take one of her hands. She held them for a moment before letting go. 'Now, would you like a cup of tea first or shall we go straight to your room?'

Edel glanced at West. 'I'd love a cup of tea,' she said apologetically.

'That would be nice,' he agreed.

Daisy waved them to seats near the fire. 'There's paperwork to do too, of course, but we'll do that later. Meanwhile, sit, relax. I'll get Tadgh to take your luggage to your room and after your tea, I'll show you up. You've booked dinner for eight o'clock in the lantern room. It should be a lovely evening. The skies are clear; there will be millions of stars.'

With that she left them and once the door was closed, Edel peppered West with questions. 'The lantern room? Seriously? We're having dinner up in the lighthouse?'

Laughing, West nodded. 'They offer it for special occasions. I thought this was special enough. We have it all to ourselves for the night.'

Tea was served with a selection of home-made cake that had Edel drooling with pleasure. 'I'd like to eat the lot,' she said, groaning after the first mouthful of coffee cake that was, she explained seriously, the best she'd ever eaten.

'After we check into our room, we can go have a walk around, give us an appetite for dinner,' West said, thinking of the meal he'd pre-ordered.

So that's what they did. They were shown to their room. 'Achill View,' Daisy told them, leading them up the curved oak stairs, pushing open the door and waving them in. 'In the morning,' she explained, closing the curtains, 'you'll see why the room was given the name. Now, I'll leave you, and we'll see you both at eight for dinner.'

Edel had a quick look around the room, admiring the furniture, the spacious bathroom. Conscious of West waiting, she opened her suitcase and hung up a dress. The lantern room sounded like it might be a place to wear something special. She'd sort the rest of her stuff out later.

Outside, it was too dark to do much exploring, but they followed a pathway for a short distance, and stood staring out to sea. There were lights in various places that may have been Achill, or the mainland or simply a fishing vessel plying its trade. 'We'll be more orientated tomorrow when we can see it all by daylight,' West said. He put an arm around her, pulling her close. 'We'd better go in, it's getting cold.'

West had a shower first. 'I'll just be a couple of minutes,' he said, 'and then you can have a long shower or do whatever it is women do in these circumstances.'

'Titivate,' she said, watching him as he took off his coat and hung it up, admiring his muscular body as he stretched for the hanger, wondering how it would feel to move her hands over it. Gulping, she turned away. Oh, yes, she decided, catching her flushed face in the mirror.

He'd only be a few minutes. Checking her watch, she saw it was only six thirty. Plenty of time. She pulled off her clothes and jumped into the huge bed, feeling the softness of the sheets, the luxurious feel of the duvet. Seriously, this was an amazing place. Dinner was bound to be just as good, why spoil it by wondering what was going to happen afterwards. Better off getting it out of the way, then they could concentrate on their dinner properly.

She could hear the shower running. Thinking quickly, she hopped out of bed again, took the duvet off the bed, put it untidily on a chair and slipped back under the sheet. She switched off the light and waited. The shower was still running. She turned the light back on, rushed to the window and pulled the curtains open. With a smothered giggle, she switched off the light again and jumped under the sheet.

She couldn't hear the shower any longer, and the stage was set.

. . .

West, opening the bathroom door, was surprised to find the room almost in darkness. It took a few seconds for his eyes to adjust. He wondered, just for a moment, if she'd run out on him. She'd done it before, after all. Then, in the light from the bathroom, he saw her, lying curled on her side, one hand extended toward him, the fine cotton sheet covering the swell of her breasts.

'I would have sworn I was only a few minutes in the shower,' he murmured, taking a few steps towards the bed.

'I hope it wasn't a cold one,' she said huskily.

He took a few more steps forward, stopping at the foot of the bed. He'd wrapped a towel around his waist after his shower. With a glint in his eye, he undid the knot he'd made to keep it in place, and let it drop to the floor.

Edel bit her lip on the sound she wanted to make. 'Well, I guess not,' she murmured and threw back the sheet.

12

Dinner in the lantern room with a canopy of stars in the sky as the main design feature and food that was beyond sublime, was something West thought he'd remember until his dying day, and very probably beyond.

He'd pre-ordered the food, hoping he'd guessed correctly. Courgette and almond soup, a combination he was curious to taste, was so good he groaned. This was followed by monkfish with a butter and Pernod glaze that had both of them oohing and aahing with pleasure.

'That was incredibly good,' Edel said once all the plates were taken away.

West smiled, stood and switched out the only light in the room, plunging them into a darkness relieved only by starlight. He moved around the table to where Edel sat, and pulled her up into his arms. Entwined, they moved to the door, feeling their way by hand, Edel giggling as they stumbled against chairs.

Opening the door onto the viewing platform was more difficult in the darkness. West silently castigated himself for not having checked it earlier. Just when he thought he'd have to admit defeat, he felt it budge and pushed the door open, almost losing it to the swirling wind outside. Cold wind. He pulled it shut again.

'Hang on,' he said, moving away from Edel, feeling his way around the curved walls to the pile of blankets he had noticed earlier. He grabbed a handful, made his way back to Edel's side and opening one, draped it around her bare shoulders.

Once out on the platform, with the door shut behind them, the breeze didn't seem so bad. The quiet of the night was broken by the thunder and crash of the waves, background music for the mesmerising canopy of stars in the clear night sky. They stood without speaking for a long time.

'It's stunning,' Edel whispered finally, moving round within West's embrace to face him and plant a kiss gently on his mouth. 'Thank you, it couldn't be more perfect.'

West returned the kiss, lingering, lips moving to open hers, tongues entwining. He moved his hands inside the shawl, found the hem of her dress and moved under, feeling the smoothness of her naked legs, rising to feel the corner of lace, brushing it aside and moving fingers to the damp warmth he found underneath, feeling his own body respond.

Groaning, he pulled roughly at the lace and felt it give. His free hand moved to unzip his trousers and within seconds he was inside her, pulling her legs up around his waist, balancing her against the railing, aware of it against her back, knowing it was probably uncomfortable, unable to stop. He came quickly, a burst of lust and tension, a release of all the months waiting that the earlier more tender lovemaking hadn't managed to assuage.

Breathing heavily, he lowered her legs. 'You okay,' he managed, kissing her softly.

Edel, remembering the gentle lovemaking of earlier, was slightly stunned by this version of West. How many layers were there to this man?

West caressed her cheek. 'I didn't hurt you, did I?'

Did he? She was definitely going to have a bruise on her back, but apart from that, and the ruin of a very expensive pair of French knickers, he hadn't hurt her. 'Surprised me, maybe,' she answered.

West drew back, trying to see her face in the starlight. All he could see were shadows. 'Good surprised or bad surprised?' he asked.

Edel didn't answer straight away. She was thinking of her late husband, Simon, a man who had become the man he thought she'd wanted, their short marriage based on deceit. Had their lovemaking just been a reflection of what he thought she always wanted? There had never been anything like this… this unbridled passion.

'I don't know,' she answered, finally. 'You puzzle me, Mike. Just when I think I have you sussed; you throw me a curveball.'

His laugh echoed into the night. Within seconds they heard a screech, as if in echo of it. 'What's that,' Edel said, turning in his arms once more to stare out to sea.

'An owl,' West said, pressing against her, feeling her warm against his belly. 'I hope you never have me completely sussed, Edel,' he whispered into her ear. 'I hope I will always surprise you.'

And before she knew what was happening, she was bent over the railing and he was inside her again, but this time gently and as he moved achingly slow, he caressed her breasts under the shawl. Oh God, she thought, feeling a heat spread upward, and she let go, and flew with it, and her call was answered by the owl who screeched again.

13

West woke early as he always did, turning on his side to watch the sleeping woman beside him, a satisfied smile on his face.

They'd left the curtains open and light flooded the room. He shuffled to a sitting position, bunching the pillows behind his head and stared out the window. Now he understood the room's name, the view over Achill Island was breath-taking. In the quiet of the morning, he enjoyed both the sight before him and the one beside him, and for the first time, in a long, long time, he felt like a man who had everything.

Hubris, he thought, shaking his head and throwing back the duvet. He crossed to the window; from it he could see down to the sea, across to Achill and over to the mainland. It was simply stunning. What a find this place was, it couldn't have been more perfect if he'd designed it himself.

Edel still slept so he headed to the bathroom, stood a long time under the powerful jets of the shower, switching it to cold for the last minute and getting out feeling energised. Wrapping a towel around his midriff, he opened the door quietly to see

Edel standing at the window, the bed sheet draped around her, looking like a Roman goddess.

She turned to smile at him. 'Some view, isn't it?'

'It sure is,' West said, not taking his eyes from her, watching as she blushed and put a hand up to fix her tousled hair. He moved to her side and ran his hand over it, smoothing down tendrils that curled gorgon-like from her head. 'Now,' he said, 'I'm starving, so if you're going to have a shower, you'd better be quick.'

Edel swept the sheet up in regal fashion. 'If some people, who shall remain nameless, hadn't taken forever in the shower, I wouldn't have to hurry,' she said, and with a grin she grabbed clothes she had laid out and vanished into the bathroom.

Breakfast was served at the refectory table in the kitchen by a pleasantly chatty Daisy. Edel chose scrambled egg with Achill smoked salmon while West had a full Irish breakfast. With home-made bread and exceptionally good coffee, they were set up for the day. As they ate, they flicked through the information folder Daisy gave them.

'I'd like to see Grace O'Malley's castle,' Edel decided. 'Apart from that I don't mind what we do.'

West, taking the folder, looked at some of the walking trails. 'This walk,' he said, tapping the page, 'goes right past it. It's the Fawnglass Loop, only three kilometres long. It says it can take from an hour to an hour and a half. What do you think?'

'Perfect,' Edel said, finishing the last of her coffee.

'Whenever you're ready,' Daisy said, taking their plates away, 'Tadgh can drop you wherever you wish to go. When you're ready to return, just ring. Oh, and dress warmly. It's sunny, but there's a distinct nip in the air today.'

They'd come equipped – walking shoes and jackets – and they were soon ready for the drive back to the quay from where they'd start their walk.

'Just give me a ring when you want to come back,' Tadgh told them. He eyed their jackets. 'You sure you'll be warm enough? Those jackets might be okay for Dublin but the wind here can be biting.'

'We'll be fine,' West said, with a questioning glance at Edel who nodded. 'If it gets too cold, we'll adjourn to the pub to warm up.'

Tadgh grinned. 'Sounds like a plan.' And with a wave he left them.

The morning ferry had left, and the harbour was quiet. They walked to the end of the pier, admired the view and returned. There was no need to linger, the whitewashed cottages were of little architectural interest, and the one pub, Ryan's, even if they had fancied a drink this early, was shut.

The castle, or to be more accurate, the tower, was only a short walk and they headed off, hand in hand. It didn't take long to explore the sixteenth-century, three-storied structure, the wooden floors and stairs to the first floor being long gone. 'Grace O'Malley was supposed to have sailed to confront Queen Elizabeth,' Edel told West, 'demanding that her sons and brother be released. She was quite a woman. Perhaps we could go to the Abbey tomorrow,' she suggested as they took a final look around. 'She's supposed to be buried there.'

Leaving the tower behind, they set off to follow the Fawnglass Loop, West armed with a map Daisy had loaned them. 'We follow the road for a kilometre and then turn right down the second bohereen,' he said, folding the map and taking a look around.

This narrow, unpaved road took them uphill, a strenuous enough walk that had Edel puffing slightly. Now and then, they stopped to admire the view and watch the birds that flew high above, trying, with little success, to identify them. 'That's definitely a kestrel,' West said pointing, 'see the way it looks as though it's barely moving? He's got his eye on something.' He laughed as they walked on. 'It's about the only bird I can name apart from the common or garden variety.'

'There's supposed to be peregrine falcons on the north coast of the island,' Edel said, 'we might see some from the guest house.'

The map was easy to follow, as were the directions attached, and they switched from bohereen to green roadway to bohereen, finally ending at a surfaced road that ran alongside a small beach. Just over an hour later, they found themselves back at the quay. Ryan's was still shut, and West wondered what time it opened. He quite fancied a Guinness and, although they'd been warm enough when they were walking, he realised it was becoming quite cold. Perhaps Tadgh had been right about their jackets.

Checking his watch, surprised to find it was only midday, he turned to ask Edel if she fancied the walk up to the Abbey when something caught his eye. A small motorboat had pulled up alongside the pier, and a uniformed garda was clambering off.

'D'you mind?' he asked Edel, nodding toward the garda. 'I'm curious as to what it's like working here.'

'As long as you don't get any ideas.' She smiled back.

Grinning at the thought, he left her and headed to meet the garda, raising a hand in greeting as he approached, getting a narrow-eyed curious glance in return. 'Hi,' he said, 'my name is West, Mike West. I'm a garda sergeant, from Foxrock, Dublin. I just thought I'd say hello.'

The uniformed garda waited a beat before extending his hand. 'The Bareton Industries drug case, a few months ago. I read all about it,' he said, catching West by surprise. 'I have a lot of time on my hands and read all the reports that come in. The name's Hall, Eamonn Hall. You here on a case?'

West smiled at the note of hope in the younger man's voice. 'Just on holiday,' he replied and nodded to where Edel stood outside the pub, 'my friend and I. We were hoping to have a pint, but the pub's shut.'

Garda Hall checked his watch. 'It's usually open around twelve. They tend not to clock-watch in these parts. It'll be open in a while. Especially,' he smiled, 'if they see customers lining up.'

'Where are you based?' West was curious as to how far this garda had to travel in the course of a day.

'Westport,' Hall replied, 'but the outlying islands are my beat. Achill has its own resident garda, but places like Clare Island, Inisbofin, Inishturk and Caher Island don't, so we get around them on a regular basis, or as needed.'

'I thought Caher Island was uninhabited,' West commented, settling back against the pier wall, interested to learn more.

Hall smiled ruefully. 'It is, but it's surprising the amount of crimes that can occur.' He too settled back against the pier, happy to shoot the breeze with another member of the force. 'We get the odd criminal thinking to store stolen merchandise there,' he explained. 'And last year a gang from Galway left a guy on the island. It seems he owed money to the wrong people. Luckily, we call there at least once a week, so he was hungry and thirsty but still alive when we found him.'

'They knew you were going to call?' West surmised.

Garda Hall shrugged. 'They may have, they may not. He wouldn't tell us who was involved, but it's not illegal to be there, just stupid, so we released him. He was reported missing by his family several weeks later. This time he wasn't found. We questioned the Galway gang, but they denied knowing anything about it.'

'Sounds like you have your share of drama here,' West said.

'About once a year or so,' Hall said with a shrug. 'Tell me the inside story on the Bareton Industries case.'

Conscious of Edel waiting, and noticing the pub had opened, West suggested he join them for coffee.

Hall nodded, obviously pleased at the invitation. 'It's not often I get to exchange work tales. You sure your lady friend won't mind?'

'Edel was involved in the Bareton Industries case,' West explained. 'I'll let her tell her side of the story.'

An hour later, they were still talking about it and other cases, swapping stories and experiences. Garda Hall seemed happy to sit and chat, until the pub door opened and a young, obviously distressed man rushed in. 'I need to use the phone,' he said to the bartender. 'There's been an accident.'

'Looks like my cue,' Hall said, standing. 'It was a great pleasure to meet you both. Thank you for the coffee and enjoy the rest of your stay here.'

West watched him join the man at the bar, listened for a few seconds to furious mutterings without hearing what was being said, the urgency of hushed tones receding as they both left the pub. He turned back to Edel who was watching him with a smile. 'You didn't mind him joining us, did you?' he asked her.

She shook her head. 'No, it was fun actually. He seems like a nice guy. It must be a lonely enough job.'

'Yes,' West agreed. 'I don't think I'd like his life. Now,' he continued, 'that fresh air has made me hungry. Would you like something to eat?'

The pub did sandwiches; but it also did seafood chowder which both West and Edel ordered. It came in a huge bowl with thick-cut brown bread on the side.

'This smells lovely,' Edel said, dipping her spoon into the creamy mixture and stirring it. 'There's loads of fish in it too.' She took a spoonful and nodded appreciatively.

A pint of Guinness washed down West's chowder, while Edel was persuaded to have a glass of white wine with hers. The landlord lit the fire and the warmth of it, the good food and the small amount of alcohol had them comfortably drowsy.

'We'll never be able to eat dinner tonight,' Edel said, putting down her spoon and relaxing back in her chair to finish the wine.

West, draining his pint and putting the foam-stained glass down with a grunt of pleasure, disagreed. 'We're going to walk to the Abbey,' he said, 'and anyway, it's only two thirty, it's a long time till dinner.'

The walk to the Abbey wasn't as far as they thought, and less than half an hour later they were looking at the supposed burial place of the pirate queen. The canopied tomb wasn't particularly impressive and bore no inscription.

'Why can't they open it and find out if it's Grace O'Malley or not?' Edel asked.

West shrugged. 'Who would they compare DNA against supposing there is any to be found? There're no living descendants that I know of.'

The walk back was leisurely, the view across to the mainland in the setting sun, stunning. They arrived back to the quay, tired and content, and ready to return to the hotel. West took out his mobile and rang the guest house to be picked up.

As they waited by the pier wall, a car came around the corner and parked outside the pub. Garda Hall stepped out and, even from where they stood, West could see the frown between the man's eyes, the grim set of his mouth.

He knew that look well; it was one he wore often enough when things had just taken a turn for the worse. 'No doubt he's calling for assistance,' he murmured to himself, relieved to see the car from the guest house arriving.

Edel glanced at him worriedly. 'You don't need to help, do you?'

West shook his head. 'No,' he said firmly, 'if he can't handle whatever has happened, there'll be someone in Westport he can call. I'm under no obligation to assist.'

Less than an hour later, however, he was persuaded otherwise.

14

Back in the lighthouse, West and Edel planned to have a walk along the clifftop but peering into the drawing room to see a blazing fire and comfortable seats, they changed their minds. A smiling Daisy offered coffee which they accepted, leaving their coats on the stand in the hallway.

They chatted, the conversation drifting into a comfortable, easy silence broken only by the crackle of the fire. And then West's phone trilled. He frowned when he looked at it, recognising the number instantly. It was the station.

Habit had made him put the phone in his shirt pocket but he didn't have to answer it. Dammit, he was on holiday. He caught Edel's quizzical look.

'Work,' he explained.

Edel grimaced and repeated what he had thought. 'Do you have to answer it? They know you're on holiday.'

West knew Andrews wouldn't ring him for something trivial. With a grunt of exasperation, he answered, expecting to hear his voice, taken aback to hear Inspector Morrison's rather clipped tone instead.

'I know you're officially on holiday, Sergeant West, but I've had a call from Inspector Duignan in Galway. It appears there's a problem on Clare Island, one of the residents has been killed in what looks like a tragic accident. The local garda rang for assistance, but unfortunately his immediate superior fell last night and broke his leg.'

West gritted his teeth. Indicating silently that he was taking the call outside, he left the lounge and headed out into the front garden. 'Sorry,' he said, 'the signal wasn't great where I was. Now, you were saying?'

Inspector Morrison continued. 'The call for assistance went to Inspector Duignan in Galway. Inspector Duignan is an old friend of mine, Sergeant West.' There was a pause as Morrison let that piece of information sink in. 'During the conversation, Garda Hall mentioned he'd been with a garda from Dublin when he was called to the scene of the accident. He mentioned your name, and Inspector Duignan thought it was very auspicious that an experienced garda sergeant was already on the scene. The accident involves the husband of Sylvia B. You may have heard of her.' He waited a moment, but West said nothing.

Morrison cleared his throat. 'Sylvia B is a very eminent artist, Sergeant. One with friends in high places. Very high places,' he repeated with exaggerated emphasis. 'As you are perfectly placed to assist in this investigation, we're asking if you would agree to do so, on a formal basis. If you agree, you will be temporarily seconded to the Westport division. I understand,' he said, 'you are there on holiday, but I don't envisage it will take up much of your time.'

West held his hand over the phone and swore loudly. He wasn't fooled; although offered as such, it wasn't a matter of choice. 'I'd be delighted to assist Garda Hall, Inspector,' he managed to say calmly, the irritation only visible on his face, in the frown that appeared between his eyes, the tightening of his lips. 'He struck me as being a very intelligent officer. Hopefully the case will be as cut and dried as you predict.'

Putting his phone away, he stood a moment looking out across the sea. He frowned at the unfairness of it, an unaccustomed bout of self-pity that he shook off before returning to where Edel sat staring into the fire.

'I'm sorry,' he said, taking his seat. 'That was Morrison.' He quickly explained, watching as disappointment flashed across her face before being hidden by a shrug.

She managed to rustle up a half-hearted smile, and said, 'It can't be helped, can it? After all, you were half-tempted to offer assistance earlier, weren't you? And I think, if I hadn't been there, you would have.'

'Perhaps,' he said. He reached for her hand. 'This wasn't what I wanted for our week away, Edel. I didn't want to be a garda, not this time.'

'Well at least this time, I'm not the victim,' she said, leaning over to give him a kiss on the cheek. 'You didn't plan this, Mike, so stop fretting. Anyway, you said it was an accident. It won't take you long, will it?'

'It shouldn't,' he agreed. 'Hall is coming to pick me up and take me to the scene. I'll be back as soon as I can.'

'You don't need to rush; I'm coming with you.'

She wasn't joking, he saw the determined look on her face. 'You'll be in the way. Seriously. And anyway, it's against policy.'

'Seriously,' she mimicked, 'I don't give a toss for your policies. They're taking you from your holiday; it doesn't mean they have to take you from me. After all, it's not like I haven't seen a dead body before, is it?'

They were still arguing when they heard the sound of a car pulling up outside. Moments later, Eamonn Hall appeared in the doorway, his face pale.

'You've heard from your inspector?' he asked West, getting

straight to the point. 'My apologies; I mentioned your name in passing, never thinking they'd involve you. I thought Duignan would let me deal with it alone. It's not as if it's complicated. Strange but not complicated.'

West nodded to a chair. 'You'd better sit down and fill me in since I've been press-ganged.'

Hall threw a glance at Edel. 'Hi again,' he said and looked back to West, one eyebrow raised in silent question.

'She's okay,' West said, deciding suddenly that giving in to her request was the least he could do. After all, as she said, she'd seen dead bodies before.

The garda shrugged, and, ignoring her, he concentrated on filling West in on what had happened. 'The man who came into the pub earlier was Finbarr Breathnach,' he began, 'he found the body. His father's body. Eoin Breathnach. There's no phone at Toormore House and no mobile coverage. He had to go to Ryan's to ring for help. It was just a lucky coincidence that I was here.'

Toormore House. West recognised the name, the car that had almost run them off the road the day before, it had come from there. 'How was he killed? You told Inspector Duignan that it looked like an accident.'

Hall closed his eyes and gulped. 'It seems he had a weird habit of dipping his toe into the fishpond to see if his fish were hungry. I think he slipped into the water...'

'And drowned,' West finished for him.

Hall gulped again and shook his head. 'I don't think so... or maybe indirectly... I'm not sure which came first.' Realising he was babbling, he took a deep breath and said, 'Lamprey eels,' nodding as if that were sufficient explanation.

Puzzled, West looked at Edel who shrugged and shook her head. He tried again. 'Garda Hall, you need to be a bit clearer with the information. What do lamprey eels have to do with anything?'

Hall took another deep breath and let it out slowly before continuing. 'The owner of Toormore House, Eoin Breathnach. He was interested in exotic fish and kept a pool full of lamprey eels. Somehow, he fell in.' He waited a beat. 'They ate him.'

West, slightly stunned, turned to meet Edel's wide eyes. 'You still want to come?'

'I'd just be sitting here thinking about it if I didn't go,' she said. 'And I've a very vivid imagination.'

They retrieved their coats and climbed into Hall's car, Edel squeezing into the back and finding a seat amongst a variety of paraphernalia, moving a lifebuoy, a bucket and raincoat out of the way.

'Sorry,' Hall threw over his shoulder, 'you never know what you'll need in this job.'

They took the road back the way they'd gone earlier, heading right rather than left at the junction, staying on the road until it ended at Toormore House.

An intricately carved wrought-iron gate opened as they approached, Hall drove through, and down a short drive. Parking the car, he nodded toward the modern one-storied building that stretched before them.

'I expected an old house,' West said, disappointed.

'It's only two years old,' Hall told them. He didn't seem in a hurry to get out of the car. 'It's hard to get planning permission to build on Clare Island, but despite objections from a variety of groups they were allowed to build this. It helped that Eoin Breathnach's wife is the artist, Sylvia B.'

'Sylvia B,' Edel said, impressed. 'I've seen her work in a gallery in Dublin.'

West hadn't heard of her but wondered if it was her idea to live in what was a very isolated and fairly desolate place. In the depths of winter, he guessed, it would be even more so. This part of the island faced the Atlantic, and there was no shelter from the wind and rain.

Even today, when Hall finally moved to get out of the car, the wind almost pulled the car door from their hands.

'It's through here,' he said, leading the way through a gap in a stone wall that extended from both sides of the house. It curved in on itself, enclosing a large courtyard area on both sides, the walls tall enough to keep out the wind so that behind it, it was quieter, and felt warmer.

In this artificial microclimate, large exotic trees flourished, their leaves obscuring the view and hiding the boundary, making it difficult to see exactly how big the area was. The pathway through the trees was narrow, forcing them to walk single file. Hall took the lead. West hesitated, caught between having Edel between them, safe, and being in front so he could see how bad the situation was and to somehow protect her from it. He'd suggested she stay in the car, but she'd shaken her head. 'Imagining monsters is far worse than seeing them,' was all she said, and he'd had to concede defeat.

Minutes later, the pathway ended in front of a large rectangular pond. Hall turned, stopping them, and looking over West's shoulder to where Edel stood said, 'This isn't pretty, are you sure you want to see?'

West, seeing the look of resignation on the man's face, knew she had nodded. There was no point in delaying things any longer. 'Let's take a look, Eamonn,' he said, and waited a whisper as the man swallowed, and with a nod, turned and stepped out into the open area around the pond.

A rough, wide stone path ran around it, a sign to one end warning of deep water. Stepping closer, West peered in, but the water was dark, murky and he couldn't see the bottom.

Eoin Breathnach lay in the water at the far end of the pond, his head bobbing on the water like a cork, his body submerged. Hall had said the man had been eaten. West felt his blood go cold. Was his body gone, his head floating unwanted?

'It's the lampreys,' Hall explained, 'they're still attached.'

Having no idea what he was talking about, West decided to ignore him for the moment. Moving around the pond, he made his way closer to the partially submerged body. The water was opaque, but when he came alongside, he saw exactly what Garda Hall meant. Attached to the man's body, were several long eels.

'What are they?' West asked, trying but failing to keep the note of fascination from his voice. 'Eels, did you say?'

Hall shrugged. 'Lamprey eels, although to be accurate they're not eels at all, they're jawless fish.'

'I'm not too sure which sounds worse,' Edel said, staring at the gruesome sight. 'They must be about three feet long. Are they attached with some kind of suckers or something?'

Hall dragged his gaze away from the sight of Eoin Breathnach's body and looked at her. 'I did an internet search on them, the first time I saw them. There are about thirty-eight types of lamprey, but only a small proportion is parasitic. They attach their mouthparts to their target and use their teeth to cut through tissue until they reach blood and body fluids. Finbarr said his father had insisted on buying the parasitic variety. He liked to starve them and then watch them attack the live fish he threw in; they'd swim around in a frenzy trying to attach their mouths to them.'

'They're still feeding?' Edel muttered, aghast.

They looked at the man's body, he was corpulent, a lot of fluids to be eaten yet.

West walked around the edge of the pool. 'You think he might have slipped in?'

Hall sighed. 'Finbarr said he hadn't fed them for a few days.

He'd ordered some live fish from the fishermen at the quay and kept them alive in a tank in an outhouse. He liked to see them eat. When he dipped his toe in, if they all came swimming toward him, they were hungry, if they didn't, he'd leave them for a few more days.' He pointed to a shoe that lay nearby. 'It looks like he lost his balance, and fell in.'

It was possible, West agreed. Possible, and nice and tidy. He could get back to his holiday. He walked around the pool again. They were losing the light; soon it would be too dark to see anything. Already, they might be missing something that may not be there tomorrow. 'Do you have a torch?' he asked.

Hall, nodding, took a torch from one of his many pockets and handed it to him. Flicking it on, West hunkered down and shone the light on the edge of the pond behind the man's head, trying to ignore the sucking, slurping sound of the lampreys as they fed. He didn't see anything for a moment; the stone at the water's edge was mossy, damp. He was just about to give up when he saw it. 'Look,' he pointed, and both Hall and Edel bent to stare at the circle of light made by the small but powerful torch.

'Ah,' said Hall, 'you're right. I see it.'
'What?' Edel asked, bending down to get a closer look.
'There,' West said, pointing, 'where the moss is disturbed.'
'Yes,' she said, seeing it now, 'he tried to climb out?'
West stood. 'Possibly,' he said, 'we'll see if they find evidence of moss under his fingernails. Assuming he has any left.'

With a shudder, Edel looked into the water.

'We need to get him out of there,' West said, turning to Hall, 'have you any idea how we can detach those creatures?'

'I do,' a voice said, approaching from the house down a different pathway.

Eamonn Hall made the introductions. 'Finbarr Breathnach,

this is Detective Garda Sergeant West, from Dublin, and Edel Johnson.'

Finbarr was a tall, thin man with extremely pale skin emphasised by a messy shock of almost black hair that looked as though it hadn't ever seen a brush or a comb. 'Did they not think you could manage, Eamonn?' he said, approaching them, his eyes darting to the body of his father, his face showing no emotion.

'Garda Hall asked for assistance, Mr Breathnach, and as I was already on the island, I came to help,' West said, drawing the man's attention to himself. 'I'm sorry for your loss; this must be difficult for you.'

The man smiled sweetly. 'That's the problem with being an outsider, Detective Garda Sergeant West from Dublin. You see, Eamonn here knew better than to offer me condolences. He knew I couldn't stand the old bastard. I'm more than happy to admit, I'm glad he's gone.' He looked at his father and sneered unpleasantly. 'You know, I couldn't have wished for a better death for him.'

'Shush, Finbarr,' Hall said, but the man merely laughed loudly and took out a packet of cigarettes.

'Right then,' West said, deciding to take charge of the matter, 'you know how we can get those creatures away from your father's body?'

Finbarr, in the act of lighting a cigarette, finished the ritual and inhaled before answering. 'Just let me finish this,' he said, 'and I'll sort that out for you.'

West clenched his jaw. He'd met lads like Finbarr before, too much money, too few manners, there was no point going up against him. Taking a deep breath, he waited as the man took puff after puff before, with a final exaggerated inhale, he threw the cigarette into the bushes. 'I'll be back in a sec,' he said, disappearing the same way he'd come.

It was ten minutes before he reappeared, accompanied by the rattle of equipment. The light had dropped, the pond now virtually in darkness. When he got close enough for them to make him out, he was wearing a grin, carrying a tall lamp with an extension lead trailing behind him. There was something else under his arm that West couldn't identify.

'Here I am,' Finbarr said, switching on the lamp and placing it so that it shone over his father's body, sending the lampreys into a renewed frenzy, their tails lashing the water. 'What a pretty sight,' he said, with a laugh.

West was tired of Finbarr's warped humour. It was getting late; he was supposed to be on holiday and this wasn't the way he'd intended to spend it. He reached in the darkness for Edel's hand, giving it a reassuring squeeze before concentrating on the unlikeable young man before him. 'What are you intending to do?'

Having set the lamp in position, Finbarr stood back. 'I'm going to switch the lamp off now. Prepare to witness magic.'

The torch West held didn't throw out enough light to show them what he was up to, but they could him hear him fumbling and muttering before a loud splash startled them all. It drew a yelp from Edel and a soft curse from Hall before sparks drew all their attention to the water.

Finbarr let out a whoop of glee. 'Yes, it worked!' He moved into the torch light, looking at West like a child looking for praise. 'I electrocuted them,' he explained. 'The old toaster in the bath trick. Only' – he pointed to the pond – 'not exactly a bath, but the same concept.'

West and Hall exchanged glances, Hall shrugging as if to say he didn't know what to make of him either.

'You've knocked out the electrics in the house, Finbarr. They're not going to be happy with you.'

'Jim will sort it,' Finbarr said dismissively as he unplugged the toaster and hauled it out.

West was about to make a comment when the sound of an engine was heard in the distance. He glanced at Hall, puzzled. 'Who's this coming?'

'I asked Chris from the garage to bring his van and a tarpaulin.' Seeing West's surprised look, Hall smiled apologetically. 'Things are done slightly differently here, I'm afraid. The only vehicle I have at my disposal on the island is the car we came in. It's a matter of making do. We'll wrap the body in the tarp, and I'll go with it to the mortuary in Westport.'

'What about the evidence here?' West asked, realising for the first time how fortunate they were in Dublin.

'I took a lot of photographs earlier and had a look around. There didn't appear to be any evidence to gather.'

West shone the torch around. He couldn't see anything but he knew that didn't mean there wasn't anything there. He was about to suggest they come back at first light and do a fingertip search when his beam caught the grinning face of Finbarr, and he knew there was no point. He was the type of young fool who would plant evidence as a joke.

Eamonn went to greet Chris and help him with the tarpaulin, Finbarr trailing behind him offering useless suggestions as to how best remove his father's body from the pond. West shone the torch over the now floating body. He didn't have any more useful ideas to offer.

'How are you going to get him out of there?' Edel asked.

'Well, I'm telling you one thing for sure,' he replied, raising the torch to see her. 'I'm certainly not climbing in there, not with those eel things. Dead or alive.'

'Lampreys,' she said with a smile.

'Them,' he agreed.

Eamonn and Chris arrived, carrying the tarp between them, Finbarr muttering advice they ignored. They dropped it by the edge of the pond. Chris took a powerful torch from his pocket and shone it over the body. If he were surprised or shocked by what he saw, his expression gave no indication. 'We need to get him over to the side,' he said. 'I've got a hook in the van; I'll go get it.'

He was back within minutes holding a long wooden-handled hook. 'It's a handy old thing, this,' he said to nobody in particular. With Hall aiming the beam of light over the body, Chris reached out with the hook. The body, free of the lampreys, bobbed like a fairground duck and it took a couple of tries before he managed to catch hold and slowly drag it to the side.

Once there, with West at the head, Chris in the middle and Eamonn at the feet, they managed with a lot of grunting, swearing and false starts to grab hold of the body and haul it out. There was little dignity in the man's death. Once on the ground, his body was rolled onto a length of tarp and rolled again to encase him in it.

Finbarr couldn't resist. 'Brings a whole new meaning to roll-your-own, doesn't it?'

They ignored him, more intent on transporting the body down the narrow, overgrown pathway to the van without causing injury to themselves or dropping the body. Edel, a torch in each hand, lit the way.

When the body was stowed in the back of the van, Hall turned to West. 'I'll go with it to Westport and wait for the post-mortem results. You can take my car; the keys are in the ignition. I'll get a lift to your guest house when I come back.' He climbed into the passenger seat and, with a nod, Chris started the engine and drove off, leaving West and Edel standing in torchlight.

Of Finbarr, there was no sign, and West, weary now, decided it was pointless going in search of the man. Tomorrow was soon enough to face that jester again.

15

Twenty minutes later, they were back in the luxury of the Clare Island Lighthouse. 'I'm sorry about this,' West said as they closed the bedroom door behind them. 'This wasn't the romantic break I had planned.'

'I don't know,' Edel replied, kissing him lightly on the lips, 'there was a lot of romance last night. This is just a blip.'

West smiled. It wasn't exactly how he'd have described the scene that had greeted them at Toormore House. A blip. 'Maybe dinner can wait a while,' he murmured, pulling her tighter against him, letting her feel what she did to him.

Edel laughed. 'You really haven't learned the concept of delayed gratification, have you?'

'And you really haven't learned how hungry I can be,' he replied, his tongue running down her neck, his hands running down her back, cupping her buttocks, moving her closer yet again.

Edel's breathing increased. Oh yes, dinner could wait.

An hour later, one appetite satisfied, they made their way to the main dining room.

There were four people already seated around one large

table. They looked up as West and Edel entered, slight smiles indicating that they knew exactly why the couple were late.

First name introductions were done, the names as quickly forgotten as the four diners carried on a conversation that had started earlier. West and Edel took their seats and browsed the menu in silence.

'I should have told you there weren't individual tables,' West whispered. 'I forgot.'

Edel smiled at him, and reached over to pat his knee reassuringly. 'It's fine,' she said.

'I can recommend the smoked duck salad,' one of the men said, addressing them. 'It's incredibly good.'

'Just what I was going to choose,' West said.

'I had the courgette and almond soup,' the woman sitting opposite added. 'It was amazing.'

'We had it last night,' Edel said, 'it was very good. Tonight, I think I'll go with the duck salad too.'

Conversation, like the wine, flowed. After dinner, they were offered an excellent smoky Irish whiskey which all of the men and Edel decided to try. It was the perfect finish to a perfect meal.

'I hope it's a bit quieter tonight,' a woman at the table commented. 'We were woken by an owl last night. I didn't know they were quite so noisy.'

Edel, in the act of sipping her drink, choked. 'Sorry,' she said, coughing, 'it went down the wrong way.'

'We heard seals barking,' West said, his face serious. 'Perhaps that was what you heard?'

The woman nodded and looked at the man beside her. 'You see, I told you I heard shouting. Seals.' She looked at West. 'That makes sense.'

'Seals?' Edel said when they returned to their room. 'I thought I was going to have hysterics.'

'Let's see if we can make them bark again tonight,' he said, pulling her into his arms and covering her mouth with his.

They woke early next morning to the sound of gulls and lay in bed watching them perform acrobatics across the sky before doing some of their own. They showered together, West soaping Edel's breasts, his hands slipping down over her buttocks with a groan. 'I can't get enough of you,' he whispered into her ear, sliding her up the wall, holding her there and slipping inside.

'You're insatiable, Mike,' Edel said, before he upped the tempo, and there was no more need for words.

∽

Two of the other guests were still sitting around the kitchen table finishing their breakfast when they arrived down. Edel hiding her dismay, greeted the couple with a smile and sat, hoping the woman wouldn't mention owls or seals.

Daisy, coming to take their order, smiled and introduced them all again. 'I know you met last night,' she said, 'but if you're anything like me with names, they'll have gone out the window. So, Mike, Edel, meet Niamh and Ciaran.' She filled coffee cups and promised to make more herbal tea for Niamh.

'Did you sleep well?' Niamh had asked the question Edel was dreading.

'Very well,' she said, refusing to do the polite thing and ask the woman the same.

She didn't need to. 'Me too, I was so relieved and today I feel full of energy. I was asking Daisy, just before you came; she said the seals aren't normally that noisy. She suggested it might be mating season.'

'Really?' Edel said, feigning interest in the life of seals, trying not to catch West's eye. She refused to look at Daisy when she returned with Niamh's herbal tea in one hand and both their breakfasts balanced in the other.

Thankfully, the other couple soon left and they were able to enjoy their meal in peace.

Everything, West thought, would have been just perfect if his position as a garda hadn't intruded. Perhaps they should have gone abroad. But then again, crime had followed him to Cornwall. There was no point in railing against it, was there? Plus, he had to admit, it was an interesting case. Killed by lamprey eels, that had to be one for the books. He'd enjoy telling Andrews about it when he returned.

There was no sign of Hall by the time they finished breakfast. Pulling on their coats they walked along the cliff until the wind and the start of a light rain drove them back.

They'd just reached their bedroom when a knock sounded on the door. 'Garda Hall,' West said, opening the door, 'I wondered when you'd get here. Let's go downstairs and have some coffee, and you can fill me in on the post-mortem. Edel,' he added, turning to her, 'do you want to wait here?'

'Can't I come with you?' she asked, sharing a smile between the two men. 'The rain looks to be down for the day and I don't fancy the idea of sitting around twiddling my thumbs. After all, I've seen the body and the crime scene. I might have something valuable to add.'

Hall, despite Edel's involvement the day before, looked to West for the *no, this is official business* he was sure would come, his mouth tightening when West nodded instead.

'Indeed, you might,' he said, and without another word indicated that the garda lead the way back down the stairs to the dining room. They passed one of the housekeeping staff on the way, and a request for coffee was met with a smile and a promise to have it sorted straight away.

'Well, bring me up to speed,' West said as they sat around the table.

Hall cleared his throat, his ruddy face turning an unattractive darker shade of red. 'We got the body back to the mortuary last night,' he said, 'but the coroner didn't arrive until this morning. That's why I was so late getting here.' His colour faded to its normal shade as he gained confidence in recounting the details of the day. 'The coroner, Bill McCullough, is the slow, meticulous type. He takes his time, doesn't rush to conclusions. The lamprey eel situation fascinated him. He wants us to bring him one.' Hall smiled. 'Not that it will make any difference, you understand, he just wants to see what it looks like.'

'It won't make a difference? So, it wasn't the lampreys that killed him then?'

Hall shook his head. 'Not accidently anyway. McCullough found a square abrasion in the middle of the victim's back. He's sent particles of wood he found in it to the forensic people. But it looks like someone used something to push him in.'

'We saw where he tried to climb out,' West muttered.

'Exactly, there was moss under the fingernails. He's sent a sample of that to forensics too; I've to send a sample from the pool edge for comparison. There's little doubt he tried to get out and someone stopped him.' Hall hesitated, gave Edel a quick glance and went on. 'There were also crush injuries to some of his fingers. There was no trace evidence, but he said it looked like someone stamped on them.'

'Not an accident,' West said, his voice grim on two counts, the murder and the end of a quick solution to the case. He looked at Hall, taking in his sombre expression. Was he concerned that he might know the perpetrator of this particularly monstrous crime? 'Murder brings a lot of nasty things out of the woodwork, Eamonn.'

Before the younger man had a chance to reply, one of the staff arrived with a tray of coffee and freshly made scones, the aroma of both filling the room and lifting the sober mood.

'These aren't going to waste,' Edel said, taking one, 'come on Eamonn. This sea air must give you an appetite.'

Within minutes the plate was empty.

'Who else lives in Toormore House?' West asked, using a napkin to wipe jam from his fingers.

'Well, there's Finbarr and Sylvia, obviously,' Hall said, putting his cup down. 'They have guests now and then; I don't know if there are any at the moment. I didn't think to ask, I'm afraid. Plus, there's a housekeeper, and gardener stroke maintenance man.' Hall clicked his tongue in irritation. 'I should have asked about guests, shouldn't I? There's no check on people coming to the island. They can take the ferry or come over in private boats, so we have no way of knowing who is here at any one time.'

West considered the situation. 'Okay,' he said finally, 'we need to get over to the house and see who is there now, find out if anyone left since yesterday, or if they had any visitors yesterday and who they were. Once we have those names, we can do a background check on them all; see if any one of them had a motive to kill Eoin Breathnach.' Frowning, West realised he usually handed background checks over to one of his team to do – it was a boring and often thankless task. He tapped a finger on the side of the cup he was holding. Couldn't he still do that? Morrison wouldn't care, as long as he got the job done, and it didn't interfere too much with the workings of Foxrock station.

'I'll get my lads back in Foxrock to do the background checks as soon as we have the names,' he told Hall. He smiled at the instant look of relief on Hall's face. 'Is there a problem with the Wi-Fi reception here?'

'I have a small cottage in Roonagh,' Hall explained. 'I rented it because I was told it had Wi-Fi. It does, just not very often, and never when I actually need it. I can go into Westport, of course, but that's a bit of a nuisance in itself.'

'Leave it to me, then. What can you tell me about the family? You seem to be on friendly terms with Finbarr.'

Hall screwed up his face. 'I was brought up in Westport; he went to the same secondary school as me for about six months. He lived with his grandparents while his mother was in Dublin trying to make it as an artist. One day, he came to school, said his mother had married someone very rich, and that he was leaving.' There was a moment's pause as the young man remembered the teasing they had given the boy. 'We never saw him in school again. Rumour had it that he went to Kylemore Abbey as a boarder.' He shrugged. 'He never said, and we never asked. His mother bought a big house just outside Westport, and she and Eoin Breathnach spent a few weeks there, now and then.

'They never stayed very long and Finbarr continued to stay with his grandparents during the holidays. When they died, within a few months of each other, Finbarr moved into the house, but I don't think Sylvia visited any more frequently. There was a housekeeper who looked out for him. We only knew he was home, because he'd turn up at the local football games and tag along when we went for chips afterwards.' Hall smiled ruefully. 'He always had money, and was generous with it, so he was accepted. But he wasn't ever liked. We used to imitate his accent and laugh at his clothes.'

Thinking back, Hall shook his head. 'We weren't very kind to him, and some of the unsavoury things we said and the practical jokes we played just because he was ever so slightly different were pretty awful, but he never complained. After I finished school, I didn't see him for a few years. When I graduated from Templemore, I requested to stay in the west of Ireland, and spent some time in Killala before getting this posting. The outgoing garda mentioned Finbarr's name, and I think I met him on my second or third visit here.'

'What did he do after school?'

'He moved to Dublin and started an arts degree in the UCD but dropped out after a year. He mentioned he'd spent a few months in the College of Art and Design too, but he didn't last there either. I'm not sure if he's ever actually worked, but he never seems to be short of cash.' Hall's upper lip lifted in a sneer. 'Of course, his mother is very successful, and he gets on well with her so I assume she funds his lifestyle.'

Living the life of a layabout probably accounted for Finbarr's irritating manner, West thought. 'What about the dead man?'

Hall shook his head. 'I know hardly anything about Eoin Breathnach; he spends little time here. He was sixty when he married Sylvia, who was only twenty-eight at the time. But they've stayed married, so I suppose they were happy. Breathnach made a killing in property, sold it all just at the right time before everything went belly-up. In fact,' he frowned, 'I gather there were some hard feelings from those who had paid a lot of money for property that was worth less than half, a few months later.'

West wondered how deep those feelings went. The property crash had left many casualties in its wake. It was something to consider in their search for a motive. But first, they'd look closer to home. 'Sylvia B, I gather, is a well-known artist so her background will be well-documented. What do you know about her personally?'

Hall blew out a breath. 'Not a lot. She left Westport when she was quite young, I think. After art college, she went to London and it was there she met Eoin. He was part of some hotel consortium, I think. Nowadays, she rarely leaves the island. Her agent comes across every few months, I know because I helped him load some of her paintings onto a very sleek motorboat a year or so ago. She doesn't encourage visitors. It was one of the reasons she left Westport, she was constantly being asked to give talks or appear at events, or had autograph hunters knocking on her door.'

'She doesn't give interviews either,' Edel added. 'Her agent, Julius Blacque, was interviewed on a talk show I happened to be watching. When asked about her, he explained that solitude was her muse. To be honest, he came across as a rather pretentious twit. But I'd forgive her anything; her work is magnificent.'

'Okay,' West said. 'Well, I suppose we'd better get over there, break the bad news and start investigating.'

'I'm coming with you,' Edel said firmly. 'An opportunity to meet Sylvia B isn't one I'm going to let slip through my fingers, despite the circumstances. I'll stay quiet, won't say a word. I promise,' she added, seeing the sceptical look in West's eyes.

West met Hall's intent gaze. 'She might turn out to be useful. We don't know how Sylvia is taking her husband's death, or how she'll take the news that he's been murdered. I don't know about you, but hysterical women aren't my forte.'

Hall shot West a doubtful look but shrugged his agreement.

The earlier, gentle rain had turned heavy and Hall's car was parked just outside the gate. Unlocking it from the shelter of the doorway, they ran to it in an *every-man-for-himself* dash.

'Goodness, it's really coming down now,' Edel said from the back seat, wiping the rain from her face with her sleeve.

'The wind is picking up too,' West said. Turning to Hall, he asked, 'Do you often have to stay on the islands, if the weather deteriorates?'

'This storm was forecast,' he replied, starting the engine and heading for Toormore House. 'I don't usually travel if the weather is bad. But Clew Bay is reasonably sheltered, so it doesn't happen too often. I'd planned to stay over tonight, anyway. I've booked a room in the pub.' Twenty minutes later he drove up to the gates, expecting them to open. When they didn't, he swore softly. 'I told Finbarr we'd be back today; I'll have to go in and get someone to open the gate.' He reached behind to grab a raincoat from the back seat. 'I hope I won't be long.'

It was ten minutes before he returned, the gates slowly opening as he climbed back into the car, sending drops of rain flying from his coat and bedraggled hair. 'Bloody hell,' he said, reaching across West's knees to open the glove compartment. He scrabbled in it for a few seconds before pulling out a cloth that was obviously used for cleaning the windscreen and rubbing it over his hair and face. 'Nobody answered the front door, so I had to make my way around to the back. Eventually, the damn door opened.'

He drove through the gates as he spoke, parking as close to the front door as possible. 'The housekeeper is going to get Finbarr. She said she'd open this door for us and let us in.'

When the door opened, however, it was Finbarr who stood there waving gaily as if they had come for a social gathering.

'I told you we'd be coming, Finbarr,' Hall complained loudly when the door shut the rain outside.

'Yes, but you didn't say what time, did you? And after all, we can't leave the gate open for all and sundry to enter, can we?'

This was patently so ludicrous Hall didn't bother to argue.

'Is there somewhere we can go to talk,' West said, refusing to stay standing in the chilly hallway.

Finbarr looked him up and down before shrugging. 'If you must,' he said, leading the way into a large sitting room where a fire had been laid, but not yet lit.

Hall, almost soaked through, shivered.

Noticing, and with a more friendly tone of voice, Finbarr

said, 'For goodness' sake, Eamonn, take off your raincoat. Give it to me,' he added, as the young garda peeled off the wet garment. 'I'll go and get you a towel.'

He returned a few minutes later, a huge bath towel in one hand. He threw it unceremoniously at Hall before dropping into the sofa with a grunt. 'Well, what did you want to talk to me about?' he said.

For all the world as if nothing out of the way had happened yesterday. West couldn't decide if he were being very clever or just extremely irritating.

'Is your mother here?' he asked.

Finbarr, with a half-smile on his face as he watched Hall trying to restore some semblance of order to his person, turned his eyes on West. 'Yes, she's always here.'

'Could you ask her to join us?'

Finbarr considered the question for a moment. 'Why?' he asked finally.

Hall threw the towel onto the arm of the chair. 'Stop being stupid, Finbarr. Sergeant West has been put in charge of the investigation into your father's death. He needs to speak to you both.'

The eyes that turned to West were suddenly sharp. 'Investigation? It was an accident.' He looked back to Hall. 'Wasn't it?'

'I'm afraid that's one of the things we are here to discuss, Mr Breathnach,' West said, watching him closely. 'We have evidence that proves your father was murdered.'

The reaction wasn't one any of them expected. Finbarr started to laugh, a rich sound of genuine amusement. 'Oh dear,' he said, wiping his eyes, 'that is just so funny. I've been wondering for years how to kill the old bastard and now you tell me someone's gone and done it.'

West, not usually lost for words, found it difficult to know what to say next. Luckily for him, the door opened to admit a tall, thin woman who was obviously the progenitor of the man who sat in the sofa, the end of the laugh still bubbling in his mouth.

The shock of black hair that sat so messily on Finbarr's head was a neatly cut cap on Sylvia's, giving her an almost elfin look. She glared at her son before turning her attention to West. 'Linda told me there were policemen here,' she said in a curiously melodic voice. 'I assume you need to speak to me.'

'Yes, Mrs Breathnach, we do. My name is Sergeant West. I'm in charge of the investigation into your husband's death. You know Garda Hall, of course, and this is a friend of mine, Edel Johnson.'

If Sylvia was surprised at a friend being invited along, she didn't say so, merely looking from one to the other before inviting them to take a seat. 'I assume my son hasn't offered you refreshments. Would you like some tea or coffee? No?' she said, as they shook their heads. 'Very well, now how can I help you?'

'They say Eoin was murdered, Ma,' Finbarr blurted out before West could speak.

'Murdered?' she said, her eyes flitting from one face to the other again as if to read the truth in one of them. Finally, they settled on her son. 'You told me it was an accident.'

Finbarr grinned. 'Seems I'm not a very good detective. I thought he'd fallen in when he was trying to see if those horrible eels were hungry enough. You've warned him often enough about the sides of the pond being slippery, haven't you?'

West looked from son to mother, unsure if it wasn't the young man's ideas of fun to muddy the water. 'Is this true, Mrs Breathnach?' West asked.

'I probably told him every day,' she said calmly. She moved to take the seat beside her son. 'But he never listened to me. He rarely did, you know,' she added without rancour. 'When we were planning the house here, he insisted on having a tropical fishpond on one side of the house and an unheated outdoor swimming pool on the other. I thought both were ridiculous. Nobody ever swam in the pool apart from him. The fishpond, on the other hand, he had heated so that he could buy whatever damn fish he wanted.'

'Did he go out to the fish pond every evening?'

Finbarr answered. 'He was just interested in the feeding frenzy. He'd no real interest in the creatures themselves.'

Having seen the lampreys, West wasn't surprised. 'Were they more active at a particular time of the day?'

The corners of Finbarr's mouth tilted upward, but there was no amusement in the movement. 'Are you trying to find out if he went to the pond at exactly the same time every day? If so, I hate to bear sad tidings,' he said with what West read as a haughty disdain for the stupidity of lesser folk, 'but he wasn't such a creature of habit. Usually, he'd go after he'd been for a swim but sometimes, he went before. And then there were days, of course, when he didn't go at all.'

West refused to be annoyed. 'Thank you, Mr Breathnach. Now, tell me please, who else was here?'

'A list of suspects,' Finbarr murmured.

'Stop, Finbarr, please,' his mother said, shooting him a quelling glance before turning back to West. 'He delights in being irritating, Sergeant, just ignore him. Usually, there would just be the three of us, and the staff, of course. Linda, our housekeeper and her husband, Jim, who does maintenance and gardening. But Eoin invited a couple of old friends to stay. Penny and Roger Tilsdale. They've been with us a week and, despite Eoin's death, I think they plan to stay another couple.' It was obvious by her tone of voice that Sylvia wasn't too happy about this. 'Oh, and Julius is here,' she added, almost as an afterthought.

'Your agent?'

'That's right. Julius Blacque. He doesn't normally stay long, but he's trying to persuade me to have an exhibition at his gallery.' She smiled, and the likeness between her and her son increased. It wasn't a pleasant smile. 'He's of the opinion that persistence pays. It doesn't. Well, not in my case anyway.'

'And that's everyone?' West asked.

'Probably,' Finbarr muttered.

'Probably? What do you mean by that, Mr Breathnach?'

'Oh, do please call me Finbarr,' the young man said testily. 'It makes you sound very pompous when you keep calling me Mr Breathnach, you know. And I wasn't, believe it or not, trying to be awkward when I said probably. Apart from the gate, this place is wide open. There's lots of hiding places where someone could keep watch.'

'So, you think some unknown person is responsible for your father's death? What motive would he have?'

Finbarr laughed. 'Tell him, Eamonn,' he said, darting a glance at the garda.

Sylvia rested a hand on her forehead. 'Oh, do shut up. This isn't the time for your warped sense of humour.' She sat forward, cutting him off. 'What my darling son means, Sergeant, is that my husband was much better at making enemies than friends. There are a number of people who will not grieve when they hear he has died. How many of them would have done the act themselves? I have no idea.'

Telling the truth or more muddying of the waters? At this stage, West wasn't sure. 'Where were you around the time he died?'

'In my studio,' she replied without hesitation. 'Alone. My routine is very regular. I go in early every morning. Linda brings me lunch, which I try to remember to eat, but otherwise I keep going until I'm done, literally and figuratively.'

'Every day?' Edel risked asking. She couldn't imagine shutting herself up in a room every day, that kind of focus was rare.

Sylvia slowly turned her gaze on her. 'My studio has floor to ceiling windows looking out over the Atlantic,' she explained, and, as if that said it all, looked back to West.

'And you didn't come out when you heard about the accident?' West asked, curious.

'What on earth for?' She looked at him with a lack of interest or concern that he could tell wasn't feigned.

Her answer drew a chuckle from Finbarr who raised his shoulders in an *I told you so* shrug.

West wasn't sure what to make of either of them. That they both disliked the dead man was plain. Someone not only pushed Breathnach in, but made sure he didn't get out, and probably stood by and watched him die. That took hatred. But from experience, he knew hatred could be a passionate, explosive type of anger or a cold, slow-burning fuse. He wasn't ruling either of these two oddly emotionless people out just yet.

'Thank you,' he said, looking from one to the other. 'We may have more questions at a later date, but if we could speak to the others now?'

'Of course,' Sylvia said, standing. 'I'll send them in to you. Come along, Finbarr,' she added, 'they can manage without your assistance.'

When the door shut behind them there was a collective sigh of relief in the room.

16

West took out a notebook and scribbled down the names he'd been given. He'd pass them on to Andrews later; get him to do some digging. 'How likely is it that someone was hiding out and keeping watch as Finbarr suggested?' he asked.

Hall gave the matter some thought. 'It's a possibility, I suppose. It was one of the conditions of the planning permission for this house that they didn't interfere with the ruins of an old settlement nearby and they didn't, but they're very close. The remnants of the walls would provide suitable cover to shelter behind.'

West thought of the drive from the quay. 'There's only one road in though. Any car would be visible. How long would it take to walk here? It's what, four or five kilometres?'

'Six,' Hall said. 'I've walked it before. It takes about an hour.'

West frowned. A determined person wouldn't baulk at an hour's walk. 'Could someone have moored a boat there without attracting attention?'

'Nobody monitors who comes and goes, if that's what you mean,' Hall said. 'There was never any reason to.'

'If a boat remained there a few days, would nobody comment?'

'Why would they?' Hall shook his head. 'Especially this time of year, boats could be tied up for weeks without being moved.'

An unknown assailant could have travelled to the island, walked the six kilometres and watched and waited for an opportunity to kill Eoin Breathnach. But why? Surely it would have been easier to have killed him in Dublin or London, or any of the other places he was reputed to spend time. Why here? And why now? No, it was much more likely to be someone closer to home. Another thought popped into his head. 'What's the population of Clare Island, Eamonn?'

'About one hundred and fifty, usually. More in the summer,' he answered and added, 'Yes, it could be someone who lives on the island.'

'We'll keep an open mind,' West said. And then, remembering something else that had been said, asked, 'What did Finbarr mean when he said, "tell them, Eamonn"?'

Hall shrugged. 'There's little to talk about on the island so the conversation turns to the more colourful inhabitants. Listening to the gossip is part of my job. It keeps me in the loop as to what's going on. I've already told you what I know and heard.'

There was something more, West felt sure of it. Suddenly he felt very much the outsider among these people.

A few minutes later, the door opened and a round, pretty face looked around its edge. 'Sylvia told us you wanted to speak to us,' the woman said, coming into the room, followed closely by a balding man of the same height. 'I'm Penny Tilsdale, and this is my husband, Roger.'

'Please come in, take a seat,' West said, and quickly made introductions, this time introducing Eamonn Hall and Edel Johnson without adding qualifications, leaving the couple to think what they wanted. Eamonn's uniform made it clear who he was, if they chose to believe Edel was a plain-clothes detective, well so be it.

'Eoin Breathnach was a friend of yours, I believe. Our condolences on your loss.'

The corners of Penny's mouth drooped and she reached, rather dramatically, West thought, for her husband's hand. 'It was such a shock,' she managed to say before holding her free hand over her mouth and squeezing out a tear.

Silent until now, Roger put his arm around her. 'It's been awful, just awful,' he said. 'Poor Sylvia, we're determined to stay as long as we can to support her through this terrible business. That son of hers is no use at all.'

'You may already know, but we are treating Eoin Breathnach's death as murder.'

'Finbarr told us. Obviously, we were very shocked.'

'Had you known the deceased for long?' West asked.

'Years,' Roger replied. 'Nearly twenty, I'd guess. We met on a flight to somewhere or other, got chatting, hit it off, discovered we were staying in the same hotel, and had dinner together a few times. We've kept in touch since. I was best man at his wedding.'

'Was this a planned visit or spur of the moment?'

'Gosh, it was planned, months ago. You couldn't call on Eoin on a spur of the moment basis; you'd never know where he was. Eoin has... had... been asking us to visit here since this place was built, but work commitments' – he shrugged – 'you know how it is.'

'What do you do, Mr Tilsdale?' West asked.

'I'm in the accommodation business,' he said vaguely.

West didn't bother to try to pin him down, they'd find out exactly what that meant when Andrews did his nosing around. 'I see. Do you know if he was worried about anything in particular?'

'He wasn't the worrying kind of man. If something annoyed him, he dealt with it.'

'Was there anything in particular that annoyed him? Anything recently? Dealt with it is fairly vague and encompassing.' Also rather worrying, West thought; a clearer picture of Breathnach was emerging, it didn't look too good.

Roger rubbed a hand over his balding head. 'I didn't mean anything in particular. Just that he wasn't the kind of man who let things slide, you know. It's like when he was having this place built, all the windows were to be triple-glazed, but the company messed up and delivered double-glazed. They promised to have them remade, but he told them they'd lost the opportunity, and he took his business elsewhere. That's the kind of man he was. He didn't believe in this three-strike business. They had one shot, they failed and were out.'

West made a mental note to look into the company who lost out. He didn't know how many rooms Toormore House had, but he guessed they were talking about a serious amount of money for the manufacture of the windows, and a hell of a lot more for transport. 'That attitude wouldn't have made him a lot of friends.'

Tilsdale gave a snort. 'Eoin's motto was, have money, have friends. Believe me, Sergeant, there were always plenty of hangers-on.' He gave his wife a sideways glance and then leaned closer and said in a lowered voice, 'Especially of the female variety, if you get my drift.'

West nodded, hiding the distaste he felt at the other man's less-than-subtle hint, regretting the need to follow the line of inquiry. 'Was there anyone in particular, Mr Tilsdale? Anyone with a grudge, perhaps?'

The man snorted again, loudly. 'That's another thing Eoin

used to say, you know, have money, have grudges. He was a very witty man.' Meeting West's unamused eyes, he put on a more serious expression. 'People in business collect grudges like flypaper collects flies.'

West had had enough. There was just one more question to ask. 'Where were you both on the morning he was killed?'

Tilsdale nodded as if it was the question he was waiting for. 'We had a late breakfast with Eoin. He was heading for a swim so we sat in here and read until lunchtime. We were just about to head out for a walk, when Linda told us the news.'

'We were devastated,' Penny said, her voice thick with tears, her eyes fixed on West.

'You didn't hear or see anything out of the ordinary?'

Both Tilsdales shook their heads and, almost in unison, said, 'Nothing.'

Standing to indicate the interview was over, West said, 'Thank you. We may have more questions at a later date.' He handed them a card. 'Just in case something comes to you later.' He waited until the door closed behind them before turning to the others, and asking, 'What did you make of them?'

'He's a little on the obnoxious side, isn't he?' Edel said. 'I wonder exactly what it is he does for a living; he was being very vague.'

Hall agreed. 'He didn't paint a very pleasant picture of Eoin either, did he? Obviously, birds of a feather.'

Breathnach was turning out to be a very unlikeable victim, West decided. It wasn't going to make their job any easier. 'You'd better find out the name of that window company, Eamonn. The maintenance man may know it. We'll need to follow that up.' Standing, he stretched, and walked to the window. The sky was still grey and ominous but it looked as though the rain had stopped. 'We'll talk to the rest later,' he said, turning to face them, 'let's have a look around outside while we can. We need to find that murder weapon.'

Outside, the rain had indeed stopped, but huge drops falling from the eaves of the house and trees along the narrow pathway forced them to duck and dive as they walked to the pond.

They entered the clearing one at a time, West and Edel following Hall's rain-soaked back. They were almost at the pond when they heard his barely disguised gasp. West reached out to hold Edel still. 'Wait,' he said firmly and stepped past her to join Hall.

The lampreys were floating on the surface of the water, their eyes opaque, their round sucker-like mouths gaping open. It was a macabre sight, but not dangerous. Looking back to where Edel stood behind a shrub, he called out, 'It's the lampreys and it's not a pretty sight.'

She joined him, putting a hand on his arm. 'How awful,' she said, grimacing.

Hall, recovering quickly from his first impulsive reaction, said, 'We need to get one for the coroner.' And with a shudder, added, 'I bet they stink too.'

'If you ask the housekeeper, I'm sure she'll be able to give you some kind of box to put one in,' West suggested, glad he wasn't going to be the one who had to transport it. 'Meanwhile,' he said, 'let's see if we can find anything that would have served as a weapon.'

The undergrowth was lush, tangled, wet and crawling with insect life. West searched slowly, moving fronds, branches and leaves aside, disturbing the creatures living there. He dropped a branch he'd picked up back onto a teeming mass of woodlice, lifting his head when he heard Edel call his name.

'What do you think?' she said when he joined her, pointing to a stake that was standing beside, but not attached to a small sapling.

He bent to have a closer look, straightening when Hall joined them. 'I said she'd be useful,' he said with a grin. 'I think she's found our murder weapon.'

Hall moved closer to get a better look. 'It fits the size and shape we're looking for,' he agreed.

Using his phone, West took several photos before pulling a pair of latex gloves from his pocket and grabbing hold of it. It came away with little effort. 'Not much of a stake, is it?' he said. 'It should have been attached with twine or something.' Peering closely at the square, flat top of the stake, he imagined he saw skin residue, but he guessed the rain would have washed anything visible away. Microscopic evidence, however, might still be there. His eyes slid along its length and looked at the hole in the ground. 'The perp pulled it out, used it to push Breathnach into the pond and just shoved it back in. Unless he was wearing gloves, he might have left epithelial cells behind.' He smiled at Edel. 'A good find.'

'Do you have an evidence bag big enough?' he asked Hall. 'If not, we'll have to improvise.'

Casting an eye over the stake, and making a rough estimate of its size, Hall wagged his head from side to side. 'It's about four feet, I think I might.' He headed to his car, returning minutes later. 'Here you go,' he said, opening one end of the large evidence bag.

West slowly manoeuvred the stake in, holding it in place until Hall grabbed it from the outside. Then he sealed the top and breathed a sigh of relief. They'd have to wait for forensics, but he was in little doubt that they had the murder weapon. It was a huge part of any murder investigation, a giant piece of the puzzle. It didn't always lead to an arrest, but it often helped to make the picture clearer. Not just at the moment, West admitted to himself, but eventually.

Hall took it from him. 'I'll lock it into the car.'

'Are you okay?' West asked Edel when they were alone. 'You know, this isn't going to be a quick and easy case. Perhaps it would be better if you went home to Dublin.'

Edel gave him a quick peck on the cheek. 'I'm fine. Really. And no, I don't think going home to Dublin is a good idea. Unless' – she looked closely at him as if trying to read his face – 'I'm getting in the way. Taking your focus off the job?'

'No, you're not in the way,' he said, reaching out to brush a raindrop from her cheek, his fingers lingering.

Edel smiled back. 'And I did find the murder weapon, after all.'

17

When they got back to Toormore House, Linda let them in on the first ring.

'Mr Blacque has been waiting in the lounge to speak to you,' she said. With obvious reluctance, she asked if they would like some refreshments.

'That would be nice,' West said, thinking they deserved something at that stage. 'I'll have coffee and...' He looked at the others.

'Coffee would be lovely, thank you,' Edel agreed.

'For me too,' Hall said, 'thanks Linda.'

Julius Blacque turned an unhappy face their way when they opened the door into the lounge. 'I've been waiting for ages,' he said, not troubling to hide the irritation in his voice.

'Murder investigations tend to be troublesome for all concerned,' West said. 'Why don't you sit down, Mr Black, and perhaps we won't have to keep you long.'

'It's Blacque,' the man said, 'two syllables, with the emphasis on the first. Spelt B-l-a-c-q-u-e.'

West sighed. 'I apologise, Mr Blacque, and for keeping you

waiting. Why don't you take a seat? My name is Detective Garda Sergeant West; I'm in charge of the investigation. And assisting me are Garda Eamonn Hall and Edel Johnson.'

The man sat, reluctance in every muscle, his face pinched. 'I heard Eoin was murdered. Well, good luck to you finding the one person who killed him among the hundreds who would have wanted to.'

'You didn't like him.' Was there anybody who did like the dead man apart from Roger Tilsdale?

'There's a lot of hypocrisy about not speaking ill of the dead,' Blacque said. 'I've been called a lot of things in my time, but hypocrite is not one of them. Eoin Breathnach was a rude, arrogant pig, Sergeant. The world is a far better place without him. But, before you ask, I did not kill him, nor do I know who did. But I hope I get to meet him, to shake his hand and say a hearty well done to the chap.'

It was a tirade of venom that left Julius Blacque exhausted, and the three-person audience exchanging glances.

'I gather you are hoping to persuade Sylvia to have an exhibition,' West said, changing the subject.

Blacque's rather dull eyes brightened. 'Did she tell you that? She said no, but I was sure she would change her mind.'

Curious, West asked, 'Will her husband's death make it more or less likely?'

The agent threw up his hands. 'I've been wondering the same myself. On the one hand, at least he can't arrive at the gallery and embarrass her, so she might do it. But on the other hand' – he waved a hand around the room – 'she has this place to herself now; he won't be banging on her studio door interrupting her, so she might be happier here.'

'He embarrassed her?'

Blacque pursed his lips and sniffed. 'She had a gallery exhibition a couple of years back, he arrived drunk and more than usually obnoxious. In a loud boorish voice he told everyone that her success was due to him.'

'Was it?'

The agent glared at West. 'Don't be ridiculous! Her talent is her success. Okay, I'll admit his money made it easier to get her work shown at the bigger galleries in the early days, but her talent would have got her there anyway – maybe a year or so later – but it was inevitable.' A sudden thought came to him. 'Have you seen her work?'

West shook his head.

'I have,' Edel said.

'Then you will agree I'm right,' he said, looking at her for confirmation.

'Her work is mesmerising,' Edel admitted. 'I saw an exhibition a few years ago. I've never forgotten it.'

How good an artist she was, was immaterial if she were also a killer. Frowning, West asked, 'There appeared to have been no love lost between Sylvia and Breathnach. Why did she stay with him?'

'Why did she marry him in the first place?' Blacque spat out. 'He hadn't changed, you know, he was just as much a boor then. I asked her why, at the time. She was twenty-eight; he was more than twice her age, a not-very-attractive sixty.' Blacque's eyes blinked rapidly as he concentrated on answering West's question. 'She was having trouble with that idiot Finbarr at the time,' he continued. 'He was up to all sorts of shenanigans. Ten years ago, after she married Breathnach, he was moved to a strict boarding school. Kylemore Abbey, I think. That takes a lot of bucks.'

'More than she had at the time?'

Blacque shrugged.

Something struck West. The ages. 'She was twenty-eight when she married Breathnach, you said. If Finbarr had started in secondary school, he must have been fourteen at least. She can't have been more than thirteen or so when she got pregnant.'

'That's not in her biographical details,' Edel said, surprised.

'Back then, these things were hushed up. It's not like today,' Blacque said. 'She's not ashamed of it, but she wants people to concentrate on her art and not on a mistake she made a long time ago.'

'Who was the father?' West asked.

Blacque looked down his nose at West as if he'd crossed the line by asking. 'I've absolutely no idea. Some pimply boy in the town, I expect. It's not something we ever discussed.'

West wondered if this was a line worth pursuing. Maybe a blackmail angle. *Give me a gazillion euro, Mr Breathnach, or I'll tell the press what your wife and I got up to when we were just children.* Unlikely, but not impossible.

'Finbarr goes by the surname, Breathnach. Was he legally adopted?' West asked, puzzled by the relationship.

Blacque smiled unpleasantly. 'Of course, he was. Just because Sylvia is an artist, don't think she's a fool. As Eoin Breathnach's legally adopted son, Finbarr stands to inherit a tidy sum of money.'

Something else that will have to be looked into. Money; the oldest motive in the book. 'He doesn't appear to have any filial feelings. Did they ever get on?'

'No idea,' Blacque said, sounding bored. 'Finbarr was in boarding school until he was eighteen. During school holidays, he went to stay with his grandparents. In those days, Sylvia spent her time between Dublin and London where Eoin had apartments, and New York where she stayed in a hotel. They bought a house in Westport, but rarely spent time there. I think she only saw Finbarr once or twice a year. Eoin, I gathered from her, spent most of his time in the Dublin apartment, but he was often away on business. He had a lot of concerns, I think, in Thailand, and the Philippines.'

'I didn't realise he was involved in property development abroad,' West said.

'I don't know that he was,' Blacque admitted with a careless shrug, 'but Sylvia often said he was in Thailand, or in the Philippines, on business.'

Interesting, but relevant? West didn't know; he'd just file it in his head with the rest of the details.

'You said he used to bang on the studio door and interrupt her,' he asked Blacque just as the door opened and the housekeeper arrived with a tray of coffee.

Linda put it down on a side table. 'I'll leave you to help yourselves. Sylvia asked me to include some sandwiches,' she said, making sure they knew it wasn't her idea to feed the gardaí.

It was late afternoon, they hadn't had lunch, and breakfast was like a distant memory of a long-ago holiday. 'Do you mind?' West asked the agent.

Blacque sighed loudly before shaking his head. 'I could do with some coffee myself,' he said.

The sandwiches were good, the coffee excellent. Soon, refreshed, they returned to the interview. 'You were going to explain why Eoin interrupted Sylvia,' West reminded him.

'Well, obviously I don't know exactly why he did it, but he seemed to take pleasure in bothering her. It was never for anything important, you know, just some nonsense or other, or to complain about Finbarr. But Sylvia immerses herself in her work; being pulled out of it was often detrimental to the finished product. She destroyed more than one painting because of the effect it had.'

'It must have made her very angry.' Sylvia had struck West as being a rather emotionless woman; maybe he was wrong.

Blacque smiled. 'You'd think so, but no. Anger isn't something Sylvia has ever demonstrated. For an artistic person, she lacks that typical over-the-top temperament. She shows absolutely no diva tendencies, at all. Something I wish I could say about some of my other clients.' His smile faded. 'It's strange, to be honest, she becomes cooler, more distant when annoyed. Almost,' he said, 'as if she were switching off.'

'Is she capable of murder?' West asked, deciding to be blunt.

Blacque's eyes widened. 'Murder? Sylvia? Absolutely not. She hasn't a violent bone in her body.'

It didn't take violence to commit murder. Often the cool, collected type were the ones to watch, their dedicated planning and calm implementation designed to fool the unwary. Anyway, West decided, Blacque was unlikely to be objective. He had a fiscal interest in ensuring Sylvia B kept painting.

Edel must have thought the same thing. 'You mentioned other clients, Mr Blacque,' she said, drawing all eyes to her. 'But I saw you interviewed fairly recently and you said she was your only client. That makes you very much a martyr to her welfare, doesn't it?'

West smiled to himself. He couldn't have put it better. He waited for the man's reaction.

Julius Blacque drew himself up, lifting his chin. 'If you're insinuating that I would lie to prevent Sylvia being brought to brook for this heinous crime just because she's my client, then you are mistaken. When I referenced other clients, I was referring to those who purchase paintings from my gallery, not those that I represent.'

'So, she is your only client?' West asked, seeking clarification.

The man nodded stiffly. 'She is my only client.'

Then he definitely had a fiscal interest in her welfare. West drew a deep breath. He'd get Andrews to dig into the man's finances, see what was under the stones. 'How did you get on with the deceased?' he asked.

'I'd little to do with him.' Blacque shrugged. 'Usually I'm only here for a few hours. This is the first time I've stayed a few days. We all had dinner together. His conversation was dull, his manner boorish. He certainly wouldn't be someone I'd choose to spend time with. But...' He smiled without humour. 'Neither would I choose to kill him. Why would I?'

West gazed at him with narrowed eyes. Sometimes the motive wasn't obvious. There was something about the slightly sleazy Julius Blacque that got his hackles up. On the mental list of suspects in his head, his name was underlined.

18

They took a break before they interviewed the housekeeper.

West tried to put his thoughts in order. So far, he was no wiser, in fact, if anything, he was more confused. Almost everybody disliked Eoin Breathnach but there was no clear motive to kill him. But then again, it was rarely that simple.

He didn't like Julius Blacque. But that didn't make him a murderer.

'It's tiring this, isn't it?' Edel said, standing and stretching.

West smiled. 'The dull plod of police work generally is.'

'Have you heard anything of interest yet?' Hall asked, looking at him hopefully.

West looked at the optimistic eyes of the garda and shook his head. 'Just because I have more experience at this kind of thing doesn't mean I am a miracle worker, Eamonn. All that I have now, that I didn't have earlier, is more questions. The biggest one, and it's probably totally irrelevant to the case, is why did Sylvia marry Eoin Breathnach? By all accounts he wasn't a particularly likeable bloke.'

'She doesn't have an alibi,' Hall said. 'She could have pushed him into the pond; it wouldn't have required a lot of strength, especially if she'd waited until he did his putting-his-toe-into-the-water nonsense.'

'But what would her motive be?' Edel asked, looking from one to the other. 'If she was tired of him, she could just have divorced him, couldn't she? She's independently wealthy now, so he couldn't have had that hold over her.'

'Maybe she did ask for a divorce but he threatened to keep this house,' Hall suggested. 'She adores it here; there's no way she'd want to lose it.'

Edel nodded eagerly. 'Yes, she mentioned her studio being her haven, didn't she?'

'Blacque said Breathnach spent little time here. I couldn't see any divorce court awarding him the house when she could easily prove she is committed to living here,' West said, putting a damper on their excitement. 'Let's keep our minds open for the moment. I'm going to phone Andrews, give him the list of names, and see if he can tell us anything more interesting about these people. I've a feeling they're not telling us everything.'

'You won't get a signal here,' Hall warned him.

West took out his phone and checked. Hall was right. No landline, no mobile phone signal. It really was an isolated place. He'd have to ring Andrews later from the lighthouse. Thankfully, they had a good signal there.

'Let's get on with it,' he said. 'Eamonn, would you go and ask the housekeeper to come in, please?'

Hall was back within a few minutes, the housekeeper at his heel, her disapproving face letting them know exactly what she thought of the state of affairs.

'Please sit down, Mrs…' West suddenly realised he didn't know the woman's surname and cursed himself for being remiss. He waited.

'Linda is fine,' the woman said. 'I'm just the housekeeper.'

The modesty was feigned and West's intuition was sharpened. 'We'll still need your surname, I'm afraid.'

She shrugged one shoulder. 'It's Higgins.'

'Thank you, Mrs Higgins.' West did quick introductions. 'We won't keep you long; there are just a few questions we need to ask.' He met her gaze calmly. 'Can you tell us your movements yesterday, as closely as you can?'

The woman blinked. 'I was here. All day. Got the breakfast, lunch, dinner, same as usual.'

'When did you last see Mr Breathnach?'

'At breakfast. He has a full fry-up every morning... or had, I should say. He never wanted lunch. He didn't even make the effort while the Tilsdales were here. I make a pot of coffee and leave it in the dining room so people can help themselves; he usually had some of that during the morning.'

'You bring lunch into Mrs Breathnach, I believe.'

'That's right. Otherwise, she wouldn't eat. She doesn't eat breakfast at all. Just drinks coffee all morning.'

'From the pot in the dining room,' West asked, trying to get a handle on where everyone was.

The housekeeper looked at him as if he was stupid. 'Of course not. Once she goes into her studio, she never comes out until late. She has a coffee maker; I fill it in the morning before she arrives.'

'Okay,' West said. 'And what time do you bring lunch in?'

'One o'clock.'

'The same time every day.'

'Every day. She unlocks her door just before one; I bring it in and leave it on the table without disturbing her. She hates being disturbed.'

'And she locks the door after you've left?'

'I guess so. I don't ask. There's no reason for me to go back.

The tray stays there until the next morning when I go to make the coffee. I take it away then.'

West decided to switch topics. 'How did you get on with Mr Breathnach?'

'I'm the housekeeper,' the woman sniffed, 'he barely acknowledged my existence.'

'Do you know why anyone would want to kill him?'

Linda Higgins crossed her arms and took her time in answering. 'You don't get to be as wealthy as he is without making a few enemies. I'd imagine there's a few who won't be sorry he's gone.'

'Are you included in the few?' West risked asking.

'I won't have to do a fry-up in the morning. For that reason, my life will be easier,' she said with a touch of a smile on her lips.

'What about his relationship with others? His son for instance?'

'You'd have to ask him that,' she replied, playing the trusted retainer role.

'He sometimes disturbed Sylvia in her studio, didn't he?'

'You'll have to ask her about that,' she said, and this time the smile was smug.

West knew when he'd had enough. 'Okay, you can go now, Mrs Higgins. We may need to ask you more questions, at another time. Perhaps you'd be so kind as to ask your husband to come in.'

Muttering that he wouldn't tell them much, she took herself off.

It was almost twenty minutes before Jim Higgins turned up. West, annoyed at the delay, had just asked Hall to go and find him when the door opened, and he walked in. 'Sorry,' he said, and with a hangdog expression he looked genuinely apologetic. 'I was just clearing those damn lampreys out of the pool when I got your message. I had waders on, and was in the middle of the pool, so it was a bit difficult.'

'What've you done with them?' Hall asked, remembering the coroner's request.

'They're in a tank. I'm going to dump them into the sea when you're finished with me.'

'Before you do, I need to take one.'

Jim looked at Hall and tilted his head. 'You can't eat them, you know.'

Hall smiled. 'No, I don't want to eat the horrible thing; the coroner wants to have a look at one. If you could put it into some kind of box for me, that would be great.'

'I'd better make it a tightly sealed box; they're starting to smell already. It'll stink by tomorrow.'

The look on Hall's face said it all. 'It's a long journey to have a stinking passenger, do the best you can to seal it up for me, Jim.'

West, tired of lampreys, brought the conversation back to the investigation. 'Can you tell us where you were yesterday, Mr Higgins, late morning, early afternoon?'

'I know exactly,' he said. 'I saw Mr Breathnach heading out to the pool for a swim just after breakfast. I knew he'd be there about an hour so I got my equipment ready, waited for him to leave, and headed over. I drain, clean and refill the pool every month. Yesterday was my day to do it. It takes a few hours, so that's where I was when I heard Finbarr scream for help.'

At last, a timeline they could work with. 'What time did you see Mr Breathnach leave the pool?'

'Eleven thirty. I remember thinking I would get all the work done before dark and have the pool refilled for his swim the next day. I made the mistake, once, of starting too late, the pool wasn't refilled and he bawled me out about it. I didn't need to be told twice.'

West nodded. 'When Finbarr screamed you went to see what was happening?'

'I did. It wasn't a pretty sight. Those bloody fish chomping away. He should never have bought them, everyone told him so.'

'You assumed it was an accident?'

Jim Higgins shrugged. 'Murder is somewhat outside the usual run-of-the-mill stuff that happens around here. I knew about his daft habit, and assumed he'd slipped. It's the bane of my life, that moss stuff, but you've seen the trees that grow in there, they cast a fairly heavy shade. He wouldn't let me spray it, you see, in case it harmed the fish, so I had to remove it by hand.

'To be honest,' he continued, 'there's just too much to do around here to spend time scraping moss. If he'd kept his shoes on, he wouldn't have slipped.' He screwed up his nose. 'Seriously, all that sticking-his-toe-in-the-water nonsense.'

'But he didn't slip,' West reminded him, 'we've evidence he was pushed. Do you know anyone who might have had a grudge against him?'

The man gave the idea some consideration. 'A few, I suppose. He had a run-in with a few of the contractors he hired to build this place. Some of them were tough nuts. He has ongoing rows with the council about the road too. He extended the road when the house was built because the council wouldn't do it, and now the council don't see why they should maintain it. I heard him on the phone one day telling them it was his democratic right.'

West didn't consider the council to be a likely suspect. He brought the conversation back to a somewhat more likely candidate. 'The window company that Breathnach originally hired and let go. Can you remember the name?'

Higgins chewed his lower lip thoughtfully. 'I'll have it on file. I can get it for you.'

'I'd appreciate that,' West said and then, as an afterthought asked, 'How big is this place? It seems to sprawl across a huge area.'

'You'd be right,' Higgins said. 'The architect advised making it one storey, although Mr B wanted it to be two. Surprisingly enough, the architect won that battle.' He smiled at the memory. 'They'd waited until that particular architect was free to work on the place before they went ahead because they heard he was the best. Anyway, it was something to do with wind erosion or whatever and the architect threatened to pull out unless he was listened to. Mr B finally caved in but insisted he wanted the same number of bedrooms, so it sprawls right across the plot.'

'How many rooms are we talking about?' Edel asked.

'Twelve bedrooms, all with their own bathrooms, plus an apartment of sorts where me and the missus live.'

'Why on earth did he want twelve bedrooms?' West asked, genuinely puzzled. 'I gather he doesn't spend much time here, and Sylvia appears to spend most of her time in the studio.'

'No idea,' Higgins said with the air of a man who didn't bother trying to understand daft decisions. 'But, generally, Mr B didn't do things without a good reason behind it.'

19

After the door closed on Jim Higgins, it opened again.

'You are welcome to stay for dinner,' Finbarr said, standing in the doorway. 'Well actually I lie; you'd be very unwelcome guests sitting in the middle of us, wondering which of us did the evil deed. But my darling mother thinks we should be polite, and ever so helpful, so the invitation is there.'

'Thank you,' West said, 'but we're finished for the moment. We'll have more questions for you and your mother, and perhaps for the others. But tomorrow will do.'

'More questions,' Finbarr said. 'Then will you do an Agatha Christie-type reveal? Call us all into a room, explain how it was done, and expose the guilty party?'

West smiled grimly. The man really was irritating. 'Real life never tends to be quite so dramatic, I'm afraid. But,' he added, 'we'll do our best.'

Finbarr stood back to allow them to pass. 'Bye now,' he said with a little giggle. 'Oops,' he added, and put a hand over his mouth.

West cast a glance over him as he passed but said nothing. There was no sign of the housekeeper so they took their coats from the stand and left, closing the front door behind them with a collective sigh of relief.

The light was fading, but it was bright enough for West to stand a moment and look back at the building. With a shake of his head, he joined the others who had climbed into the car away from the cold sea wind.

'It must be really miserable here in the depths of winter,' Edel said, shivering a little.

'It gets pretty cold,' Hall admitted. 'But I don't think they leave the house much. At least, Sylvia doesn't. Finbarr spends some time with friends in Galway and Dublin, and I've seen him in Westport too, now and then.'

He started the car and headed out the road, turning left when they reached the turn-off for the lighthouse.

West was silent during the short journey, his head buzzing with all he'd heard. He needed to look through his notes and try to make sense of it all. He missed Andrews and realised how much he had come to depend on him. They'd have sat and chewed over the information for hours. There was Hall, of course, he'd have to work with what he had.

'You said Finbarr was only in school with you for a few months before being moved. There wasn't any indication he was in trouble of any sort, was there?'

Hall shook his head. 'I don't remember hearing anything.'

'Did you both attend the same primary school?'

Pulling up outside the lighthouse, Hall switched off the engine and turned to face West. 'No, he went to a school several miles away. I don't know why.' He frowned, and then shrugged. 'It wasn't private or anything. His gran used to drive him there and pick him up in the afternoon. We were only in the same school for three or four months, at the most. Why?' Hall asked, shuffling in his seat. 'Have you thought of something?'

Instead of answering, West asked, 'Did you notice his eyes when we were leaving?'

'His eyes?' Hall said, surprised. 'No, to be honest, I didn't really give him much attention. What did I miss?'

'His pupils were pin-pointed, and he was giggling inanely. My guess is he'd taken something.' West shrugged. 'It may be prescription meds of course, but I just wondered was there a history of drug abuse. It might have been the reason he was sent to boarding school.'

'You think he might have been on drugs back then?' Hall asked, taken aback. 'He was just a kid.'

'Ten years ago. It wouldn't have been unheard of. You've never heard rumours of drug use?'

Hall shook his head. 'Never a word.' He leaned forward to peer out the window as a strong wind buffeted the car. 'It's going to be a rough crossing,' he said, 'I'd better get going. I'll have that wooden stake sent to the forensic lab in the morning. I'll have to go into Westport to have it sent through official channels, so I won't get back here until early afternoon sometime.'

'That's fine,' West said. 'Higgins gave you the name of that window company, didn't he?'

Hall nodded. 'Yes, they're located just a few miles from Westport.'

It was a long shot, but it had to be covered. 'Why don't you call to see them while you're in the area? See if anyone holds a grudge? I'll talk to Andrews when I go inside, get him working on those names. He's not going to be able to do anything until tomorrow anyway. Ring me when you're on your way.'

Another gust of wind hit, shaking the car dramatically. West turned to speak to Edel who was wedged uncomfortably in the back seat. 'Be careful getting out,' he warned.

They made a rush for the front door, the rain-laced wind

pushing them along. 'Gosh, that's a wild one,' Edel said, shaking raindrops off in the hallway.

A laugh drew their attention. Daisy stood in the doorway of the drawing room, smiling. 'That's just a little squall,' she informed them. 'Wild is when you can barely open the door, and when you do it takes two of you to stop it being ripped off its hinges. It makes every day a challenge.'

'We East Coasters have it easy.' West smiled.

Daisy didn't move away. 'I hear you're helping Garda Hall investigate Eoin Breathnach's death.'

West took a deep breath. 'That's right.'

'He was murdered, I hear.'

'How did you hear that?' he asked, surprised how fast the news had spread.

Daisy gave a throaty laugh. 'Just because we're isolated, and half the island doesn't have phones or mobile coverage, doesn't mean news doesn't get around. Tadgh was down at the quay earlier, he met the postman... Oh yes,' she said when she saw West's surprised look, 'we have a postman. Granted, he only delivers once a week and in the winter, it can be a bit hit and miss whether he gets here or not, but we have him, and he's as good as a town crier. He was out at the house, just after you arrived there, heard the news from Finbarr and brought it with him on his deliveries, dropping off post and gossip at the same time.'

So now everyone knew, and if the killer was somewhere on the island, he was forewarned. *If* he was on the island. There was no point going down that tricky path, West knew, he'd continue the investigation the way he always did. Methodically and by the book.

. . .

Back in their room, he checked the time. It was almost seven. He'd have to phone Andrews at home.

'Peter, hi, it's Mike.'

'Mike, I wondered when you'd ring. Mother Morrison filled me in; he said you might be in touch. Honestly, trust you. You go to one of the most remote places in Ireland, and still find a dead body.'

West smiled, relieved that Andrews already knew the facts of the case, if not the truth. 'I didn't actually find a dead body,' he said. 'You make it sound as though I go out looking for them.'

'Hmmm,' Andrews replied. 'Well, go on, tell me all about it.'

West gave him a quick run-down of events including the details of the lamprey eels.

'Eels,' Andrews said, his voice an equal mix of fascination and revulsion. 'Well, that's a new one. It's definitely murder then?'

West grunted an affirmative. 'There's a fine cast of potential suspects too. I've done preliminary interviews, and I think they're all lying to some degree. Whether it has any bearing on the case, I don't know. But I need you to do some digging for me; internet access here is a bit erratic.' He read the list of names, spelling out Blacque's.

Andrews repeated them back. 'Okay, I'll see what we can find out and get back to you as soon as we have anything.' They chatted for a few minutes more before West hung up.

He grinned over at Edel. 'Peter says hello. He doesn't think much of our romantic break away.'

She laughed. 'Well, it's an unusual one, I'll give you that.'

West's eyes went soft.

She held her hands up. 'I know that look,' she said. 'Forget it, I'm starving.'

West reached for her, pulled her close and buried his nose in her hair. 'You smell so good. Okay,' he said, putting her at an arm's length, 'dinner.'

She looked down at the jeans and shirt she was wearing. 'Is it okay to go like this, d'y'think or should I change?'

West let his gaze linger on her curves. 'You look delicious.'

As it happened, they were the only ones in the dining room that evening, the other guests having left. Relieved to be spared conversation about seals or owls, they sat and relaxed. Dinner was, once again, amazing and they chatted about this and that as they ate the delicious food and drank superb wine. It wasn't until coffee was served that the conversation circled back to the day's events.

'It's going to take longer than you hoped, isn't it?' Edel asked, reaching a hand out for his.

He held it and let out a gusty sigh. 'A tragic accident, Morrison said. Well, by all accounts, it appears to have been neither tragic nor an accident. Yes, I'm afraid it's going to take a lot longer.'

'What's the next step in the investigation?'

He hesitated a moment, reluctant to turn their evening into an examination of the day's goings-on. But she looked interested, not bored or irritated, so he humoured her. 'The victim appears to have been an extremely dislikeable chap. Roger Tilsdale seems to be the only person who had any time for him. But being disliked isn't generally a motive for murder. We need to find one. We don't have enough information as yet, so we have to keep looking, and digging. Andrews may turn up something tomorrow.'

'What does your gut tell you?' Edel asked

He could see she was genuinely fascinated. She'd been involved in two cases with him before, of course, but each time had been too closely involved to have enjoyed the process. This was different. He smiled at her. 'My gut? Okay, you watch way too much television. But you're right, my gut feeling is that nobody I spoke to today was telling me the truth.' He tilted his head, reconsidering. 'No, that's not quite right. They weren't lying, as such, but they were all hiding something. Whether or not it's relevant, remains to be seen.'

'How do you know?' Edel asked. 'I read somewhere once that people look in one direction if they're lying, is that true?'

West drank some of his coffee. 'Yes, that's true. Or it can be. But it's not foolproof. I prefer to look at people's body language, the slight hesitation before they speak, the twisting of fingers, the white knuckles because they're gripping something too hard, or just a reluctance to tell us something.'

'Like Roger and his "accommodation business",' Edel said, making inverted commas in the air.

'Yes,' he said, 'and Sylvia's white-knuckle grip on the arm of her chair when we were speaking to Finbarr.'

Edel's eyes widened. 'She thinks he did it?'

'He consistently attempts to cloud the waters,' West said, 'but whether that's just his way, or the drugs he's on, or whether he did indeed kill his father, I don't know. Not yet.'

'Mr Blacque seems to think he'll inherit a lot of money.'

West's eyes narrowed. 'Breathnach was under no obligation to leave him anything. Finbarr isn't a child. They didn't appear to have any kind of father/son relationship, so why would he leave him money? Unless, of course,' he said with a frustrated groan, 'Blacque knows more about the will than he's letting on.'

Daisy opened the door. 'How about a whiskey?' she asked. 'I have a lovely smoky single malt. A sixteen-year-old Lagavulin. Tempted?'

'Yes,' they said in unison.

With a grin, Daisy left, to return moments later with the bottle in her hand. She took two small glasses from a cabinet and placed one in front of each. 'I buy Irish products mostly and

Irish whiskey too, but this is something special. It's from the Isle of Islay and, according to the distillers, it is a complex mix of seashore and moor. It seemed to me the perfect choice for here.' She opened the bottle and filled the two glasses. 'Have a taste.'

West lifted the glass and took a sip. 'Wow,' he said, truly surprised, 'smoky is right.'

Edel sipped hers. 'Goodness,' she said, 'it's delicious.'

'Why don't you join us?' West said.

Daisy smiled, fetched another glass and sat. She half-filled her glass and took a miniscule sip. 'I don't really drink,' she said, 'but I do like a bit of this now and then.'

'It's quiet tonight,' West said, wondering how successful they were.

'Sunday night often is. People come for Friday and Saturday night, and then head home on Sunday. It gives us a bit of a breather and allows us to catch up.'

'Are you full most weekends?'

'Most,' she said. 'We do close for Christmas, but that's all. We've been so lucky; people want to stay somewhere that's a bit different, a bit unique. And these days, when people are so inundated with technology, they want somewhere that doesn't have too much of it. We don't have television, for that reason.

'There'll be more competition when they open Toormore House. But perhaps that won't happen now that Eoin Breathnach has died.'

West looked at her sharply. 'He was going to open it as a hotel?'

Daisy looked at him, her brow creased in puzzlement. 'I thought you knew that. You were there yesterday, didn't someone say?'

Remembering Higgins' remark about Breathnach never doing anything without a good reason, West wondered if he'd known about the hotel idea. The man didn't appear to have been dissembling, but maybe he had his own reasons for not offering the information. Or maybe Breathnach had kept his plans quiet. 'How do you know?'

'I saw that man Tilsdale arriving, when I was down at the quay last week. I've seen his photograph in the trade magazines. That's what he does. He buys old houses and converts them into luxury or boutique hotels.'

'He said he was a friend of the deceased,' West said, taking another sip of the Lagavulin. 'He didn't mention anything about converting it into a hotel. Are you just jumping to conclusions?'

'Perhaps,' she admitted. 'But, you see, Eoin Breathnach approached me about three months ago, and asked if I'd be interested in running Toormore House in conjunction with the Clare Island Lighthouse. I told him I wasn't. I like it here; the owners give me a free hand and don't interfere in how I run the place.' Daisy's normally pleasant face became troubled. 'He didn't take too kindly to being rejected, you know. He told me that he'd other irons in the fire, and that I'd better look out.' She stopped a moment and then said quietly, 'His voice was mean and spiteful. So, when I saw Roger Tilsdale at the quay, I guessed why he was here.'

'But he still would have needed someone to run it, wouldn't he?' Edel asked.

Daisy nodded. 'It isn't as easy as people think. It's a tough job. I wouldn't do anything else but then, we're lucky. This place is something special.'

West caught Edel's eye. It was indeed special.

'Not quite the romantic break you'd hoped for though, is it?' Daisy asked.

'Not quite,' he agreed with a smile.

Daisy finished her whiskey and stood. 'If you want to go back up to the viewing platform at any time, by the way, help yourself.

We don't have anyone booked to use it until Friday. I'll leave the key on the hall table.'

A flush of colour swept up Edel's neck and cheek.

West didn't notice. He was filing away the information Daisy had contributed, trying to see where it fit, or if it did. Why was Tilsdale being so secretive? He'd have to find out. Nasty things often hid behind secrets.

Sylvia had moved to Toormore for the isolation. Against all odds and no doubt using Sylvia's fame and her connections to put pressure on the planning authority, Breathnach had obtained permission to build the house. West doubted that Sylvia knew of his plans, but with twelve en-suite bedrooms he guessed the idea to convert it to a hotel had been there from the beginning. All Breathnach needed to do was to wait a couple of years and apply for consent for change of use. West had been a solicitor; he knew the law. All Breathnach had to do was cite precedence – they'd converted the old lighthouse into a hotel, hadn't they? And that would probably have been that.

He'd deceived Sylvia. West wondered if he'd deceived her in other ways.

He lifted his preoccupied face and met Edel's questioning look. 'I think we'll head back to Toormore House in the morning,' he said.

Edel, colour still in her cheeks, had been wondering if he were planning another amorous encounter on the viewing platform, and was trying to think of a way to explain that talk of seals and owls had put her off the idea without offending him. Discovering that he'd not been thinking of her at all struck her as funny and she started to giggle, dissolving into infectious laughter when she saw his surprised look.

. . .

The laughter snared him and without knowing the reason for it he joined in, all thoughts of work driven from his head. And when she stopped for long enough to tell him what she'd found so funny, he laughed even harder. It was the perfect antidote; he didn't think of work again that evening.

20

Next morning, when they came down for breakfast, West asked for a lift to Toormore House.

'Tadgh will take you whenever you're ready,' Daisy said with her usual smile.

'After breakfast would be grand.'

She nodded and turned away, looking back as a thought crossed her mind. 'The weather's going to be very cold today, would you like to borrow some warmer jackets? We have plenty to spare.'

'I'm okay,' West said. 'We're not going to be outside much today.' He smiled at Edel. 'What about you?'

'I think I'll be fine,' she said, throwing Daisy a grateful smile.

'Well, if you need them later in the week, just ask,' she said, turning away to start breakfast.

An hour later, they headed out to the waiting car. Tadgh nodded a greeting and took off as soon as the doors were shut, rattling down the road at speed. 'I used to come out here before the house was built,' he said, taking the turn for Toormore House without slowing down.

West, who'd been in some hair-raising car chases in his day, gripped the sides of his seat and heard Edel's loud gulp from the seat behind.

Tadgh, oblivious to their reactions, carried on talking. 'I'd take a tent and set it up on the leeward side of the ruins. Tourists rarely went that far so it was a great place to be alone. At night,' he said, 'it was amazing. There were only the millions of stars to give light and the crash of the waves for music.'

Edel risked leaning forward from the back seat. 'It sounds magical.'

Tadgh turned to give her a sad smile. 'It was. Very special.' There was silence for a few minutes as the car bumped along the road. 'I went to university in Belfast,' Tadgh explained, 'and then did a diploma in tourism in Dublin. Altogether, I was away for almost five years, only getting home for the odd weekend. When I came back permanently, the house had been built. You can still set up a tent among the ruins, of course, but the house lies between them and the clifftop, spoiling the view.' Shaking his head and swerving to avoid a rabbit that sat heedlessly in the middle of the road, he added, 'They should never have got planning permission, of course. But that's money for you.'

When they reached the house, the gates were shut. Tadgh tooted but there was no answer. With a grunt of exasperation, he climbed out and went to find someone to open them.

'Money or Sylvia B's contacts?' Edel asked.

West turned to her. 'So cynical,' he said with a smile before looking back at the house. It had been well-designed, and was an attractive-looking house, but even low-lying as it was, it was an anomaly in this place where in the distance, the early morning sun glinted on the remnants of ancient stone walls still wet from the previous day's rain. 'I'd guess it was money to the right people, so a bit of both,' he said as Tadgh approached from the other side of the gate waving a key.

Moments later, he climbed into the driver's seat, handed

No Past Forgiven

West the key and drove the short distance to the front of the house. 'Just give the key to Linda, please. Jim said to leave the gate open. You want me to pick you up later?'

'We should be okay, thanks,' West replied. 'We're expecting Garda Hall to join us eventually. I've left a message with Daisy telling him where we are.' Agreeing to contact him should the need arise, they got out and headed to the front door. West waited until the car moved away and silence was restored before ringing the doorbell.

It was opened a moment later by the housekeeper, who stared at them with an assumed lack of recognition. 'Yes?' she said and stood with her hand on the door as if any moment she was likely to shut it in their faces.

'Good morning, Mrs Higgins,' West said, holding out the key.

She looked at the proffered hand and sniffed. 'That's Jim's department.'

'Well that's all right, I wanted to have another word with him anyway.'

The housekeeper's mouth tightened.

'But for the moment,' West said, keeping his voice friendly, 'I'd like to speak to Mrs Breathnach, please.'

With obvious reluctance, Linda stepped back, taking the door with her like a shield she was afraid to relinquish.

Deciding to forestall any further interaction with the less-than-hospitable housekeeper, West headed for the room they had occupied the day before. Edel threw the woman a weak smile that was not returned before following him. 'What is wrong with her?' she said quietly as they heard her footsteps fade away.

'Some people just don't like dealing with the gardaí,' West said with a shrug. 'Sometimes, it's because they've had a bad experience. Sometimes, it's because they're hiding something and we're pretty good at finding out people's secrets.'

Edel looked towards the doorway through which the housekeeper had vanished. 'I can think of another reason.'

'And what would that be?' West asked.

'She's just a bad-tempered old bat.'

West was still smiling when the door opened. Sylvia stood a moment in the doorway before moving forward, a multicoloured silk dress floating around her as she walked. 'Good morning,' she said, reaching to shake both their hands. 'Please, sit down.'

She waited until both sat before sitting herself, arms outstretched, looking just like a butterfly. Her dress definitely couldn't be described as funeral attire, in fact there wasn't the slightest air of mourning about the woman.

But people reacted differently to death. He knew that only too well, the memory of Brian Dunphy's death never far from his mind. 'We're sorry to trouble you again, Mrs Breathnach,' he said gently, deciding to give the woman the benefit of the doubt, 'but, in a murder inquiry, I'm afraid, there are always more questions to ask.'

Sylvia nodded her understanding. The gesture was almost regal and imparted a decorum on her that defied the frivolousness of her dress. And then she grinned, and the effect was lost. 'He'd have loved all the attention, you know. He always thought it was his due.'

West decided the grin allowed him to proceed without caution. 'Why did you marry him, Mrs Breathnach? If you don't mind me saying so, you didn't appear particularly suited.'

The grin widened. 'Well, you see, Sergeant West, that's where you're wrong. We were eminently suited. His money and my fame got along very well indeed.'

'By all accounts, he was a difficult man,' West said. 'He can't have been easy to live with.'

Sylvia laughed. 'He wasn't, but then neither am I. Artists tend to inhabit a rarefied world that is difficult for outsiders to understand. Are you thinking I might have killed him? Perhaps,' she admitted, 'I would have, if I'd had to live with him all the time, but we rarely spent time together, you know. Ask anyone.'

'You have fame, and your own money,' Edel asked, genuinely curious. 'Why did you need his?'

Sylvia's smile faded. 'There's a line from a movie that suits. *Fame costs*. The more famous I became, the more money I needed to spend to get away from my adoring fans. Even retiring to our home in Westport didn't help; I just couldn't get the privacy I needed. This' –she waved her arms dramatically – 'was the answer. Have you any idea how expensive it was to get planning permission? Or to build a house when everything, and I mean every little thing, had to be brought in by sea?'

'A lot,' Edel guessed, unable to estimate how much money it would cost.

'Millions,' Sylvia admitted. 'Way more than Eoin expected when he finally agreed to come here.'

'It was your idea?' West asked, surprised. Having learned of the man's aspirations, he assumed the opposite was true.

'We stayed in the Clare Island Lighthouse a few years ago,' Sylvia explained. 'Eoin stayed in front of the fire reading papers, while I explored the island on foot, walking miles every day, searching for inspiration. I found it here and painted my first seascape.' She ran a hand over her hair and smiled at the memory before shaking it away. 'It was incredibly successful, but I found more than inspiration here, I found the isolation I craved. I wanted to stay here.' Her smile faded and her face became hard. 'So, I made it happen.'

So, I made it happen. Was she being stupid or arrogant, West wondered, thinking that perhaps he'd been wrong, that maybe she and Breathnach were very well suited indeed.

'Was turning Toormore House into a hotel also your idea?' he asked bluntly, watching her reaction closely.

If he expected drama, he was disappointed. 'No, it wasn't but there was no question of that happening,' she said calmly.

'But Eoin *was* looking into the idea?' West persisted.

'He could look into it all he liked but believe me it was never going to happen.'

There was no hint of doubt in her voice but thanks to Daisy, West had more information. 'Did you know he'd approached the manager of the Clare Island Lighthouse and asked her if she'd run it?'

Sylvia shook her head but made no comment.

'Roger Tilsdale' – West hammered in the final nail – 'that's what he does. He converts stately homes, and the like, into boutique hotels. But you still maintain you knew nothing about these plans?'

'Sergeant West, believe me,' Sylvia said firmly, 'Eoin could plan until the cows came home, and often did, but there was no way he was ever going to turn Toormore House into a hotel.'

'So you keep saying. But what was to stop him?' West asked.

She looked at him without answering.

'Is the house in your name?' Edel asked.

Sylvia slowly turned her head to look at her. 'As it happens, it's not, but that doesn't make any difference to what I said.'

'Who owns Toormore House now?' Edel pushed.

'The will has yet to be read,' she said with an elegant shrug that sent a ripple down the silk of her dress. 'You will remember, Eoin only died the day before yesterday.'

West saw something in the woman's face, a certain knowledge. 'But you know what it says, don't you?' he ventured. The silence stretched uncomfortably long. West, impressed by Edel's astute questions, hoped she wouldn't spoil it by jumping in with another. He needn't have worried; Edel sat tight, watching the play of emotions on the woman's face.

Finally, with a sigh that said she admitted defeat, she said, 'He's left his estate, apart from a few minor bequests, to me and Finbarr. This house, as you've guessed, will be mine.'

'Does Finbarr know?'

Sylvia shook her head. 'Definitely not. He and Eoin didn't get on, as you may have guessed, so I doubt if he has any expectations.'

West would have thought the same. The will was generous to the young man, and he wondered why.

Sylvia obviously felt the situation needed explaining. 'Eoin liked the idea of having a son, that's why he adopted Finbarr. He wanted to have a son to carry on his name.'

West would have liked to ask why they didn't have children of their own, but that was straying too far over the line marked invasive curiosity, so he didn't. As it turned out, he didn't need to.

'Did he never want children of his own?' Edel asked.

Sylvia's face hardened. For a moment, they didn't think she was going to answer, but then, through tight lips, she said, 'Finbarr's was a difficult birth. There were complications. The doctors told me they had no choice, they had to do a hysterectomy.'

Colour flushed Edel's face. 'I'm so sorry,' she mumbled, 'I had no right to ask.'

'If that's all the questions you have,' Sylvia said, ignoring her, 'I'd like to get back to my studio. Perhaps you'll see yourselves out.'

'We'd like to speak to Finbarr again,' West said quickly.

She turned, a sudden anxious look on her face. 'He doesn't know about me, about the hysterectomy.'

'That's not something we need to discuss. Ever.'

Sylvia stood a moment, her eyes fixed on his and, as if what she saw reassured her, she nodded, and opened the door. 'I need to get back to my studio, I'll have Linda send him to you,' she said without turning around.

West's eyes flicked to where Edel sat, colour still flying in her cheeks. He hadn't asked the question; but he would have found out anyway. This is what he did for a living, after all, constantly intruding into people's private lives to find out and pick through their secrets.

He guessed she didn't think his job was quite so glamorous anymore.

21

They waited about fifteen minutes in an uneasy silence before the door opened again. Whether the delay was caused by Linda's inability to find Finbarr, or her reluctance to help, West wasn't sure. Her attitude was beginning to irritate. He wondered what she hoped to gain by it.

Putting the housekeeper's manner aside for the moment, he took a hard look at the young man who slouched in the door. It was difficult to believe he and Garda Hall were the same age; Hall showed maturity and a level of authority, whereas Finbarr Breathnach was the epitome of the spoilt wastrel that he possibly was.

Possibly. West tried to put aside any preconceptions; an open mind was a better sponge than a closed one.

Finbarr dropped into the same seat his mother had vacated not long before. Long legs clad in tightly-fitting black jeans, stretched out before him, a black shirt hung loosely each side of his too-thin frame. His lips, girlishly red, were stretched in an unamused grin as he looked first at West and then, appreciatively, at Edel. 'What've you done with my pal, Eamonn?' he said.

'Garda Hall is following up some leads; he'll be joining us later. We've a few questions we'd like to ask you.'

Finbarr yawned. 'Okay, fire ahead. I'll try to be entertaining with my answers.'

'Why did you take Breathnach's name when he and your mother married?'

If Finbarr was surprised by the question, he hid it well. Yawning again, he waved a hand in apology before answering. 'Sylvia insisted,' he said.

Sylvia, not Eoin. She'd lied. Or Finbarr was lying.

'Do you know who your biological father is?'

Finbarr held the smile in place, but his eyes grew hard. 'I assume you have your reasons for delving into such things; it might be interesting to know what they are.' He waited a moment, and when West remained silent, sighed heavily. 'It was some boy. I don't think his name was ever mentioned. Certainly, she never told me. Perhaps, if I didn't look so much like her, I might have been curious, but as it stands, I'm almost a clone of her, aren't I?'

It was pretty much what West had thought when he'd seen them both together. Whoever had sired Finbarr had left little to show for it. He nodded in acknowledgement of the man's comment before moving on. 'Were you aware of Eoin's plans for converting Toormore House into a hotel?'

'Yes,' Finbarr said to his surprise.

'How did you find out?'

'My father rarely did anything without an ulterior motive,' he said, echoing what Jim Higgins had already told them. 'When he invited the Tilsdales here, I knew there was something going on so... and you'll be impressed with this,' he added with a glint in his eye, 'I did some investigative work.'

'You researched them?' West asked.

Finbarr shook his head. 'No internet access here, I'm afraid, I had to do it the old-fashioned way. So much more fun, really. I waited until they were in the middle of dinner and made my excuses. Their room wasn't locked, of course, so it didn't take a lot of ingenuity to poke around and find what I was looking for.'

'And what exactly was that?'

Finbarr's smile faded. 'Plans. Detailed plans to turn the house into one of those boutique-type hotels. Mum's studio, with its stunning view, was going to be the central lounge. It would have broken her heart.'

'She's adamant it would never have happened,' West said.

'We wouldn't have let it happen,' Finbarr said, careless of the consequence of his words. 'Painting is her life. That studio is her sanctuary, her inspiration and her solace.'

'But it won't happen now, will it?'

'Have I just provided myself with a motive to kill my father?' Finbarr said, amused. 'How silly of me.'

West wasn't the slightest bit amused. Nor did he think the young man was silly; he did, however, think he was a clever bastard. 'Did you tell anyone about what you found?'

Finbarr looked at him, the amused grin still playing about his lips. 'Well, actually, yes. I told Julius. He was horrified.' The amused grin grew. 'Oh dear, is that someone else I've provided with a motive. How careless of me, and how difficult I'm making it for you.'

'You certainly have a knack for muddying the waters, Mr Breathnach. The question is, of course, why you would want to do that?'

The only answer was the lazy shrug of one shoulder.

West, tired of the man's game, brought the interview to a halt. 'I've no more questions at the moment, thank you. You can return to whatever it was you were doing. Perhaps you could tell me where I might find Mr Blacque?'

'He's in the library,' Finbarr said, getting to his feet. 'I'll tell him you're looking for him.' At the door, he stopped and turned back with a smirk that made him look almost demonic. 'Perhaps he'll make a run for it, now wouldn't that be fun?'

As his footsteps faded away, Edel glanced at West. 'I don't know what to make of him. Do you think he did it?'

West let out a heavy breath. 'I don't know. He seems fond of his mother. He might have killed Breathnach to stop the hotel business, but she seemed quite sure it wasn't going to go ahead anyway.'

'They all seem pretty sure about that,' Edel said.

West rubbed a hand over his face. 'Finbarr's "we wouldn't have let it happen" was a careless throwaway comment with no weight behind it. But Sylvia was very adamant the hotel wasn't going to go ahead. She refused to tell us why, which beggars the question why she was so sure.'

'Because she planned to get rid of him?'

'Get rid of him?' he repeated, looking at her with a crooked smile. 'That's rather sanitising what happened to the poor man.'

Edel shrugged. 'He didn't sound like a particularly nice man.'

He had to admit she was right; Breathnach didn't. But that wasn't a motive to kill him.

'Do you think stopping the hotel business was the motive?' Edel asked him, just as West was thinking the same thing.

He tilted his head, side to side. 'People kill for a variety of reasons. The motive can be something as stupid as *he looked at me funny*. People kill because they can. Often the motive doesn't make sense. But...' His brow furrowed. 'It was the way he was killed here that puzzles me. It was cold-blooded and determined. Whoever killed him would have had to hit his fingers hard to prevent him climbing out, would probably have looked him in the eye while he was doing so. That strikes me as needing a lot of hate. The hotel business just doesn't seem like something that would generate that level of emotion.'

Just then the door opened and Julius Blacque stood there, looking none too happy at being summoned once again. 'What more can I possibly tell you?' he said from the doorway.

West took a deep breath. 'Please come in and sit down, Mr Blacque.' He waited until, with a huff of irritation, the man moved from the doorway and perched on the side of the chair, as if to say he didn't intend to stay long.

'Did Finbarr tell you about Breathnach's idea to convert Toormore into a hotel and the plans he found in Roger Tilsdale's room?'

Blacque looked from one to the other; his eyes narrowed. 'He might have done.'

'Did he or didn't he, Mr Blacque?' West said sharply, tired of their attempts to avoid telling the truth.

Blacque crossed one knee over the other. 'Yes, he told me. What of it?'

'Were you surprised?'

Blacque laughed uneasily. 'Nothing Breathnach did surprised me. But, if you pardon me saying, I know Sylvia better than you, she'd never have permitted the plans to go ahead.'

'Even though the house was in his name?' Edel asked.

Blacque shrugged. 'Whatever Sylvia wanted, Breathnach did. That's all I know.'

'Did she mention it to you?' West asked, wondering if Sylvia had told them the truth.

Blacque frowned in concentration, and then shook his head. 'No, I don't remember her doing so. Finbarr only did so in a sneering comment about Tilsdale. I don't think he thought it would go ahead either.'

West frowned as Blacque left the room. He had hoped Eoin Breathnach's idea of converting the house into a hotel would be a motive for his murder, but it was proving more and more unlikely. He had a feeling that a chat with Roger Tilsdale would finish the idea off.

The Tilsdales were found in another lounge reading the papers and enjoying a coffee. They looked up with a welcoming smile when West and Edel appeared. 'We heard you were here,' Roger said with the enthusiasm of one for whom three-day-old newspapers held little allure. 'Bringing us some news from the outside world, are you? I don't know how they survive here. No television, barely a radio signal and newspapers that are past their sell-by date by the time we get them. Unbelievable.'

The room was larger, cosier than the more formal room they'd been in. The well-worn furniture hinted that it was the room usually used by the family. Turning towards the window, West could understand why. It overlooked the sea, the view dramatic. He guessed it was the same view Sylvia had from her studio; suddenly, he could fully understand why she needed it.

They took a seat opposite the Tilsdales, sinking into a comfortable two-seater sofa overloaded with cushions.

'A few things have arisen during our investigation that we need to clear up,' West said.

The Tilsdales were united in presenting a blank appearance.

'Your accommodation business,' West said pointedly. 'It appears it is more to do with buying stately homes and converting them into boutique hotels, is that correct?'

'Stately homes, old schools, old churches. A wide crosssection of buildings convert nicely into upmarket small hotels,' Roger explained without hesitation.

'Is that why you were here? To convert Toormore House?'

Tilsdale laughed, his belly wobbling. He took out a folded handkerchief and dabbed his eyes before answering. 'Oh dear, Sergeant West, wherever did you get that idea? I told you why we were here. Eoin invited us. We were friends. I will admit,' he said, 'Eoin did mention the idea, he'd even gone to the trouble of having plans drawn up and sent to me but my response was the same. I laughed. He quickly gave up the notion, if he'd ever seriously entertained it, when I explained why.'

'And why is that exactly?' Edel asked. 'Clare Island Lighthouse does extremely well, why wouldn't a hotel here?'

'Internet access for one,' Tilsdale replied. 'There isn't any this side of the island and bringing it would be prohibitively expensive, and even then, it would probably be unreliable. People who visit upmarket boutique hotels want to get away from it all, but not that far. Plus, and more importantly, this area is more exposed than where the lighthouse is; there's a problem with erosion. They should have built the house much further back than they did. It seems that's what the architect advised, but Sylvia insisted it be built where it is. I would be more than reluctant to invest money in a hotel that may not be here in twenty or thirty years.'

So that was it. West's idea for a motive was finally and most definitely shot down.

'Are you disappointed?' Edel asked when they returned to the other lounge.

West smiled. 'Only in the hope that I could settle this quickly. It often happens this way, you know. We follow crumb trails for days or weeks only to find they lead nowhere. Sometimes, one trail will intersect with another and we follow both for a while. It's all part of the job.'

'So, what now?' she asked.

West was wondering the same himself. One trail had dead-ended. Problem was, there didn't appear to be another. Just a few scattered crumbs. Standing, he took her hand. 'Let's get a lift back to the hotel and see if Andrews has come up with anything. I'm sure Higgins wouldn't mind dropping us back.'

22

Jim Higgins was found out in his workshop. He looked up when West and Edel blocked his light, putting down the secateurs he'd been sharpening. 'You want me?'

'We were wondering if you could drop us back,' West asked. 'We could wait until Garda Hall arrives, but that could be hours yet.'

Higgins wiped the oil from his hands with a rag that hung from a nail. 'Happy to,' he said. 'To be honest, you put the missus in bad form when you're here, and when she's in bad form it makes my life hell, so I'd be happy to drive you away.'

Taken aback, West asked, 'Why doesn't she like the gardaí?'

Higgins reached for car keys that hung on another nail and indicated with a nod that they precede him down the narrow path to the garage. It wasn't until they were sitting in the car that he answered West's question. 'It's not the gardaí she dislikes; she likes young Eamonn, right enough. No, she just dislikes you Dubs.' Whether he shared his wife's sentiments, he didn't say. There was no further conversation, he hummed as he drove and pulled up outside the lighthouse.

'Thanks,' West said, getting out.

The car pulled away immediately. 'She dislikes us because we're from Dublin,' Edel said, staring after it. 'Honestly, how ridiculous. I was right; she's just a grumpy old bat.'

West put an arm around her shoulder. 'We can't arrest her for that, unfortunately.'

They walked into the lighthouse. Looking into the lounge, they saw the fire had been lit. 'I'll go and get some tea while you're ringing Peter,' Edel said. 'Would you like something to eat?'

'A sandwich would be great,' West said, and sitting down in front of the crackling fire, he took out his mobile. He noticed a few missed calls, all from Andrews. Hoping he had some encouraging news; he pressed the speed-dial button.

Andrews answered immediately. 'Where've you been?' he complained.

'Sorry, I decided to go back to Toormore this morning, follow up something.'

'And?' Andrews asked. 'Any luck?'

West grunted and explained his morning's pursuits. 'Just a dead end,' he said.

'Yes,' Andrews agreed, 'I had a word with the powers that be in town planning. No application was made for a change of use. So that fits with what you've said.'

West stretched his legs out, feeling the heat of the fire and wishing he could just sit there with Edel, maybe drink some more of that Lagavulin and forget about the outside world. But that wasn't going to happen. 'Tell me you learned something useful,' he said. 'I've run out of ideas.'

The phone crackled loudly. 'Hello?'

'I can hear you, Peter, go ahead.'

'Sorry, the line went funny for a moment. Anyway, I did some digging on the names you gave. Some interesting facts came out. Eoin Breathnach was worth, by the least computation, twenty million euro. Most of that is in property, with an apartment in London, one in New York, and a villa in Portugal being the most valuable of what he owns. He also has shares in hotels in a few countries, all of which are doing well and adding to his coffers on a weekly basis. There's no record of any criminal activity, but you know better than I do that that doesn't mean there wasn't any. But that's all – so far. Seamus is working on it; he has a few leads yet to follow.

'The info on the young lad, Finbarr, is more interesting. You asked me to check his record. There was one. A sealed, juvenile record. I did some digging, rang a mate who works in Galway who contacted a friend who works in Westport who...'

West interrupted him. 'Peter, I'm already lost. Just tell me what you found out.'

'Fine,' Andrews said, unperturbed. 'It seems your Finbarr was caught selling cannabis in the playground of his primary school. He was kicked out. He was sent to a different primary school, further away, and later he started in the secondary school in Westport. A few months later, he started in Kylemore Abbey. Following school, he came to Dublin, to UCD, but dropped out after a year. I spoke to someone there who remembers him well, mainly because of who his mother was, of course. Anyway, he didn't drop out really, he was pushed.'

'Drugs,' West guessed.

'Yep,' Andrews confirmed. 'Just using though, no hint that he was dealing so it never led to a conviction. And the same thing in the College of Art and Design. He was told to leave after several warnings.'

'No convictions?'

'Not one.'

'I did think he was on something yesterday when we were leaving. He was all giggly and his pupils were pin-pointed.'

'Maybe Eoin Breathnach found out and threatened him?' Andrews suggested.

West wasn't convinced. 'I don't know, Peter, from all accounts he and Finbarr weren't close. Why would he care if the lad was using?'

'Maybe the mother cared. You said they were close. Maybe she asked Breathnach to have a word with the boy, and things went wrong.'

'This wasn't spur of the moment, this took some planning. And a lot of hate. I got the impression Finbarr didn't care for the man, but not that he hated him. Breathnach didn't spend that long in Toormore, just a few weeks now and then.'

'On that note, I did as you asked, or to be correct, Sam Jarvis did. Breathnach spent approximately three months in Ireland in the last year. The rest of his time was divided between his London apartment and the villa in Portugal, with one trip to New York and several weeks spent in Thailand.'

'Three months in Ireland; were they all spent on Clare Island?'

'Impossible to say.'

West remembered something Sylvia had said. 'The wife said he didn't spend long here, so possibly not.'

'You're thinking that rules out someone from outside your cast of characters?'

West smiled. Andrews could read his mind even at a distance. 'I wish you were here for this, Peter. Yes, I think it is closer to home. You had to have seen it, Peter, it was pretty horrific. Someone really hated the poor bastard. By all accounts, he wasn't a very likeable man, but this was something more.'

'Well, we'll keep digging our end, Mike. Maybe we'll turn up something more pertinent.'

'Fine,' West said. He was about to hang up when Andrews spoke again.

'By the way, we've had a forensic psychiatrist's report on Ella Parsons.'

'Already! That was quick work.'

'Her husband wanted it done as soon as possible.'

'And?' Although West didn't really have to ask, he'd known from the beginning how this was going to fall.

'The report states she's currently unfit to plead.'

Just as West had expected. 'And I suppose she's been discharged from the clinic?'

'Yes, the same afternoon,' Andrews said. 'We can have the state psychiatrist see her but that's going to take a few weeks to organise.'

'We'll have to follow due process; it's never speedy.' West tried not to think of the frustrating and time-consuming series of reports that would possibly go backwards and forwards for years.

Hanging up, he put Ella Parsons out of his head, drummed his fingers on the table and thought about Finbarr. He didn't think his drug habit fitted into the equation anywhere. Nor could he imagine Sylvia requesting her husband's help in sorting him out. Maybe she hoped being on Clare Island would isolate him; keep him away from his source. It didn't seem to be working. West wondered where he was getting it. There was a time when it was only the cities where drugs were freely available. Unfortunately, as he knew only too well, that time had long gone. There were no doubt drugs available in Westport, especially if you had money. He'd have to ask Garda Hall when he arrived.

It was Edel who arrived first, followed by Daisy holding a large tray. She set it down on a table beside the window and offloaded a pot of tea and a plate of sandwiches. Setting out cups and saucers, she added a jug of milk and a sugar bowl before leaving with a final request that they tell her if they needed more of anything. Edel put down the plate of cake she'd carried in and they looked across the table at each other and grinned.

'This is almost normal,' she said with a laugh.

West agreed. 'Definitely more along the lines of what I had planned.'

'You get through to Peter?' she asked, pouring the tea.

West took the cup and saucer she held out to him and nodded. 'Yes, he says hello, by the way. He's envious, would you believe it, says it will go down in the records as being the weirdest murder ever. They've been looking lamprey eels up on the net, him and the lads, and studying photos of them.'

Edel smiled. 'He's a nice man. It's a shame he's not here. You two make a good team.'

West, who'd been thinking the same thing, said nothing. Instead he reached for a sandwich. They were good; fresh crusty bread and roast chicken. 'We'll never eat all these,' he said, finishing one and reaching for another. He was wrong and soon the plate was empty. Neither was tempted by the cake, so they sat back, relaxed and finished their tea.

'I'd like to come back here again someday,' Edel said.

'Despite everything?'

She smiled. 'There aren't going to be dead bodies everywhere we go, are there?'

He reached across the table and caught her hand. 'No dead bodies, drug barons, blackmailers, or anything else will spoil our next holiday, I promise.'

Edel gripped his hand. 'This holiday hasn't been spoilt, Mike. It's not what I expected, true, but we're together, and I'd be lying if I didn't say I'm finding it a little fascinating.'

They were still holding hands a few minutes later when Garda Hall walked into the room. He stopped in the doorway, looking a little embarrassed at interrupting what had all the marks of a romantic moment.

He went to back away but was stopped by West's wave.

'I can come back when you've finished lunch,' he said apologetically.

West shook his head. 'That's okay, we're done. Sit down. Have a cup of tea if you want, I think there's still some in the pot, and I'll fill you in on the morning we've had.'

Hall sipped the almost cold tea while West took him through the information he had learned from Daisy and their resultant interviews with the people at Toormore House.

'Garda Andrews put the final nail in the coffin of that idea when he found out that no change of use application had been made. He also found some information for us on Finbarr.' West quickly summarised the other man's drug history.

'You were right,' Hall said, looking at him with admiration.

'It's not getting us any nearer to finding Eoin Breathnach's killer though, is it?' West said. 'I hope you have some news from the window company to cheer us up.'

Hall smiled ruefully. 'Well I have, and I haven't,' he said, putting his cup down. 'I did an internet search for the company but, unfortunately, it folded last year. There weren't any details, so I decided to visit the industrial estate where it had been to see if I could learn anything. The office next door to it was open and they were happy to tell me.' He stopped a moment and when he continued, he spoke more quietly. 'Losing the contract with Toormore broke them. They couldn't absorb the loss and had to close down shortly afterward. There were eighteen people working there, they all lost their jobs.'

'What happened to the owner?'

Hall drew a deep breath, threw a sideways glance at Edel and wiped a hand over his face. 'He...' – a loud exhale – 'hung himself.'

'Damn! Had he a family?'

'A wife and three children. The man I spoke to said she was

racked with grief. Doubly so, it seems, because she was the one who heard about the job and encouraged him to put in a quote. She'd heard about it from her sister.'

Hall pressed his lips together as if unwilling to go on and then sighed, a long, low hiss of regret. 'Linda Higgins.'

23

Nobody spoke for a few minutes, each of them digesting the information. It wouldn't have taken much strength to push Eoin Breathnach into the pond, nor to bash his fingers to prevent him getting out. A woman fired with rage could have done it. And Linda Higgins would certainly have hated the man who'd caused her sister such grief. It fitted. Motive and opportunity. Now they just needed proof or a confession, or preferably, both.

'Okay,' West said. 'Good work, Eamonn. Let's go and see what the lady has to say for herself, eh? We'll get a DNA sample too and send it to Dublin. If she handled that stake with bare hands, she may have left trace epithelials.'

'You really think it could be her?' Edel asked.

West and Hall exchanged glances. 'It could be,' West said at last, 'but we'll continue to keep an open mind. Let's see what she has to say for herself. So far we only have supposition.'

'She kept it all quiet. Did she think you wouldn't look into it?' Edel said.

'Not every garda is as efficient as Sergeant West,' Hall said with an admiring glance toward the older man. 'I wouldn't have thought that something that happened almost two years ago would have been relevant.'

'Revenge is a dish best served cold, isn't that the saying?' Edel remarked. 'She bided her time until she was ready. Maybe she thought, like you, that two years was long enough to put people off the scent.'

West frowned. 'Let's not get carried away, please. This is still just supposition. We need a lot more before we can go accusing the woman.'

Edel shot Hall a sideways look and winked. He smiled and they headed out to his car.

For a change, the gates to Toormore House were open. They drove straight through and parked near the front door. It was early afternoon, but the light was already fading, the sky behind the house streaked with the orange of the setting sun.

'The Higgins' have an apartment around the side,' West said, indicating a path that curved around the house. They followed it, passing the beautifully draped windows of Toormore House until they rounded a bend and came to a plain front door with a net-curtained window to one side. There was no knocker or doorbell. West rapped lightly with his knuckles. When there was no answer, he knocked again, a little harder. This time, they heard the faint sound of footsteps approaching, and the rattle as a key was turned in the lock.

It was Jim Higgins, his face a mask of puzzlement. 'You back again? Why didn't you knock on the main door?'

'We want to speak to your wife,' West explained. 'May we come in?'

'She won't be happy about that,' the man said, shaking his head, a grim expression on his face.

'Unfortunately, Mr Higgins, we do need to speak to her. May I remind you; we are investigating a murder? In fact, we've a couple of questions for you too.'

Jim Higgins stared at him, grunted and stood back to allow them in. He directed them to a small, comfortable room dominated by a TV. The shelves on either side held a collection of movies. Crime movies mostly, West noticed, peering at the titles.

'You didn't tell us of your connection to the window company, Mr Higgins, why was that?'

Higgins poked a finger through a hole in the fabric of his flannel shirt and scratched his chest. 'It's not something we speak about. It happened. It's done. What's the point in dragging it up and causing more grief?'

West gave him a sharp look. 'Your wife's brother-in-law committed suicide because Eoin Breathnach withdrew his business. Now he is dead, and you didn't think the connection worth mentioning?'

The man drew back, eyes wide. 'Now hang on just a minute! You can't think Linda had anything to do with his murder. That's ridiculous.'

'Is it?' West asked softly.

Jim Higgins ran a hand through his hair. 'Of course, it is. She didn't like the man, but she wouldn't have murdered him. Murder. For goodness sake.'

'Perhaps we should talk to her.'

'She's in the house,' he said. 'I'll go fetch her. We have a connecting door for convenience.'

Just then they heard a door opening and the tap of quick footsteps along the hallway. Linda appeared, her eyes searching for her husband's. 'I saw your car from the bedroom window,' she said, turning to West. 'I waited for you to ring the front doorbell. When you didn't, when you came straight here, I guessed you'd discovered about my brother-in-law.' As she saw the truth on their faces, she turned a sickly shade and reached a trembling hand out to steady herself.

'Why don't we sit down?' Edel said gently.

Surprised by her unexpected sympathy for a woman who'd only ever been rude to them, West watched Edel reach for the woman's hand and lead her to a chair.

There was a bit of fuss as they all tried to find seats in the small room. It relieved some of the tension, and colour had returned to Linda's face by the time they were all seated. 'We don't speak about it, at all,' she said quietly. 'Never have done. Jemma, my sister, is barely holding it together.' Her eyes met West's. 'She never held it against me, you know, never once said if it weren't for me, Dave would still be alive.' She sniffed. 'She doesn't have to. I've felt guilty every day since.' She smiled sadly at her husband. 'Jim tells me I'm being silly, and he's right, I suppose. I told Jemma about the job with the best intentions. But' – she bit her lip – 'Breathnach was a nasty piece of work. I knew what he was like, had seen his dealings over the years. I should have known better than to get involved, to have encouraged Dave to have anything to do with him.' She stopped and pinched the bridge of her nose. Her voice under control again, she continued. 'But business was slow, and it was a big contract. Windows,' she said with a shake of her head, 'you'd think it couldn't go wrong.'

'But then it did,' West said.

Linda nodded. 'A hiccup. They were made double-glazed, not triple. It was just a hiccup, easily remedied. But Breathnach blew a gasket and cancelled the contract. Dave tried everything, offered him a discount, then a bigger discount. Breathnach laughed in his face. Kept saying he was a one-strike kind of man. He took pride in saying it. As if that made it all okay.'

'Couldn't you have asked Sylvia to intercede?' Edel asked.

Linda sighed. 'She was away. In New York, I think. She didn't move here until it was all done, and never knew about the fuss. A couple of weeks later, a company from Dublin came and installed the triple-glazed windows. They laughed when they heard about the previous company's mistake. Laughed,' she repeated grimly.

Edel and West exchanged a glance. Now they understood her dislike of Dubs.

An air of sadness settled over the room. The light was almost gone outside, but no one moved to switch a lamp on and they sat in increasing darkness. The room was becoming chilly too, a set but unlit fire beckoning vainly for a match.

'Why did you wait until now to kill him?' West asked gently.

Linda lifted her chin with a jerk that disturbed an unshed tear. It ran down her cheek and plopped onto her shirt. 'You have no idea how happy I am that he is dead, and that he died in such a horrible way. It seemed fitting, somehow. But I didn't do it.'

West looked at her closely. 'You had motive, means and opportunity, Mrs Higgins.'

'Yes, I had,' she acknowledged, 'but I didn't kill him. Why would I have waited two years? I had means, motive and opportunity any time he was here. Every time he was here. Why wait? If I didn't kill him when Jemma found Dave's body hanging in their garage, when the grief and guilt were an all-consuming agony, I wouldn't have killed him now when they've receded to a constant ache.'

Remembering the sight of Breathnach's body, the lampreys sucking the life out of him, West knew the killer was filled with rage, anger, hate. Not a constant ache.

'You do believe me, don't you?' she asked.

West met her eyes. Yes, he did. 'If we can take a DNA sample, we can send it off and that should help settle the matter.'

Linda gripped her husband's hand and nodded.

'Garda Hall will take the sample,' he said, getting to his feet. 'We may have more questions, of course.' With a final nod, he took his leave of them, Edel following close behind.

'She didn't kill him, did she?' Edel said as they made their way back to the car.

'No, I don't think she did.'

'I'm not sure I'd have blamed her if she had,' Edel said, climbing into the back of the car. 'What a horrible man Breathnach is proving to be.'

'Chaos,' he said, turning to look at her. Seeing her puzzled face, he smiled. 'It's what would happen if everyone decided to kill horrible people.'

He turned back to look out the windscreen only half-listening to her muttered justification for murder. No, he didn't think Linda was guilty, but it was the second trail that had run cold.

24

'But you do think Linda's telling the truth, don't you?' Edel asked, Lagavulin in hand, her feet stretched toward the fire.

West took a sip of his whiskey. 'Yes, but it will be better to have proof of her innocence. Hall will send her DNA off to Dublin. If they find something on the stake, they'll be able to compare it.'

'The killer might have worn gloves.'

West grinned at her. 'Yes, Garda Johnson, the killer may indeed have worn gloves.' His grin faded. 'If the lab does find some trace, we'll have to get DNA samples from everyone.'

'Higgins' will already be on it, won't it?' she asked. 'He planted the trees, so he'll have handled the stake.'

'True,' West muttered. The whiskey and the glowing embers had succeeded in lulling him into a state of relaxation where Eoin Breathnach's death was a fading irritation.

'So, what next?' Edel asked, finishing her glass.

West finished his and stood. 'Next job,' he said huskily, 'is reminding you that I'm not just a guard.'

It was good to keep reminding her, he thought, over an hour

later, her warm body curled up beside him. 'You have me bewitched, Edel Johnson,' he whispered into her hair, his lips curving into a smile as he heard her sleepy chuckle.

∼

Breakfast was, as usual, delicious. Edel ordered eggs Benedict, and West, with a comment about all the exercise he'd had the previous day giving him an appetite, ordered a full Irish.

'What happens now?' she asked, putting her knife and fork down on the empty plate. 'That was divine, by the way, you should have it tomorrow.'

West speared his last piece of sausage and popped it in his mouth. 'We'll wait and see if Andrews has turned up anything of interest. He has Seamus Baxter working on it, if anyone can find anything it's Seamus.'

'Will we be returning to Toormore House?'

West looked at her over the rim of his cup. 'That sounds like a loaded question to me. Why do you ask?'

'It was, I suppose. It's just that having seen some of Sylvia's paintings, I'd love to see around her studio, and maybe have a peek at what she's working on now. Do you think it would be okay to ask? Or totally inappropriate considering the circumstances?'

West gave her question some thought. It wasn't as if Sylvia was consumed with grief, after all. 'There's no harm in asking,' he decided, finally.

Daisy came over to clear away their plates, accepting their compliments with a gentle smile. 'More coffee?' she asked. Both declined. The empty plates balanced in one hand, Daisy hesitated and looked at West. 'Do you mind me asking?' she said, 'Did you find out was there any truth in the plans to convert Toormore into a hotel?' She shrugged. 'I'll understand if you can't tell me, it would just put my mind at ease. I know competition isn't necessarily a bad thing, but we could do without the stress to be honest.'

West understood her concern. He didn't think it would hurt to let her know. After all, if she asked at the planning office, they'd tell her the same. 'There appears to be no truth in it at all, Daisy.'

When he saw the woman visibly relax, he realised it was worrying her more than she had admitted, so he decided to go further. 'In fact,' he said, 'I spoke to Roger Tilsdale and he thinks the site is unsuitable for a high-end hotel. Something to do with lack of internet access.' He didn't mention Tilsdale's concerns about erosion, it wasn't necessary.

Daisy nodded. 'We didn't have access initially. We thought people would like to get away from it all. It turns out that people are quite happy not to have television, but not so happy about the lack of internet. It wasn't difficult for us though, there are several homes on this part of the island, but Toormore is just too far away.' With that, she smiled and headed away with the plates.

West finished his coffee and suggested they go for a walk. 'Andrews will ring eventually, but until he does, we have nothing to do. Let's get some fresh air.'

His mobile rang just as they were about to leave. It was Hall. 'I've sent the sample Linda gave us to Dublin,' he said. 'While I'm in Westport, I've some other work I need to get done, if that's okay.'

'That's fine,' West said. 'I'm waiting for Garda Andrews to get back to me. When you get here, we can discuss our next step.'

Pocketing his mobile, he joined Edel who waited out by the gate. The day was lovely, warmer than it had been, with a blue cloudless sky and a slight breeze. They left their coats unbuttoned and strolled along the clifftop, holding hands and stopping now and then to admire the scenery.

West was pointing out what he thought were seals far below when he heard Edel take a deep breath. 'You okay?'

'I'm not sure I've ever felt better. I love you, Mike.'

She walked on before he could respond and in that inopportune moment, his mobile chirped. 'Great timing,' he said, as he heard Andrews' voice on the other end.

'I know you're being sarcastic, and I don't want to know what I've interrupted, please,' Andrews said caustically.

'We're out for a walk,' West replied. 'That's all. I wasn't sure I'd get a signal this far from the house. It's not the best though, so I'll head back that way.' He waved to Edel, pointed to his mobile and turned to retrace his steps. 'Have you anything interesting for me?'

'I spoke to Bob Phelan, as you asked. He's very interested to hear where your lad Finbarr is. They've nothing concrete on him, but his name has come up a few times. Now here's the interesting bit. You know that new designer drug, Zombie Zee? Well, it's flooding the Galway drug scene. Phelan says the coastguard have stopped a number of boats and confiscated thousands of euros worth of the stuff. But it's all small scale. They think someone is getting larger amounts in by sea, but they don't know where.'

'They think it might be here? That Finbarr's involved?' West asked. He wondered if they were right; using was one thing, and Finbarr definitely looked like he did that, but dealing was a different ball game. Okay, he had history, but he'd been a child. And there had been nothing since. Nothing in ten years. Or had he just got clever, and not been caught.

'When I told them he was living on an island, they did,' Andrews said.

'He's not taking it in at Toormore, Peter. There's no access to the sea from there, it's on a cliff. He'd have to take the stuff in at the main harbour, but the coastguard patrols the sea between Clare Island and the mainland. He'd never be that stupid.'

'Stupid enough to be using though, isn't he?'

West grunted. 'I'd bet on it. I just can't tie his using drugs to Breathnach's death. I don't think the man would have cared one way or another.'

'Maybe Breathnach threatened to stop him?' Andrews suggested.

'We're clutching at straws. I'm getting tired wandering down dead ends.' He filled him in on the events of the previous day. 'That was the second; I'm not keen to try another.'

'Seamus is still digging into Breathnach's past. Nothing much has come up yet. I'll get him to have a look into Finbarr's finances. See if there's any unusual activity.'

West was about to trot out the official line about invasion of privacy but changed his mind. Seamus was a wizard on the computer; he could find out anything. *Let him see if there is anything to find*, he thought.

He hung up with a sigh. It was the way the job was. One step forward, two steps back. Red herrings, dead ends, wild goose chases. Normally, he enjoyed untangling it all but not this time.

Shaking his head, he looked for Edel. She hadn't walked far and was looking out to sea, one hand holding her hair back, the other buried in her pocket. Leaning against the wall of the house, he watched her and thought about what she'd said. He'd waited for this moment for so long. He loved her; had done almost from the beginning.

Walking over, he put his arms around her waist and drew her back against him. They stood that way for some time, just staring across the sea to Achill Island, watching birds whirl by, listening to the waves crash on the rocks below. It would have been easy to have said *I love you too,* but he wanted to wait, for the words to be more important, separate from hers, and not merely a reflex.

The moment had passed, anyway. When she turned in his arms, her hands stayed on his chest, keeping him at a distance. 'What did Andrews have to say?' she asked, all notion of romance vanished.

He wondered if she'd regretted saying those three words, and inwardly cursed Andrews and his damn phone call.

With a shrug, he told her about the possible drug connection.

'It's a bit of a stretch, isn't it?' she said. 'There's nowhere for a boat to land near Toormore. We've seen the cliffs.'

He'd said the same thing but now he wondered. 'Unless there's a way down we don't know about. Do you fancy a long walk? We could go over and explore the clifftop.' He shrugged. 'The case seems to have stalled, so for want of something better to do we may as well have a look.'

'A long walk sounds like a good plan. And perhaps we may see something we'd not noticed by car.'

'I'll just tell Daisy where we're going, in case Eamonn arrives,' he said, heading back into the lighthouse. He returned a minute later. 'She says there isn't a way down to the sea from Toormore as far as she knows, but I still think it's worth having a look for ourselves.'

Minutes later, hand in hand, they were heading down the road.

The walk was quiet and peaceful. No cars passed them; no other walkers crossed their path. Following the road, it was just under an hour before they saw the low profile of Toormore House appear.

They were almost at the gates when West spotted a well-worn grassy footpath heading off at an angle. 'I bet that leads to the coastal path,' he said, 'let's try it.'

The path skirted the grounds of Toormore House and did, as West thought, lead them to the coastal pathway. The wind was stronger here, coming in gusts from the sea, flattening their clothes, tossing their hair. The path followed the cliff, keeping several feet from an edge that was raggedly eroded, parts of it jutting out like giant decaying teeth with gaps in between to trap the unwary.

'We'd better be careful,' West said, repeating the words when they were swallowed by the wind, watching her nod and grin as they left the path and headed over to the edge. When they were almost a foot away, the wind buffeting them, Edel shook her head and pulled back.

'It's not safe to get any closer,' she shouted.

He released her hand and pointed back to the path, giving her a gentle push when she was reluctant to leave him. 'I'll be careful,' he shouted, and he was, feeling the ground in front of him with his foot before stepping closer to peer over. The cliff face was almost straight down to the rough wild Atlantic. There was no way any boat could land here. He said as much to Edel when he returned to the path.

'We can go back,' he said, catching hold of her hand. A little further inland, he saw the ruins that Tadgh had mentioned and pointed to them. 'Let's have a look,' he said.

The ruined settlement was spread over a wide area but apart from the low remnants of walls, there wasn't much to see. Only two or three walls higher than a few feet still existed. They stepped behind the tallest and were immediately sheltered from the wind. 'This must be where Tadgh camped,' he said, 'incredible the difference one wall can make.'

'It's unbelievable they were allowed to build so close to these ruins,' Edel said, running her hand along the rough stone. 'It must have been a big enough settlement; it seems to spread from here to the house.' She looked around, peering into the distance, estimating the size. 'Of course, they would have had to build from stone; there are hardly any trees on Clare Island. I suppose that's why it survived as long as it did.'

They wandered around, trying to guess the layout. 'It's a shame no records exist,' West said, standing beside one isolated low wall, trying to figure out which way the building would have gone, searching the ground for any evidence of size or direction.

Edel, walking around the edge of a pile of rubble, tripped and almost fell, swearing loudly enough to attract West's attention. He hurried to her side. 'You okay?' he asked, putting an arm out to steady her.

'I tripped over that stupid thing,' she said, rubbing her ankle.

'Be careful where you walk. There's been a lot of rubbish dumped here over the years.' He looked at the pallet she'd tripped over, wondering how on earth it had ended up there. About to turn away, something caught his eye. He bent down to look closer.

'Is there something there?' Edel asked, seeing an intent look on his face.

'I don't know. Something caught the light. But I can't see what. Probably a piece of glass or something.' Curiosity made him investigate further. Reaching down, he gripped a corner of the pallet and gave it a tug. It lifted easily. 'It's not heavy,' he told her, 'just awkward. Stand back, and I'll move it.'

He bent, took a firmer grip, and pulled it out of the way, his eyes widening at what he uncovered. 'Well now,' he said, straightening, 'what do we have here?'

Edel stood behind him. 'It looks like a hatch,' she said, puzzled.

'It does indeed.' West knocked on it. The sound rang dully. Metal. It was covered in moss and lichen and had obviously been there for a long time. A handle of sorts was set into one end, and here the moss and lichen had been rubbed away, exposing the metal to the sunlight.

'A secret passageway,' Edel said, her eyes shining. 'I bet it was an escape route from the house.'

West stood. An escape route? Perhaps, but to where? The land around was flat as far as the eye could see. 'It might have been a military route,' West suggested. 'If the settlement was under attack, it could take soldiers behind their attackers, fight them from two fronts.'

Edel bent, and putting her fingers under the handle, gave a firm tug. It didn't budge. 'It might have been found when the house was being built. They probably put the cover on it for safety.'

'Perhaps, but why hide it?' West looked around the edges. 'See,' he said to Edel who bent down to follow where his finger was pointing. 'The moss and lichen, they break along the sides. This has been opened recently. And more than once, I'd say.' He looked back toward Toormore House. 'I think we'll find this runs down to the sea,' he said. 'It's just too much of a coincidence. We should cover it up again and wait until Hall is with us. See what he thinks.'

Edel's face fell. 'Can't we just have a look?'

West shook his head but seeing her disappointment, changed his mind. 'Okay. Just a quick look. Stand back,' he warned her, and gave the hatch a yank. There was no movement. Standing astride, he tried again, this time applying continuous pressure.

'It's moving,' Edel cried, clapping her hands together. 'Keep going.'

West grunted and kept pulling and then, suddenly, the hatch lifted easily and he dropped it back to expose the gap beneath. They peered down. There was a staircase, roughly hewn from the rock, the steps uneven and narrow. But it looked solid.

'You ready for a bit of exploration?' West asked, meeting her eyes. 'It's probably going to be dirty and damp.'

Edel eyed the darkness. There'd be spiders. Probably big ones. But a secret passage, it was the stuff of adventures. She grinned at him. 'Absolutely. But I hope you have a torch?'

West smiled, and reaching into an inside pocket, he pulled out a small torch. He switched it on, the powerful beam lighting up the interior, showing a tantalising curve in the steps. 'Let's go down a little bit,' he said. 'I'll go first, if I say go back, go back, okay?'

He took a tentative step down, keeping his hands on the edges, ready to retreat if the steps were less trustworthy than they looked. He'd reached the turn before Edel took the first step down. 'Can you see anything?' she asked.

West took another step and suddenly the patch of sky vanished. The torch, small but powerful, lit up a few steps ahead of him, and then hit wall. 'There's another turn,' he called back. 'I think I'm right. It's a spiral, going downward.'

It was cold, but surprisingly dry inside, and the air was fresher than West expected. It strengthened his belief that someone was using the passage regularly. 'We should go back,' he said suddenly. What on earth had possessed him to be carried away on a whim? They should have waited.

'Oh, not yet, Mike,' Edel pleaded from a few steps above. 'Let's go on a bit more. I bet you're wrong. It'll level off soon and we'll pop up like rabbits from a warren.'

But it didn't, it continued its downward trajectory.

'Okay,' West said, a few minutes later, 'we have to go back. It's still going downward, Edel. It isn't an escape route to land; it's one to the sea.'

'It can't be,' she said, 'there's no beach, no coves along here.'

'When this was dug there probably was. We're talking about

hundreds of years of coastal erosion; we've no idea what the coast of Clare Island was like then.'

They stood in silence as both considered the changes that time had made. Even in the shelter of Clew Bay, the Atlantic was rough.

'It makes sense, I suppose,' she agreed. 'Where do you think this passage ends now? High up on the cliff somewhere?'

Sense told West they should turn back, but curiosity was stronger. 'I suppose we could go a bit further and see. If someone is using it, it has to go somewhere.'

They moved on, the silence only broken by their footfall on the rock or the occasional grunt as one or other of them stepped awkwardly on the uneven surface. West didn't bother reconsidering when each turn led to another, figuring it had to come to an end soon.

Twenty minutes after they'd entered the passage, he heard a distinct sound that made him stop. 'Listen,' he said to Edel. 'Do you hear it? It's the sea.'

The next turn brought them to a small, shallow cave. 'Wow,' Edel said, moving past him to stand near the edge, peering down to the sea just a few feet below.

'Careful,' he warned, coming to stand behind her, slipping an arm around her waist and drawing her back against him.

'This is amazing,' she said. 'It must, one day, have continued to a cove. What a great escape route. They probably had a boat waiting here and sailed off to Achill or the mainland.'

'It's probably not visible at a distance,' West surmised, releasing Edel and looking around. The entrance to the steps, set at a slant in the rock, was barely visible even from where he stood. To one side of the cave there was a small concavity. Curious, West moved to examine it.

'What is it?' Edel asked, joining him.

West used his foot to push the equipment that was untidily

stowed at the back. His voice was disparaging. 'A pulley system. I think we've found how they're bringing drugs in.'

Edel's face fell. 'It was so magical; now it's tainted and sordid.'

'Let's get out of here,' West said. 'We can let the drug squad know; they can close the place down.' He took a last look at the sea before turning to start back up the steps, directing the beam of light at her feet as she walked. It took them longer on the return, their steps slower, the excitement that had driven them to the bottom missing from the climb upward. It was thirty minutes later when West stopped, puzzled. 'Hang on, Edel,' he said.

When she stopped, he switched off the torch. The darkness was dense. Turning the torch back on, he said, 'Let me change places with you.'

Edel waited until he brushed by before asking anxiously, 'Is there something wrong?'

'Let's just keep going.'

When they rounded the next curve in the steps, he stopped again and switched off the torch. Still no light from above. He gritted his teeth but said nothing. A minute later, he saw it, a crack of light, just the merest glimmer. He was right underneath the hatch.

Someone had shut it.

25

West pushed at the hatch, but it didn't budge. Handing the torch back to Edel, he used both hands to push as hard as he could and swore loudly. 'I think someone has put something on top,' he said. 'Switch off the torch for a sec.'

In the darkness, the problem was clear. There was a crack of light around the edge of the hatch, but in two sections it was missing. Someone had laid something over it. Something heavier than the pallet that had been there earlier.

'Maybe if both of us push, it will work,' Edel said, moving up to stand beside him.

West put the torch in his pocket. 'Okay, on three,' he said.

They strained for several minutes, grunting and groaning with the effort, desperation giving them the adrenaline rush to continue even after they knew whatever it was, it was too heavy to push away.

'Is someone playing a trick on us?' Edel said, and lifting her chin shouted, 'hello' at the hatch door.

There was no reply. Perhaps whoever had done it was up there laughing. But West guessed, whoever it was, he was leaving them to their fate.

'What do we do?' Edel said, putting her arms around him.

He held her tightly, saying nothing, ideas running through his head. 'Okay,' he said finally, 'this is what we're going to do. We're going to sit tight here until it gets dark. Maybe whoever did this is playing a practical joke on us. If so, they'll probably come back and let us out. If not, when it gets dark, we'll go back to the cave and use the torch to try to signal a passing boat.'

'Send an SOS, you mean?' Edel said with a smile in her voice. 'Honestly, this is very James Bond, isn't it?'

It was cold in the passage, and as the afternoon turned to evening and the light faded, it grew colder. They alternated standing arms around one another for warmth and comfort, with sitting one step apart, Edel resting her head on West's knee.

Trying to signal a passing boat wasn't much of a plan, but it was all West could think to do and, once they were certain nobody was coming to let them out, they headed back down the steps.

'The islands of Inisbofin and Inishturk are nearby,' West explained to Edel as they moved into the shallow cave, 'there may be someone sailing from either of them to Achill. They're more likely to pass this way, the channel between Clare Island and the mainland is a busy one. I'm going to flash an SOS every fifteen minutes for as long as I can.' He stood close to the edge and flashed the sequence once. He was tempted to do it again, but it was going to be a long night. He had no idea how long the battery would last and it was their only hope.

'Well, I hope someone does save our souls,' Edel said, looking around for somewhere to sit. Picking up the rope attached to the pulley system, she curled it around to make a mat and sat on that. It didn't help much, it was cold, and it was going to get a lot worse.

'It doesn't actually mean that, you know,' West said, switching off the torch and sitting beside her, wincing as he sat on a part of the pulley by mistake. He wondered if they should move into the stairwell, but they needed to keep an eye out for an answer to their signal.

'Save our ship?' Edel ventured.

West laughed. 'Nope, keep guessing.'

He felt her shake her head and knew she was struggling not to cry.

'Spoilsport,' he said, giving her a hug. 'I'll tell you the answer. It doesn't actually mean anything. In international Morse code, three dits form the letter S, and three dahs form the letter O. *SOS* became an easy way to remember the sequence, three short, three long, three short.'

'Save our souls sounds better,' Edel muttered.

They sat huddled together in silence for a few minutes, their eyes adjusting to the almost complete darkness. The clear skies of earlier hadn't lasted; thick cloud had drifted over during the afternoon and it obscured the moon and stars.

'We could have done with a full moon tonight,' Edel complained.

'Our signal will stand out even more in this darkness.' West tried to sound positive, even as he felt the cold creep under his skin. 'Next time someone offers us warmer coats to wear, we'll take them,' he said.

Edel gave a forced laugh. 'We hadn't planned to get locked down a secret passageway by some deranged murderer.'

West took his jacket off, pulled Edel closer and draped it around them both, fastening the top button to stop it falling away. 'Better,' he whispered into her ear.

'Much,' she said and kissed his cheek.

He heard the lie in her voice and held her tighter.

Every fifteen minutes without fail he undid the button, stood, and sent the signal. The regularity was important. If it had been seen and reported, someone might be looking for it.

By the sixth time, it was becoming more difficult, his numb fingers struggling with the small, awkward on/off switch.

Looking down at the sea, he wondered, by daylight, if it would be possible to climb down and swim until he reached a place where he could get out. He was a strong swimmer. It may be their only option if nobody answered their distress call. The battery wouldn't last for another night.

'Who do you think did it?' Edel asked, when he sat down.

West, who had been wondering the same thing, shrugged. 'My guess is Finbarr. He has history, he's obviously taking drugs. This, I think, has his stamp all over it.'

'Yes,' she agreed, 'he'd be my bet. Do you think he killed Eoin Breathnach too?'

There was a long pause before West replied. He wasn't sure if she understood the implications of what Finbarr had done here. If he were responsible, his intent was clear. He wanted them to die. If they weren't rescued, he'd come down in a few days and roll their bodies into the sea. When they were found, *if* they were found, people would assume a tragic accident. If there were enough of their bodies left intact, a post-mortem might show they'd died of hypothermia, and that would be a puzzle. But there would be no link to Toormore House, no link to Finbarr.

'I wouldn't have said so before, but after this… well, I think he probably did. Eoin might have found out about the drug-running somehow, and whereas I don't think he cared much about Finbarr's welfare, he seems to have cared about Sylvia. Having her son arrested wouldn't have pleased her. He might have threatened Finbarr in some way to make him stop. Problem is,' he added, 'drug-running is a very lucrative business. Even if Finbarr wanted to stop, the people he was dealing with may not have wanted him to.'

He moved to signal again, and this time it took several

minutes. His fingers felt thick, clumsy and even using both hands it was a struggle to finish. He stood for a few seconds, staring out at the dense blackness, wondering if he were wasting his time. He checked his watch, taking a minute to understand what the luminous dial was telling him. It was eleven, they'd been down here... he tried to calculate, but couldn't, and knew they were in more serious trouble than he'd realised. Hypothermia.

Quickly, he moved back to Edel's side and snuggled up to her, trying to absorb some of her heat. She was shivering. Minutes later, so was he.

The wind picked up... and it started to rain... grey sheets of cold water blown in on each gust and soaking them to the skin. 'We have to move into the stairwell,' West said, opening his coat and pulling Edel to her feet. 'Edel,' he said, shaking her gently until she opened her eyes. 'We have to move.'

She didn't help or resist and he half-carried, half-pulled her to the stairwell. They should have moved further up, away from the wind that had started to wail, but their coordination seemed to have gone and neither could manage the steps. They sat on the lowest one, wrapping their arms around one another. West looked for his coat to pull around them and realised he had dropped it. Rain had soaked through the thin jumper he wore, but strangely enough, he didn't feel cold anymore. Except for his fingers. They were so numb he didn't bother trying to send any more signals.

'Anyway,' he whispered into Edel's ear, 'I can't remember what the sequence is, isn't that crazy?'

He'd stopped shivering but started to feel increasingly sleepy and knew they were both reaching the more serious stage of hypothermia. They should probably get up and walk, he thought, making a half-hearted attempt to wake Edel, but she didn't answer.

He had one moment of clarity before he passed out.

They were going to die here, and he hadn't told her he loved her.

26

Garda Eamonn Hall arrived back on Clare Island just after two. He'd tried West's mobile several times to let him know he was on his way, but there was no answer. Arriving at the quay, he tried again and then rang the lighthouse. Getting an engaged tone, he cursed the mobile phone coverage on the island and decided the best thing to do was to go there. If West had gone to Toormore House, he'd have left a message.

Minutes later, he pulled up outside the lighthouse. Daisy, who'd been standing on the doorstep polishing the brass knocker, stopped and turned when she heard the car.

'Hi,' he said, walking up the short path from the gate.

'Hi yourself, Eamonn.' She smiled.

'Is Garda West here?'

She shook her head. 'No, they left here a few hours ago to walk over to Toormore and have a look around. They said they'd only be gone a few hours so they're probably on their way back.'

Thanking her, Hall returned to his car and sat. He tried West's mobile, unsurprised when it went directly to voicemail again, and left a message saying where he was.

It was sit there and wait, or drive the road to Toormore

House and hope to meet them on the way. Not a man for sitting around, he decided on the second option and headed off at a leisurely speed, enjoying the blue-sky day.

∼

The gate to the house being shut, he parked on the road and made his way down the pedestrian entrance to the house. Knocking on the front door, he whistled as he waited.

'Hi Linda,' he said, when the housekeeper opened the door. 'Is Garda West here?'

'No, thank the Lord, he isn't.'

Assuming she was going to say yes, Hall was temporarily lost for words. 'Perhaps he's out in the grounds, maybe with Jim?'

Linda shrugged. 'I suppose he could be. I haven't seen Jim since lunch.'

Hall thanked her and headed around to Jim's workshop. When he wasn't there, he went looking for him, eventually finding him removing leaves from the swimming pool. 'Jim,' he greeted him, 'have you seen Garda West?'

'Not today,' he replied, lifting the net and dumping leaves on the side. 'Was he supposed to be here?'

Hall shook his head. 'Not really, I called to the guesthouse. Daisy said he and Edel had planned to walk here. Maybe they changed their mind and I'll find them there when I go back.' He frowned, not sure what he should be doing. 'Is Finbarr around?' he asked, thinking since he'd come here, he may as well do something constructive.

Jim jerked his head toward the house. 'He's playing pool with that Tilsdale man.'

Linda, looking less than pleased to be disturbed again, let Hall in and directed him to the games room.

'Eamonn,' Finbarr greeted him cheerfully, 'come and play

the winner. Me, of course,' he added as he pocketed the final ball.

'I'm working,' Hall said, picking up Tilsdale's abandoned cue. 'But I suppose I could classify this as building community relationships.'

'Of course, you could,' Finbarr agreed.

They spent the next hour shooting pool. A casual question as to how Sylvia was coping caused Roger to shrug and Finbarr to raise an eyebrow. With no idea what West had discovered from his colleagues in Dublin, Hall didn't know what else to ask and was feeling slightly aggrieved. After all, it was his patch; West shouldn't have gone off without involving him in the investigation. He needed to know what was going on.

It was getting dark by the time he left. Returning to Clare Island Lighthouse, he expected to find West there, and entered with a scowl on his face, ready to show his annoyance.

The scowl faded when Daisy told him she hadn't seen West or Edel since they had left earlier. 'And they're only wearing light jackets,' she added, looking worried. 'What should we do?'

'Leave it with me,' Hall said and went back to his car where he sat in silence for a moment. He checked the time, made a quick call, jotted down a phone number and, taking a deep breath, rang West's Foxrock Station, and asked to speak to Garda Andrews.

'Garda Andrews, it's Eamonn Hall. On Clare Island. I was in Westport this morning but arranged to meet Sergeant West back here when I finished. I haven't been able to contact him. And nobody seems to know where he is. I know he expected to hear from you this morning, I'm just hoping you can tell me where he may have gone.'

Andrews caught the anxiety in the man's voice. 'I did speak

to him, but that was at 11am. He didn't mention he was going anywhere.'

'Did you have any new information for him? Perhaps if you tell me what you told him, I might be able to figure out where he went.'

'There wasn't anything definite. We heard from the drug squad that Zombie Zee is flooding the Galway area, and they were interested to hear that your friend Finbarr was living on the island, but Mike didn't think it warranted following up. We're still digging into Breathnach's life but, to be honest, we don't really have anything yet.'

'I've been out to Toormore House and spoke to Finbarr. West hasn't been there today. According to the manager here, he and his friend, Edel, went off on foot in that direction. I'm beginning to worry.'

Andrews frowned. This was out of character for West. Gripping the phone, he spoke calmly to the island garda, trying to keep anxiety and frustration from colouring his voice. The man needed support, not more pressure. 'Can you gather a few people, head out in a few different directions? If he was definitely heading toward Toormore House, is there a shortcut, or would he have gone by road?'

'By road, I'd say. You'd need a good map and proper walking boots to go over land. He might have had a map; I'll check with Daisy. But he certainly didn't have proper walking boots.'

Andrews thought a moment. 'Right, you'll need to do that walk. Are there houses along that route?'

'Just a few on the road, and a couple of farms just off it.'

Farms, that meant numerous outhouses to search. 'Okay,' Andrews said. 'You need to get help. Call on every house, check every outhouse. Let me know when you're organised and ready to set off. I'll stay by the phone.'

· · ·

Hall hung up and headed back inside. There were no other guests staying that night so Daisy, Tadgh and the chef, Tibor, were only too happy to lend a hand, all of them worried about what might have happened to West or Edel.

Daisy, when asked about the map, shook her head. 'No, they didn't take one.'

Hall nodded grimly. 'Okay, so they probably stuck to the road. Ring anyone you can, we're going to need more help. And if you can contact the owners of the farms and properties between here and Toormore, get them to search their properties.

'I'll ring Joe Callaghan, and Leo Murphy,' Tadgh said, taking out his phone, 'they own the two farms.'

'Okay, what about the houses?'

Daisy looked at the others and shook her head.

'Right,' Hall said, 'we'll have to call on them.' He turned to Daisy. 'Can you rustle up some blankets to take with us? If they're outside somewhere, they're going to be cold. And torches too.'

Daisy nodded and ran off to collect what they needed. Tibor suggested hot tea might come in handy and went to fill a couple of flasks.

'It's bloody cold out there, Eamonn,' Tadgh said bluntly. 'If they've been out in this since morning, they're in big trouble.'

Hall bit his tongue on the abrasive comment he wanted to make and rang Andrews with an update. 'We're going to set off in a few minutes. I think you should have a helicopter standing by; it's been cold all day, but since the sun went down the temperature has dropped dramatically and it's starting to rain. If they've been outside for hours...'

'I've already been in contact with emergency services,' Andrews said quickly. 'There'll be a helicopter standing by to airlift them if necessary. I've also notified the coastguard. They're going to patrol from the quay to Toormore just in case they fell or followed a pathway down and got stuck on the cliffside somewhere.'

It happened, but Andrews just couldn't imagine West being that stupid. Hanging up, he shook his head. It was frustrating to be so far away. He checked his watch and saw it was almost six. He could be in Galway in around three hours. He wasn't sure how long it would take to get to Clare Island from there. Maybe another two?

He'd filled Morrison in after Hall's first call. Lifting the phone, he dialled his extension and gave him an update. 'I'd like to go, to make sure they're doing everything necessary. I could be there in about five hours.' He waited for an answer while mentally planning his journey.

'Okay,' Morrison said, 'get going, take one of the lads with you. I'll give Galway a ring; get them to meet you somewhere en route. That'll get you there faster.'

'Thank you,' Andrews said and hanging up, headed out to see who he could find. Both Sam Jarvis and Seamus Baxter were in the general office and instantly volunteered to go with him, worried looks on their faces.

'Just one of you, I'm afraid. Seamus, you're needed here, keep digging on Breathnach. When we find West, he'll want good news.'

Andrews made a quick phone call to his wife, Joyce, and then he and Jarvis headed out to the car park. Rush hour traffic was the usual chaos; Andrews did something he rarely did, he activated the strobe lighting and siren, and sped along bus lanes. Twenty minutes later, when his phone buzzed, he pulled it out and handed it to Jarvis.

'Garda Jarvis here.' The younger officer listened intently. 'Okay. Great. We'll see you there.'

'A car is going to meet us in Athenry. There's a small station there, they'll be waiting and will drive us the rest of the way.'

Andrews nodded, keeping his attention on the road, and his foot to the floor. Ninety minutes after leaving Dublin they pulled into the car park of Athenry's small garda station, locked their car, and jumped into the back of a squad car that had started its engine as soon as they'd arrived.

'Thanks lads,' Andrews said, fastening his seat belt. The car took off immediately. 'You know the story, I assume,' he asked.

Both uniformed gardaí nodded. 'Yes, we've been asked to put ourselves at your service. I'm Shane Rourke, and my partner here is Darrick Costello. We'll take the quickest route to Roonagh Pier and there'll be a motorboat waiting to take you across to Clare Island.'

'How long?' Andrews asked.

'An hour and a half, if we're lucky,' Rourke replied. 'And then twenty minutes on the boat. We'll go across with you and help with the search. Garda Hall contacted Westport; a few lads from there have already gone over.'

Andrews breathed a sigh of relief. All that could be done was being done. They'd find them.

They reached Roonagh Pier in exactly an hour and a half, pulling up beside a large gathering of people. 'It's lads from the local GAA,' Rourke said, recognising familiar faces. 'They'll be going across to help.'

Andrews and Jarvis exchanged appreciative looks. They weren't going to be short of manpower if they'd called in the local Gaelic Athletic Association.

Getting out of the car, they were approached by one of the men. 'Tadgh gave us a shout,' he said, introducing himself to the uniformed gardaí, and then at their nod, to the two plain-clothes detectives. 'I'm Aidan Gibney. Tadgh Sullivan is in our GAA team, he asked for help. We're going over in groups; about ten have gone already. We're happy to do whatever we can to help.'

Just then the small motorboat arrived back from the island, and he left them to arrange the next group. Andrews turned to Rourke. 'Who's Tadgh Sullivan?'

'He's married to the manager of the Clare Island Lighthouse where Sergeant West is staying.'

'Ah, okay,' Andrews said, nodding. Obviously, community spirit was strong in these parts. He approved.

'Our boat is just over here,' Rourke said, leading the way to where another uniformed garda stood beside the pier.

The boat was small. 'Will it take all of us?' Andrews asked, as the boat dipped lower in the water with each added body.

The uniformed garda who was driving it nodded reassuringly. 'Relax,' he said, 'it can take up to six.'

The boat pulled away from Roonagh Pier and headed across the black sea toward the lights of the island. Twenty minutes later they heard the chat as the boat pulled up alongside Clare Island Pier, a general hullabaloo of greetings being shouted, directions being given, worried voices and grim faces.

Leaving the boat, Andrews headed to what appeared to be the operational centre of the crowd, relief crossing his face when he saw the uniform. 'A Civil Defence team,' he said to Jarvis. He introduced himself to the man in charge. 'Garda Peter Andrews, from Dublin. I work with the missing man. He's also a friend.'

'Gareth Dunne,' the man replied, taking Andrews' hand in a firm grip. 'We're the Civil Defence search and rescue team. We were on a training exercise a few miles away when we got the word and came to help.' He indicated the group of men standing not far away. 'We've had a lot of volunteers; it took me a while to get them organised to stop the search descending into disorganised chaos. A co-ordinated search of the entire island is now underway.' He pointed to the map he'd laid out on the bonnet of a car. 'Have a look,' he said. 'We'll find them. There isn't an area we're not searching and we're also liaising with the coastguard.'

Andrews and Jarvis peered at symbols and abbreviations that meant nothing to either of them. Dunne moved a finger over the map, showing them how it worked. 'I've divided the island into sections; each section is covered by a team. That,' Dunne explained, pointing to the first number, 'is the size of the team; that one, the time they headed out and that, the expected time it will take them to cover their allotted area.'

Impressed, Andrews nodded. 'Where do you want us to go?' he asked.

'We've everything covered,' Dunne said, tapping the map. 'To be honest, I've never seen such a turnout for a search and rescue. It appears every garda and GAA member within a twenty-mile radius has turned up to help. It's very impressive.' He pointed toward the pub. 'The owner has given us permission to use Ryan's as a base. It's getting too cold to stand out here. If all the teams come back without locating the missing people, we'll send fresh teams out using a different grid, just in case.' He folded his map and led the way into a pub filled with grim faces and sombre voices. It was much colder. 'Minus four,' Andrews heard someone say as they pushed inside.

Dunne, seeing his worried face, offered reassurance. 'Your friend is young and fit. He'll have sought shelter, and he and his friend will have huddled together to preserve heat.'

'Can they last the night?' Andrews asked. 'They must be hurt or trapped somewhere; otherwise we'd have found them by now.' He rubbed a hand over his jaw. 'Maybe I should contact his parents and warn them.'

The pub staff had set up flasks of tea on the bar. Dunne poured a cup for each of them. 'There'll be no harm waiting till morning for that,' he said, slurping the hot drink. 'It won't achieve anything by giving them a worrisome night.'

Andrews acknowledged the truth of that. Hadn't he said much the same thing to people in his time? The morning might bring better news; he'd wait.

Turning to talk to Jarvis, his attention was caught by a uniformed garda with a worried expression who approached them hesitantly. 'Eamonn Hall?' he guessed, stretching out a hand.

Hall took it. 'Yes, I heard your name mentioned. You made good time getting here.'

Andrews weighed the younger man up. A good officer, he'd been told. He saw a flicker of guilt in his eyes. 'It's not your fault, you know,' he said with a smile. 'Mike West tends to follow his own path even if it does lead to dangerous places.'

'If I hadn't mentioned his name to Inspector Duignan, he wouldn't have been dragged into this mess,' he said.

A frown creased Andrews' forehead. 'You think whatever has happened to him is mixed up with the murder of Mr Breathnach then?'

Hall huffed a sigh. 'I'm trying to keep an open mind, you know, but I don't like coincidences.'

Neither did Andrews. He took Hall by the elbow and led him to a quieter corner of the room. 'Jarvis and I are going to hang around for a few days. Our Inspector Morrison is going to clear it. Why don't you fill me in on everything?'

At midnight, Dunne's phone rang and his suddenly alert face quickly silenced conversation around him. 'Okay,' he said, and listened for a few minutes, nodding. 'Hang on and I'll ask the locals.' Lowering the phone, he looked around the room. 'Does anyone know of any caves in the south cliffs?'

Higgins, who had joined them after walking the road from Toormore, shook his head. 'It's a sheer drop around there.'

'What have you heard?' Andrews asked, pushing through the crowd to get closer to Dunne.

'There's been report of a distress signal,' Dunne explained. 'A fisherman sailing home to Achill saw it, he thought he was imagining it, but fifteen minutes later he saw it again. When he got home, he reported it to the local coastguard who transmitted a message to the vessel searching the coast between the quay and Toormore. They carried on to the south coast to see if they could see anything, but all they can make out is a very faint light a few feet above sea level.'

There was a collection of indrawn breaths as they all looked at one another. 'Can they get closer and investigate?' Andrews asked, feeling the first stirring of hope.

Dunne shook his head. 'Way too rough for them, I'm afraid. They've used their searchlight but can't see anything apart from that faint light.'

Andrews, his face creased with worry, said, 'You think it might be them?'

'The search teams are all reporting back in the negative,' Dunne said. 'There was a distress signal reported, and now a light where there shouldn't be one. I've no idea how your friend might have got there, but I'd say it's a possibility.' Narrowed eyes scanned the room, picking out members of his team. 'It looks like we're going to have to descend from the clifftop to find out; the coastguard vessel is going to stay where it is to direct us.'

'If it's them, why wouldn't they have kept signalling?' Andrew asked, as they prepared to leave.

'Probably suffering from hypothermia at this stage,' Dunne said. 'It causes confusion. Okay,' he said, heading out the door behind his team, 'who do we have with us that can abseil in the dark?'

An hour later, with the equipment organised, they headed en masse to Toormore House, parking on the road outside. With powerful torches lighting the coastal path ahead, they made their way along it. The wind had picked up, howling in from the sea and it was bitterly, teeth-chatteringly cold. It was difficult to speak, so nobody did.

They did a lot of thinking instead. Andrews was wondering how West could have been so stupid and, if he had but known it, the Civil Defence team were agreeing, wondering how many times they'd have to rescue careless tourists before they learned some sense.

Dunne held a large torch and signalled the coastguard when the path reached the cliffside. The vessel flashed its huge light and kept it on while the group moved along the rough, uneven surface of the path, careful not to stray from it. In the darkness, the edge was difficult to see.

Then the coastguard light flashed several times. They were there.

For the next several frustrating minutes, the coastguard, as prearranged, flashed its light to send simple left and right directions to position them exactly.

'Is that Morse code?' Jarvis asked quietly.

Andrews nodded. 'I learned some when I was a Boy Scout. He's spelling out either left or right. See, dot – dash – dot. That's right. If he wants us to move left, he'll flash dot – dash – dot – dot.'

Dunne was a careful man. He knew there was little margin for error. A final signal from the coastguard and he waved his team forward.

Andrews nudged Jarvis. 'They've flashed a Y for yes.'

It took several minutes to get it all set up. The two climbers nominated for the task donned the regulation safety apparel and tested the powerful torches fitted into their helmets. Light also came from several handheld torches, their beams criss-crossing as the owners moved about. Out at sea, the coastguard vessel continued to aim its powerful beams at the cliff face.

Finally, they were ready. It had been decided that one would go down first, assess the situation, and report back. With shouts of 'good luck' blowing in the breeze, the first man vanished over the side, the ropes playing out slowly as he descended.

Andrews and Jarvis exchanged worried glances but said nothing.

It seemed a long time before Dunne's handheld radio crackled into life. 'Go ahead, Kev.'

The radio crackled again and then, clearly, they heard Kevin's voice. 'They're here in a shallow cave. Alive, but unconscious. There's no sign of any injury.'

The words were greeted with shouts of relief from the gathered group. Andrews turned to Jarvis and grabbed him in a brief hug. 'He's alive.'

Dunne quietened them all down with a wave of his arms. 'We've a long way to go yet,' he said. 'We need to get them out of there.'

Kevin's voice came again. 'There appears to be a stairway heading from the cave. It's narrow and steep though and would be too difficult to manoeuvre bodies up. I think our best option would be to ask the coastguard to send a dinghy. The drop from the cave to the sea is only three or four feet at most; we'd easily lower them down.'

Dunne agreed and sent a message to the vessel. It was quickly answered. They were happy to oblige and would await a signal to proceed.

Andrews and Jarvis stood looking on as Dunne gave quick commands to his team. Specialist rescue equipment was lowered down to the cave and a second climber descended to assist Kevin in making West and Edel transport-ready. The signal was sent and within minutes a dinghy was bobbing in the rough seas at the base of the cliff.

Dunne kept the handheld radio in his hand and Andrews and Jarvis huddled close to listen as the dinghy crew and the Civil Defence officers organised the safe transfer from the cave.

'Nice and slow. Tie the rope tightly around something. That's better, but it's still like a bloody rollercoaster down here. Okay, that's it, slowly, slowly, easy does it. Okay, we have him.'

It took several minutes to lower each gurney. They listened to the continuous calls back and forward between the cave and the dinghy until finally, both were on board.

'Okay, that's us ready. Off we go.'

Andrews moved closer to the cliff edge. In the powerful coastguard light, he could see the dinghy as it navigated the waters back to the vessel and tied up alongside. A short while later, a final Morse code message was sent. They were safe on board.

Dunne joined him. 'Try not to worry; the coastguard has experience in treating hypothermia. Your friends are in good hands. They'll be met by an ambulance when they get to Galway and be transferred to Galway University Hospital.'

Andrews huffed a sigh of relief. 'Your team has been great. We owe you.'

'All in a day's work,' Dunne said, turning back to monitor the safe return of his men from the cave.

Most of the search team had left as soon as the good news had spread. Andrews and Jarvis got a lift back to the quay with Tadgh and found Rourke and Costello drinking coffee in Ryan's.

'We heard the good news,' Rourke said. 'You want to have some coffee, and then we'll take you to Galway and drop you at the hospital?'

Andrews patted him on the arm. 'Yes, thank you, much appreciated.'

Almost four hours later, a pale Jarvis, and an even paler Andrews, bid their uniformed gardaí colleagues a grateful goodbye as they were deposited at the door of Galway University Hospital. They'd been in contact on the way, both West and Edel were doing fine, both were awake and almost back to normal.

'What a night,' Andrews said, pushing through the swing door. 'Let's just see for ourselves that he's okay, and then we'll get the hell out of here.'

They followed the directions they'd been given, stopping in front of the ward and exchanging glances before going in. They found themselves in a small corridor with numbered doorways on each side.

'What number were we told?' Andrews asked.

'Seven,' Jarvis replied, walking ahead. 'Here it is.' He pushed the door open, and spotted West in the far corner of the four-bedded unit. 'He looks okay,' he said.

West heard the whispers and turned his head, lifting a hand in acknowledgement when he saw who it was.

'What a run-around you gave us,' Andrews said, his face brightening when he saw Jarvis had been right. He did look okay.

West grinned, and reaching out, caught Andrews' hand in a strong grip. 'Believe me, it wasn't intentional.'

Andrews dragged over a chair, and Jarvis perched on the edge of the bed. 'Where's Edel? We heard she was okay.'

'She's next door; I'm just back from visiting her. She's fine. They gave us both some intravenous therapy on the coastguard vessel. It was amazing; within a few minutes we both woke up and before we got here, we were feeling fine. They insisted they needed to do some tests, but they've all come back normal. They said we could leave whenever we wanted.'

Andrews shook his head, hearing the unspoken request. 'Wait until later, eh?' Then, seeing that West was going to argue, added, 'I bet Edel is exhausted after it all.'

West relaxed back against the pillows. 'If I'm honest, I'm pretty shattered myself.'

Andrews gave a satisfied smile. 'Why don't you tell us what happened, before you fall asleep. The Civil Defence team who found you said there was a passageway from the cave. Nobody else in the group knew it existed, not even the locals. I don't know what possessed you to go down it, but what happened, did you lose your way back?'

West's expression grew grim. 'No, we didn't. There's a direct passage from the surface to the cave, we found the entrance by accident.' He ran a hand over his face. 'We'd only meant to have a quick look but got carried away and ended up at the bottom in that shallow cave. We went straight back up only to discover someone had pushed something across the hatch. We waited, but whoever it was didn't come back.'

Andrews and Jarvis exchanged startled glances. *Someone tried to kill them.* This wasn't what they'd expected to hear. 'Luckily you left that torch pointing out to sea,' Andrews said, putting his thoughts into words.

'I don't remember doing that,' West said, 'I'd been sending an SOS every fifteen minutes, but eventually my hands got too cold, and then I couldn't seem to remember the sequence. I don't remember putting it down at all. Maybe I dropped it.'

'Or,' Jarvis said, 'it was the last rational thing you thought to do.'

'Possibly,' he agreed.

Andrews, looking grim, said what they were all thinking. 'If you hadn't, we'd never have found you, you know. They'd have put the SOS down to a prank and forgotten about it, and we'd have gone on searching.'

There was silence for a few minutes.

'You know who's responsible, don't you?' Andrews asked.

West grunted. 'I think it might be Finbarr, but I can't be sure. The passageway is obviously being used for something. I found a pulley and ropes which would indicate something is being brought in, or perhaps sent out. Put that together with what you found out about him, and what Bob said about Zombie Zee, and it seems to make sense.'

'How did he know you'd gone down?' Andrews asked. 'Is the entrance visible from the house?'

West frowned, thinking of the area. 'No, I doubt if he'd had a clear line of sight to it. We must have just been unlucky.'

'Or maybe he was checking it out because a shipment was due?' Jarvis suggested.

'That makes sense,' West said, looking sombre, 'and when he found the hatch open, he did what he did to protect his business. It would be way too lucrative to lose.'

'Do you think he knew it was you?'

'If he didn't know when he closed the hatch, he'd have known as soon as the search for us started. He could have gone back and opened it, that early we'd have still managed to climb out. No, he was protecting the passageway.'

A nurse, coming to check on West, admonished the two visitors. 'This is not visiting time, gentlemen. Perhaps you could come back later?'

It wasn't really a question. The nurse waited, hands on hips until the two men stood and made their goodbyes. 'We'll come and get you later,' Andrews said, smiling at the surprise on West's face. 'Did you think we were going to leave you here?' he said, and with a wave and a nudge for Jarvis to move, the two men left.

Jarvis stayed silent until they exited the hospital, their breaths pluming in front of them. 'We're staying?'

Instead of replying, Andrews took out his phone and seconds later was speaking to Inspector Morrison. 'They're both okay,' he said, 'but I think we need to stay a bit longer. This case has developed legs.' He filled him in on how West and Edel had been locked inside the passageway. 'It's attempted murder, Inspector.'

Morrison breathed heavily into the phone. 'This is going to be a jurisdictional nightmare but okay,' he said. 'I'll clear it with Westport and Galway. You'll need a car; I'll organise one for you at the nearest garda station. Remember,' he finished, 'Garda Hall is keen, just lacking experience; make sure you keep him in the loop.'

Agreeing to follow protocol, Andrews hung up. 'Right,' he said to Jarvis, 'let's go find somewhere to sleep for a few hours.'

They didn't have to wander the city. Jarvis, with a shake of his head, took out his phone and within a few seconds had the co-ordinates of the nearest hotel. Five minutes later, they were facing a suspicious receptionist who looked at them askance.

Jarvis blushed when he realised what the older woman was thinking and quickly took out his identification. 'We're working on a case; we just need rooms for a few hours.' His heavy emphasis on the plural seemed to settle the woman's over-vivid imagination, and she handed him two key cards.

'She thought you were a rent boy, did she?' Andrews asked yawning, as they walked toward the lift.

Jarvis coloured again. 'I suppose you see it all when you work in a hotel.' Checking his key card, he laughed. 'Suspicious cow,' he said. 'She's put us on different floors.'

27

Andrews and Jarvis were used to long hours and little sleep when on a case. Neither thought three hours sleep was bad, and the late breakfast in the hotel was certainly worth getting out of bed for. 'What's the plan?' Jarvis said, swallowing the last of his sausage with a mouthful of tea.

Andrews placed his knife and fork across the plate and groaned with pleasure. 'That was something,' he said. 'Okay, we'll pick up the car, collect West and Edel and head back to Clare Island. I want to catch the bastard who left them for dead.'

'Pretty keen to get my hands on him too.' Jarvis drained the last drop of tea from the pot. 'We're not staying in the same place as them, are we?'

'You want Morrison to have our guts for garters? There's rooms to be had in that pub, Ryan's, we'll stay there.'

The local garda station was a ten-minute walk from the hotel. Within minutes of identifying themselves, the station sergeant came out to greet them. 'I've been asked to offer you every assistance,' he said, handing them a set of car keys. 'If you need uniform backup, we can let you have a few men.'

Andrews took the keys with a shake of his head. 'Thanks,

appreciate that, but we have a local man, Eamonn Hall, with us. We should be okay.'

'I know Eamonn, he's a good officer. As is your Detective Sergeant West, by all accounts. The best of luck in catching the bastard you're looking for.'

With a final agreement to leave the borrowed car in Athenry when they were done with it, Andrews and Jarvis took their leave and drove the short distance to the hospital.

West and Edel were sitting in the reception area waiting when they arrived. Both looked pale, but they smiled when they saw the two men coming through the door. 'About time,' West said, standing. 'We're starving. Have you seen what they serve for breakfast in hospitals?'

'We've eaten,' Andrews said, giving Edel a hug before standing back and looking her over. 'You sure you're okay?' he asked, seeing the dark circles under her eyes.

Edel patted his arm. 'I'm fine, honestly. Thank you both so much for staying, and for... well, for coming to our rescue, I suppose. Someone always seems to be rescuing me.'

'If a certain detective sergeant took better care of you, we wouldn't have to,' he said caustically, taking her by the elbow and guiding her out, ready to provide more support if he felt her waver.

West, walking side by side with Jarvis, followed behind. He gave the younger man a cordial grin. 'I'm never going to hear the last of this, am I?'

Jarvis smiled. 'Baxter and Edwards send their regards. Now that they know you're safe, they think it's hilarious that you did something so stupid.'

West decided it would be better not to make a comment.

'If you don't mind me saying,' Jarvis added hastily.

It would be a seven-day wonder, West hoped. He'd just have to put up with it.

They had something to eat in a local cafe before starting on the journey to Clare Island. 'I contacted young Hall,' Andrews told West as they drove, 'he's going to meet us at Roonagh Pier and take us over. I had a long conversation with him this morning. After they'd seen you off last night, they went looking for the entrance to the passageway. Someone had dragged a huge piece of masonry over it. He left Higgins guarding it until they can get hold of a garda forensic technician to go over and try to get some trace off it. He's an efficient officer, isn't he?'

West grunted a reply. It was a difficult thing to think of someone deliberately setting out to kill you. He twisted in the seat to look at Edel. 'You doing okay?' he asked.

'Sam is keeping me entertained,' she replied, smiling at him. 'Stop worrying, I'm fine.'

He had to be content with that. Turning back, he said, 'Hall hasn't gone to speak to Finbarr, I hope.'

Andrews threw him a glance. 'No, he hasn't. I told him last night to keep him under surveillance, but not to approach. Finbarr helped with the first part of the search, heading home when the Civil Defence people arrived. But Higgins was there; he'll have told Finbarr everything, I'd imagine.'

Jarvis leaned forward. 'Those Civil Defence guys were brilliant. I've never had dealings with them before. We were so lucky they were doing some training in the area. They even had two Rope Rescue Responders with them. They're the ones who abseiled down to you.'

West hadn't known the details of what had occurred. 'I don't think there was anyone on the island who didn't help in some way,' Andrews said. 'Daisy and Tadgh are a popular couple. Tadgh has contacts in the GAA, so we had an influx from the local club as well. You'll owe a lot of pints in the pub, Mike.'

When they pulled into the car park beside Roonagh Pier, they saw Hall standing chatting to a couple of elderly women. Seeing the car, Hall headed over, reaching it as West climbed out.

'There was a moment when I didn't think I was going to see you again,' the young garda said, reaching for West's hand and shaking it. 'Lord, what a night you gave us.' He bent to peer into the car. 'You okay, Edel?'

She smiled and nodded. 'Honestly, I'm fine. Don't forget, when all of you were running around, we were both asleep.'

Nobody had looked at it from that point of view. West laughed, and the others joined in. The two elderly women, who still stood watching them, put their heads together.

'We're shocking the locals,' West said, leading the way to the pier where the garda boat was docked.

∾

Twenty minutes later, they were disembarking on Clare Island. 'The pub has rooms, doesn't it?' Andrews asked Hall.

'You're staying at the Clare Island Lighthouse, both of you,' West said. 'You too, Eamonn, if you're staying over.'

'Morrison will have a heart attack,' Andrews said. 'We'll stay in the pub; we'll be fine there. And you two can have a bit of privacy.'

West reached across and gripped his arm. 'I wasn't asking you to share our room, Peter. I insist, it's my treat, and the least I can do after you both rode to my rescue.' He waited with bated breath, hoping Andrews wouldn't see it as some kind of charity. He was sensitive when it came to things like that, as West knew only too well. 'Please, Peter,' he said, 'I owe you.'

Edel added her persuasive skills to the mix. 'Oh, do say yes, it's a fabulous place and the food is amazing.'

Andrews glanced at Jarvis. 'What d'you think, Sam? Will we spend a night watching these two making cow eyes at one another, for the sake of a decent meal?'

'Cow eyes,' West said in disgust, putting an arm around Edel's shoulder. 'We do not do that.'

'I don't know, we'll start getting a reputation if we check in together again,' Jarvis commented.

'You've told Baxter and Edwards that story, haven't you?' Andrews said with a baleful look at the younger man, knowing by the glint in his eyes that he had. 'My reputation is ruined. Well, I suppose we may as well stay at this posh place to compensate.'

West and Edel exchanged a confused look.

'I'll tell you about it someday,' Andrews said, 'when you're in need of a laugh.'

'I'll be heading back,' Hall said, 'but thank you, I appreciate the invite. Do you want to go into the pub and we can discuss the next step?'

It was agreed by all to be a good idea. Heading inside, they took over a corner near the fire, moving chairs to make themselves comfortable.

'Pints all round?' West asked.

'And a coffee for me,' Edel said.

Minutes later, West returned with a tray holding four pints, three Guinness and a Heineken for Andrews. 'He's bringing your coffee in a sec,' he said to Edel before sitting beside her. 'It would be nice just to stay here drinking excellent Guinness all day, wouldn't it?'

Andrews shook his head. 'Not with that bastard on the loose. I'll enjoy a pint more when he's locked away.'

'You think it was Finbarr?' Hall asked, before picking up his pint and taking a long pull.

West shrugged. 'We were discussing this last night. I wasn't sure about his involvement before. His criminal drug history is just that... history... but he is a user, and the local drug squad have been keeping an eye on him, so they've had their suspicions. Someone was definitely using the passageway to smuggle something in or out.'

'Eoin Breathnach probably found out. Maybe he threatened to turn him in. So, he killed him,' Andrews said.

Hall looked from one to the other. 'It all ties together.'

West, in the act of lifting his pint, stopped and held it for a moment. 'It seems to, doesn't it?'

'But you're not convinced?'

'I'll be happier with some hard evidence.' West smiled and took a drink. 'When's the local garda technician coming?'

Hall checked his watch. 'She should be here in about an hour. She'll ring me when she gets near. I can take her to the passageway myself, if you'd prefer not to go back.'

West shook his head. 'I have a vested interest in making sure she does a thorough job, Eamonn, but thanks.'

They chatted about the case as they waited. Jarvis, still fascinated with the workings of the Civil Defence, asked Hall if he had worked with them before.

'Yes, we use them quite a bit. With the islands and mountains to cover, we get a lot of search and rescue calls. They're a huge asset; they have medics, the Rope Rescue Responders you saw in action last night, and search and rescue people. They have ultra-high frequency handheld radios that work on parts of the island where we can't get signals. They have boats too, and have inter-boat communication.'

'Why didn't they use their radios to contact the coastguard last night?' Jarvis asked. 'Morse code is a bit slow.'

Hall took another mouthful of Guinness. 'Their handheld radios are for on-site use, to communicate within a disaster area, that's all. They could communicate with each other, but not the coastguard vessel.' He drained his pint just as his mobile rang. He answered it, checked his watch and said, 'I'll be waiting.' Hanging up, he smiled at the attentive faces watching him. 'That was Fiona Wilson, the local garda tech. I'll head back to the mainland and pick her up. We should be back in about an hour.'

After he left, West thought he'd better ring the inspector and get the no doubt sarcastic comments out of the way.

To his surprise, Morrison seemed genuinely pleased that he was all right. 'Are you sure you are cleared to be back at work?' he asked.

'I'm feeling fine, sir. We both are, thank goodness. I've more reason to get this case settled now, anyway.'

Morrison grunted down the line. 'You're thinking it's the same person?'

'Clare Island is small, Inspector. The average population is one hundred and fifty people. I think it's highly likely.'

West's next call was to Seamus Baxter. 'Seamus,' he said, 'any more info for us on any of the characters here.'

'Sergeant West,' Baxter said, 'you okay?'

West was tired of answering the question. 'Fine, Seamus, I'm fine. I could do without any smart remarks though.' He guessed Baxter had been just about to make one when there was an extended silence. He knew the irrepressible man would get whatever dig he was about to make in at a later date.

'I've dug around a bit but so far, nada,' Baxter said. 'But I've other places to look. I'll give you a shout if I come up with anything.'

'Okay, thanks Seamus,' West said, hanging up. 'Nothing,' he told Andrews. 'But he'll keep digging.'

'Like a mole,' Edel said, sipping her coffee.

Both men smiled. The description suited the slightly chubby Baxter perfectly.

'You don't need to come to the passageway with us, Edel,'

West said, 'why don't I drop you at Toormore House? Maybe Sylvia will be feeling sympathetic and offer to show you her studio. I know you're dying to see more of her work.'

Edel's eyes lit up. She hadn't wanted to return to the passage and now she had a way out. 'I'd love that,' she said, giving him a warm smile.

∼

A little over an hour later, Hall pushed through the door followed by a slight, pretty woman who looked, at first glance, to be in her late teens. Hall made the introductions. West, grasping the woman's firm dry hand, decided his first impression was off by at least twenty years. Up close, she was still pretty, but faint lines told a story of experience, adding rather than subtracting from her looks. She was, he decided, an interesting-looking woman.

Offered a coffee, Fiona Wilson shook her head. 'Thanks, but I'd prefer to get on, if that's okay. I'm heading to Dublin immediately after, so I'll take the samples with me.'

Nothing else needed to be said. With a wave to the barman, they headed out just as Tadgh pulled up outside the pub. 'I gave him a shout,' Hall explained, 'we'd never all fit into my car.'

'Well done,' West said. 'We'll go with him. I want to drop Edel at Toormore House first. We'll catch up.'

Tadgh brushed off any attempts West and Edel made to thank him for his part in their rescue. 'We pull together here,' was all he said, and took off up the road at his usual speed, leaving Hall's car still standing by the harbour wall.

The gates to the house were closed. 'Hang on here, Tadgh, I'll take Edel inside and come back,' West said.

They walked round the garden and up to the front door.

'You'll be okay, won't you?' West asked. 'I should be back for you in about an hour.'

Edel kissed him lightly on the cheek. 'Stop worrying, I'll be fine. If Sylvia isn't in the mood to show me her studio, I'll just persuade Linda to make me some coffee.'

When the door opened to a less-than-welcoming Linda, West grinned at Edel. 'Good luck with that,' he said and headed back to the car.

Edel fixed a smile on her face. 'Hi, Linda, I was hoping to have a word with Sylvia.'

The housekeeper looked her up and down. 'You look pale,' she said, her voice more friendly than Edel had ever heard it. Standing back, in an invitation for her to enter, she continued, 'I'll go and see if she's free.' And leaving her standing in the hallway, she vanished through a door.

Looking around the large hallway, Edel wondered why it wasn't filled with Sylvia's paintings. Instead, there were a few dull landscapes, a heavy, rather ugly hall table and nothing else. No chair. And she would really like to have sat down. Her recent experiences had taken more out of her than she'd expected.

She was still standing several minutes later when Finbarr came down the stairs, his eyes brightening when he saw her. 'Someone to play with,' he said cheerfully. With a wicked grin, he added, 'perhaps not hide and seek though, eh?'

Resisting the impulse to punch him, Edel offered a forced smile. 'Perhaps not,' she agreed and tried to ignore him, hoping he would continue to wherever he was going, wishing Linda would return and rescue her.

She was in luck. Just as Finbarr reached the final step the housekeeper returned and shot him a baleful glance. 'You're supposed to be entertaining the Tilsdales,' she said, her voice tight with annoyance. 'Go and do something with them, will you?'

Finbarr sighed dramatically and with a wave at Edel, disappeared through another doorway.

Linda stared after him, her ears cocked. Only when she heard the sound of voices, did she turn her attention back to Edel. 'He'll stay five minutes and leave again, and they'll be after me asking for coffee and herbal teas. They'd never dream of helping themselves,' she went on, 'unless it's to wine and whiskey. The sooner they all go the better.'

'They must be a support to Sylvia, though,' Edel suggested.

In a return to her usual acerbic manner, Linda glared at her. 'You know nothing.'

Edel clearly heard the unsaid, *you stupid girl*.

As if reading her mind, Linda ran a hand over her face. 'I'm sorry. It's not your fault they're driving me crazy. They don't bother Sylvia; she never comes out of her studio. I don't think she's even seen them since Eoin died. They're just sitting around like vultures.'

'Like vultures? They're not expecting anything in his will, are they?'

Linda looked momentarily confused and shook her head. 'No, I meant they're eating and drinking at his expense. We're using four or five bottles of wine a night, and I've lost track of the amount of whiskey we've gone through. Good stuff too.'

Edel smiled to herself.

'Anyway,' Linda said, shaking her head, 'you didn't come to hear my woes. Sylvia will see you.'

Edel felt a shiver of excitement as she followed her to the studio. She was going to see paintings by a famous artist that had never been seen before.

At the studio door, it was several seconds after the gentle knock before they heard the rattle of a key. The door opened and Linda, with a quick look around, nodded at Edel and stepped back and was gone before she could offer her thanks.

Sylvia B stood to one side and waved Edel in without a word. The studio was far bigger than Edel had expected but what caught her breath was the wall of glass on the far side – floor to ceiling windows giving a stunning view of the wild grey sea. It was mesmerising. Her gasp of awe was involuntary and raised a low chuckle from the woman who stood watching her. 'It has that effect on me every day.'

'It's breath-taking,' Edel said, walking towards the window. Closer, the cliff was visible, but only a few feet stood between this part of Toormore House and the sea. Remembering Roger Tilsdale's comments, Edel thought she could see his point. How soon would this amazing room be at risk?

'It's inspiring,' the woman behind her said.

Turning, Edel looked to see if grief had impacted on the artist. If it had, there were no visible signs. But then, the woman was already pale and thin. Her black cap of hair was tousled, and, as before, she wore no make-up. Her dress, another of her favoured floating, gauzy numbers was liberally speckled with paint, as were her face and hands.

Edel gave a surreptitious glance around to see what she was working on. Unfortunately, she was in the wrong position and all three canvasses on the easels had their back to her. Did she work on them simultaneously, she wondered, waiting for the opportunity to ask, afraid to alienate the artist by jumping in too soon with questions.

'You had a terrible ordeal,' Sylvia said, approaching her. 'I've heard all about it, the basic facts from Linda, and a rather more dramatic account from Finbarr.'

Edel tried to smile. 'It was pretty awful.'

Sylvia narrowed her eyes. 'It was awful, and all you want to do is forget about it, don't you?'

Edel was surprised. 'Am I that easy to read?'

'Artists are good at seeing the subtle nuances,' Sylvia said with a shrug. 'Come and look at my paintings, maybe they will help replace bad memories with good ones.'

Edel held her breath as she walked round, letting it out in a gasp of sheer pleasure.

Sylvia, her melodic voice perfectly in harmony with the subject matter, explained. 'I had originally planned a bigger, single painting, but the logistics of such a size were beyond me so, instead, I decided on a triptych. Apart from a few minor changes, it's finished.'

It was the view from the window. Sea and sky painted in hues of blue and black. The beauty, power and destruction of nature untamed. It was thrilling, overwhelming. Edel was speechless.

As if pleased with her reaction, Sylvia smiled and then, moving to a corner of the room, she poured two cups of coffee, adding milk to both. She took them over, held one out to Edel who took it automatically, and stood with her staring at the paintings.

'They're stunning,' Edel said eventually.

'People look at art in different ways,' Sylvia said, 'some will look at these, and see sky and sea, nothing more. Others will see it as an allegory for something or other. I'd be interested to know what you think.'

Edel shivered suddenly. She gave the question some thought before answering, the artist standing quietly beside her, waiting. 'It would be easy to dismiss them as very good paintings of the sea, easier, perhaps, than seeing what they represent.' She turned to face Sylvia. 'Good and evil. The power of each, and how focusing on one can fool you into ignoring the other. The sea can be stunningly beautiful, but you ignore its destructive capability at your peril.'

Sylvia smiled.

Edel looked at her curiously. 'Is that what you were trying to express?'

'I never share what I'm trying to express, it ruins it for some. People buy paintings because they like what they see, or because it means something to them. They don't really want to know what it means to the artist.' She gestured to the far corner of the room. 'Come, and I'll show you some other pieces I've done recently.'

There were several smaller canvasses, mostly seascapes, gentler, less threatening versions than that portrayed in the dramatic triptych. There were also a couple of landscapes with the sea as a backdrop. Edel exclaimed over one depicting the lighthouse. 'That's where we're staying. How lovely.'

When she had seen them all, Sylvia invited her to sit and poured more coffee.

'Will your agent take all your completed canvasses with him when he goes?' Edel asked. She would love to know how much they cost, wondering if she could afford to buy the one of the lighthouse. If he were taking them with him, perhaps she could visit the gallery and find out.

But Sylvia merely shrugged. 'Tell me,' she asked, changing the subject, 'who does your policeman friend think is responsible for locking you inside the passage?'

It was Edel's turn to shrug. And then, because she suddenly, inexplicably felt sorry for the woman who had lost her husband, and who might very well lose her son, she said, 'They think the passage was being used to smuggle drugs.'

Sylvia caught her gaze and held it. 'Finbarr?'

She tried to look away but Sylvia reached out a hand and caught her wrist. 'You're hurting me,' Edel said, surprised to hear a quiver of fear in her voice.

Sylvia must have heard it too. Letting go, she stood abruptly and walked to the window. 'It was inevitable, I suppose. They'd have dug into all of our lives, our histories. They've probably found out about Finbarr's bit of trouble in school. It's hard to keep secrets in this part of the world; people have long memories when they've nothing else to do.

'He's been in trouble with drugs on and off ever since. The psychologist I sent him to described him as having an addictive personality type, if it weren't drugs it would be alcohol or gambling or sex. Or a combination of them all.' She smiled, making the resemblance to her son more striking. 'Thankfully, Finbarr is mono-addictive. It's only drugs and even then, it's a bit of weed or the occasional foray into the latest designer drug. He's never, to my knowledge, done heroin.'

'Did you know he was bringing them in?' Edel knew she should stop, but curiosity kept her going. Anyway, it wasn't doing any harm and she might learn something she could pass on to West.

Sylvia ran paint-spattered fingers through her hair. 'I don't think he's the one you're looking for. Finbarr is absolutely useless at keeping secrets, you know, he could never have pulled it off. And if the gardaí think whoever is bringing the stuff in murdered Eoin, I tell you straight, it wasn't Finbarr. He'd never kill his father.'

She wouldn't be the first woman to be fooled by a man, Edel thought, with a sudden bite of bitterness. 'They didn't get on, did they? Finbarr made no secret of that.'

'A lot of fathers and sons don't get on; they don't all kill them.'

'But he wasn't his father, not really. Maybe that made it easier.'

Sylvia looked at her with her head tilted. 'What makes you think he wasn't his real father?'

Edel's mouth fell open. 'What?' She laughed uncertainly. Sylvia was pulling her leg. Wasn't she?

'Eoin *was* Finbarr's real father.' Sylvia laughed with genuine amusement. 'Do you know how good it feels to say that? To be able to say it at last.'

Stunned, Edel struggled to find words, finally saying, 'But he's years older than you.' She tried to remember what she'd heard of Sylvia's past; all she could think of were two statistics. She'd been fifteen when she had Finbarr. And Eoin was thirty years older than her.

'It wasn't a spotty-faced boy in the town,' she said quietly.

Sylvia smiled. 'That was my cover story.' The smile slowly faded, replaced by a look of deep sadness. She hesitated, as if afraid to say more and then, with a look at Edel's sympathetic face, she continued. 'There was a shortcut home from school that took me across fields, but planning permission was given to build houses and it was fenced off. Within a few weeks, the fence had holes everywhere and me and other kids still used the shortcut.' She sighed. 'I was daydreaming about one of the boys in school. It was almost Easter, there were lots of parties, and I was hoping to bump into him.' Her laugh was brief and bitter. 'Daydreams. Innocent daydreams.' It was a few minutes before she spoke again. 'Off in a world of my own, I wasn't paying attention, and he caught me as I came through the fence. He said he was going to call the police, and dragged me into one of the almost finished houses.' Sylvia wore a stricken look as she remembered what had happened, and Edel felt her heart begin to pound.

'He told me he'd let me go, but he'd have to spank me first and told me to bend over a bench. I thought it was better than him calling the police, so I did what he said.' She smiled sadly. 'God, I was an innocent fool. Even when he pulled my skirt up, I thought he was just going to hit me. When I realised what was going on, it was too late. He held me down, tore my knickers off and pushed himself into me. The pain was excruciating, I can still remember it.' She sighed again, a long mournful sound that made Edel shiver.

'I thought that was it; that that was the worst that could happen to me. But he wasn't finished. I lay there, still stretched over that damn bench, afraid to move. I could hear him behind me and then... I don't know how many minutes later... he was on me again, his hands, pulling my blouse out to feel my breasts. I could feel his hard penis poking, and then he buggered me.' There was silence for a few seconds. 'I thought he was going to rip me apart.'

'Oh my God!' Edel, stunned, couldn't think of another word to say.

'He left me there,' Sylvia said, her voice trembling, tears running down her face.

Edel wanted to move, to offer some kind of physical support. But she couldn't, all she could think of was the horrifyingly clear image of the young girl bent over the bench.

Sylvia's voice still trembled. 'It was at least an hour before I could move. I was in luck, there were some old paint-spattered rags lying around and I used them to clean the blood away. I managed to tidy myself enough to get home and up to my bedroom without anybody knowing.'

'You didn't tell your mother? Ring the gardaí?' Edel was appalled, imagining the traumatised girl dealing with the rape alone.

Sylvia shook her head. 'I was ashamed and just wanted to forget about it. A month or so later, the housing estate was finished and there was a big write-up in the local paper and there he was, Eoin Breathnach. I saw his name, and I remembered it. I swore someday he would get what was coming to him.

'And then I discovered I was pregnant.' She laughed without humour. 'Actually, my mother did. She noticed the bulge and questioned me. It had never entered my head, you know. My periods had only just started and it wasn't something I'd considered. She wanted to know who it was. I spun her the story of a boy in town, but refused to name him. I was lucky; she and my father supported me, stood by me, watched over Finbarr when I went to college, while I established myself as an artist.

'I saw Eoin in the newspaper and magazines over the years and finally met him again at a gallery opening in London. He didn't recognise me. I chatted him up, invited him to dinner and made him a proposition.'

Edel waited to hear what it was. When Sylvia appeared to have become lost in her silence, she couldn't help herself, she asked, 'What was it?'

Sylvia shrugged and smiled. 'I'd already discovered how difficult it was to make it in the art world without a wealthy sponsor. I offered him a deal: I wouldn't tell the world he raped a fourteen-year-old child and was the father of her son and, in return, he would marry me, allow me full access to his wealth, and adopt Finbarr officially.'

28

Edel shook her head. It was all pretty unbelievable. 'Why marriage? Why not just ask him for money?'

Sylvia smiled wickedly. 'He'd never married. In interviews over the years, he always said it wasn't for him, that he liked his freedom too much to be shackled to one woman. I decided to shackle him.'

It seemed a bit crazy to Edel.

Sylvia saw the reaction on her face. 'You don't understand,' she said. 'I was a well-known, well-regarded, slim and elegantly attractive woman who mixed with a very arty set. Men were always coming on to me, women too, and I couldn't bear any of them to touch me. Being married was such a relief. All I had to do was wave my wedding band, and the huge, incredibly expensive engagement ring, and they left me alone.' She laughed. 'You didn't think I slept with him, did you? Oh, my dear, that wouldn't have worked. He liked them young. Very young. A thirty-year-old woman didn't do it for him. And as for me, that rape, all those years ago...' She shrugged.

Edel walked back to the triptych. It had unsettled her, but it made more sense now. She thought she understood. It wasn't beauty overwhelming darkness that it depicted, but the opposite. 'It's your life,' she said at last, feeling the artist come to stand beside her once more. 'You've never come to terms with it; it's behind everything you do. Dark and cold.'

'My most autobiographical piece, definitely.'

Edel turned to her. 'You killed him, didn't you?'

Sylvia opened her mouth to speak but closed it again as a sharp knock sounded on the door. Without another word, she smiled at Edel and went to answer. It was Linda, and at her back, West and Andrews.

'Wilson has finished collecting samples,' West said, his eyes flicking between the two women. 'If you're ready to go, we'll head back.'

What rotten timing, Edel thought, turning to say goodbye to Sylvia.

'I'm glad you came to see me, Edel,' Sylvia said, 'and please don't worry. There is another way of looking at the triptych, you know. Things aren't always what they seem.'

And what was that supposed to mean? Edel wondered as she followed the two men from the house to where Tadgh was waiting with the engine running. She climbed into the back, keeping her thoughts to herself despite a concerned look from West and a quizzical glance from Andrews. She needed time to process what she'd learned.

∽

Back at the quay, they stood while Eamonn Hall loaded the samples they had collected onto the boat. They had watched, surprised, at the speed and efficiency of Fiona Wilson. She'd gone alone down the passage, taking samples as she went, collecting several from the shallow cave, and from the rope and pulley system. Back on the surface, she'd smiled grimly at West. 'We'll get this bastard, Sergeant.'

Hall was ready, the samples safely stowed. 'Ready to go.'

Fiona nodded and turned to say goodbye. 'I'll get these to the forensic lab tonight. They've promised to push them to the front of the queue. You should start to get preliminary results tomorrow afternoon.'

She jumped into the boat and seconds later it was bouncing toward the mainland.

West was about to suggest a pint before they headed back, but he noticed Tadgh checking his watch. With a sigh, he herded the others towards the car and they bundled in, Edel sitting between West and Jarvis in the back, Andrews in the front.

~

At the guesthouse, West went in search of Daisy while Edel showed the two men into the drawing room. The fire had obviously just been lit; there was a lot of smoke, but not yet much flame. Andrews reached for a poker and started to move the coals about.

West came back, a smile on his face when he saw him. 'You'll put it out,' he said, sitting beside Edel. 'Luckily for us, Daisy said they have a few rooms free for a couple of nights. She'll bring your keys through when she's bringing the beer I ordered.' He turned to Edel. 'Our room is free until next weekend, so we can stay until then.' He saw her pensive face and frowned. 'You okay? You've been quiet since we left Toormore House. Did something happen?'

'Did you get me a drink?'

'Yes, a glass of wine.'

'Let's wait until we get our drinks, and I'll tell you. I think it might be important.'

Daisy came a few minutes later carrying a tray laden with drinks. Balancing it with practised ease, she placed a pint before each of the men and the glass of wine in front of Edel. From her pocket, she took two keys and handed one to Andrews and Jarvis with a brief explanation of where their rooms were. 'Dinner will be in an hour,' she said, and with a smile left them.

The fire had taken hold, small flames flickering. Edel kept her eyes on it, as she sipped her wine and told the three silent men Sylvia's tale.

West shut his eyes. He'd thought looking at paintings would be a pleasant change for Edel. Instead she'd been dragged even further into a case that was starting to stink. Eoin Breathnach was a rapist. Sylvia, his victim. Finbarr his biological son.

'She didn't answer you,' Jarvis said, his eyes wide.

Edel shook her head. 'Unfortunately, not. I don't know if she would have done. She did say something strange at the end.' She explained about the painting. 'Just as I was leaving, she said, "things aren't always what they seem".'

Andrews screwed up his face. 'Okay, so you had thought the painting was biographical, everything beautiful in her life buried by the darkness of her past, right?'

Edel frowned and nodded.

'Well, what did her weird comment mean?'

Draining her glass, she sighed heavily. 'I don't know. Why would she kill him after all these years? Surely she'd had plenty of opportunity.'

'Muddying the waters,' West said, 'just like Finbarr was doing the first time we met him. I wonder...'

'If she thinks he did it?' Andrews finished his thought.

Jarvis frowned. 'If they are both muddying the waters, perhaps each thinks the other did it.'

West slapped a hand to his forehead. 'Enough,' he said. 'My brain cannot take any more. I suggest we give it a rest until tomorrow. I need a shower.' He glanced at the two men. 'I always bring too much clothes with me, I can lend you both a fresh shirt, if you'd like.'

Jarvis, conscious of his grubbiness, was relieved and accepted immediately.

Andrews, who rightly guessed West was stretching the truth, asked, 'Are you sure?'

'Absolutely,' West replied, and stood. He planned to have a quick word with Daisy to see if she could have their clothes laundered. Shirts he could lend, but he drew the line at offering his underwear.

By the time he'd spoken to Daisy, and dropped the shirts off to Jarvis and Andrews, twenty minutes had passed. Edel was still standing in the same place when he got back, staring out the window. He put his arm around her, pulled her to him, feeling the sigh before he heard it. 'My plan to give you a nice break didn't go too well,' he said.

Edel gave a chuckle and lifted her face to look at him. 'I was really enjoying it, Mike. She is an amazing artist. There was one smaller painting with this place in the background. It was stunning. I was going to ask Mr Blacque how much it would sell for, but she was being a bit mysterious about whether or not he was taking them.' She smiled. 'It's probably too expensive anyway.'

West thought she was right but didn't say so. He wondered at Sylvia's unwillingness to commit her work to Blacque. He'd been her agent for years. Interesting, he thought, and then gave himself a mental kick. No more work this evening. 'Let's go have a shower,' he said, taking Edel by the hand, ignoring her comments that they hadn't much time. In the spacious bathroom, he pulled her to him again and lowered his mouth to hers, his tongue seeking, his hands moving over her, opening buttons, unhooking her bra, feeling her skin with a thrill of pleasure. Edel moaned when his hands stopped, but it wasn't for long. He undressed and led her into the shower cubicle.

It was top of the range with a huge square showerhead from which the water fell like rain. It was just what they needed. They stood under it for a long time, letting the water wash away the stress of the day. Then slowly, gently, West kissed her.

Suddenly, Edel pushed him away. 'We'd better get dressed,' she said, kissing him lightly. She saw his surprised look and kissed him again. 'I'm sorry, Mike. I just can't get what Sylvia told me out of my head.'

West closed his eyes. What an idiot he was. He gave her a kiss on the cheek and stepped out of the cubicle. With a towel around his waist, he went into the bedroom and sat on the bed, dropping his head in his hands. Mixing business and pleasure was never a good idea, especially his business.

He was dressed before Edel appeared, an overlarge dressing gown making her look small, fragile. 'I'm sorry,' he said. 'I was being particularly insensitive.'

Edel smiled and shook her head. 'It's okay. Really,' she said when his face remained sombre. 'Why don't you go ahead and have a pint with the others, I'll be down in about ten minutes.'

West hesitated, then with a brief smile, left the room.

∽

Jarvis and Andrews were sitting in front of the fire when he went into the drawing room. Half-finished pints in front of each showed they'd been there for some time.

'Edel will be down in a few minutes,' he said, when they greeted him. He sank into a chair and stretched his legs out. 'She's been through so much in the last year that I sometimes forget she's a civilian. Sylvia's story has hit her hard, I'm afraid.'

Jarvis grunted. 'She gets locked in a passage, almost dies from hypothermia, and to top it all hears a terrible story about an artist she admires. It's not surprising, is it?'

And then her boyfriend had expected sex, as if everything was rosy in the garden. West closed his eyes. He hadn't been insensitive; he'd been a pig.

Edel chose that moment to appear. She was wearing a turquoise dress that hugged her bust and waist before falling in gauze panels to the ground. She looked pale, but she was smiling as she stood in the doorway. 'I hope you're all ready for dinner. I, for one, am starving.'

∼

The dinner was superb and following West's orders nobody spoke about the case. Instead, they chatted about nothing in particular, drifting from topic to topic. Jarvis, a little uncomfortable at first, relaxed after his third pint and regaled them with an account of his holiday to the Grand Canyon the previous year.

'It sounds amazing,' Edel said, 'it's somewhere I've always wanted to go.'

Jarvis smiled broadly. 'Honestly, it's incredible. You should do what we did. A couple of days in Las Vegas, then hire a car and drive from there. We visited three national parks, Bryce, Zion and the Grand Canyon. It's an easy drive from one to the other, no problem at all.'

He was so enthusiastic and painted such a fascinating picture of his travels that Edel turned shining eyes to West. 'Why don't we do that?'

West grinned. 'Sounds like a plan.'

Just make sure not to find any dead bodies, Andrews wanted to say but he bit his tongue on the comment. They looked so damn happy together.

29

Next morning, they waited until after breakfast to discuss their next step. 'I can bring some more tea and coffee through to the drawing room if you'd like,' Daisy said, and if it was a subtle hint that she needed to them to move from the table, nobody took offence.

They declined her offer and left, meeting Eamonn in the hallway shaking raindrops from his coat. 'It's miserable out there,' he said, hanging his coat on a hook and wiping a hand over his face.

West gave him a concerned look. Recent events seemed to be taking their toll on him. He looked pale. 'We're heading into the drawing room. Why don't you ask Daisy for a hot drink?'

Hall smiled and shook his head. 'Thanks, I'm grand.'

The fire hadn't yet been lit, but from habit they sat in chairs surrounding the empty grate. 'We've some information to share with you, Eamonn,' West said, just as his mobile rang. Answering it, he said, 'Hi Seamus, we're all here listening, I'll put you on speaker.' He put the phone down on the coffee table between them.

Baxter shouted 'hello' resulting in a noisy few seconds as

everyone returned the greeting. 'Get on with it, Seamus,' West said finally. 'What do you have for us?'

'Something interesting for a change,' he answered. 'I had a call from Bob Phelan yesterday, he'd heard about your experience down the passageway. He wanted to know was there any proof that Finbarr was involved.'

'We don't have anything yet,' West said. 'Fiona Wilson, the garda technician was here yesterday, she took a lot of samples. Until we get something back from her, we have nothing.'

'That's not quite true,' Seamus said mysteriously, leaving a dramatic pause before continuing. 'While I was talking to Bob, I mentioned some of the other characters I was looking into. One name got his attention. Julius Blacque.'

'Julius Blacque,' West repeated, surprised.

'You know how it goes,' Seamus said, 'a couple of punters were caught under the influence and were offered a deal if they coughed up the name of their supplier. Blacque's name, or rather the name of his gallery, had been given a number of times, but when the drug squad investigated, they found nothing. Blacque told them he couldn't be responsible for people who attended his gallery showings.'

'Well he can't really, it doesn't sound very substantial, Seamus,' Andrews said, unimpressed.

A chuckle came down the line, reverberating off the wooden table. 'Ah, but you don't know the rest. I had a look into Blacque's finances. His gallery is successful, but he is broke. Very broke. I visited it in person last night and spoke to the assistant who works there. She doesn't like him much. It seems the very debonair Julius has a big cocaine problem, and that's where all his money goes. She also said there'd been some very shifty people calling on him, every month or so, for the last year.'

'Okay,' West said, 'that's certainly something to think about.

Thanks, Seamus, keep digging.' He cut the connection and pocketed the mobile, frowning. 'Well, thoughts on that?'

'Maybe not Finbarr then,' Hall said slowly.

'Maybe not, but if we're going on the assumption that the drug smuggler and the murderer are one and the same, what's Blacque's motive for killing Breathnach?'

'He impacted on Sylvia's productivity. Less paintings, less money,' Jarvis suggested.

'I don't think that's it,' Edel said, shaking her head. 'She has several finished paintings in her studio and was very cagey about whether she was giving them to him to sell for her.'

'Maybe she's heard about his drug problems. You said she was very protective of Finbarr, perhaps Blacque supplied him with drugs, she found out and wasn't happy?' Andrews said.

'Maybe Breathnach found out and he threatened to tell the gardaí?' Jarvis suggested. 'Losing his main client would be bad enough, maybe losing her and being arrested for drug trafficking would've been the last straw.'

There was silence for a moment as they all considered this option. West groaned. 'It's all supposition. We need that magic ingredient, cold hard proof. Or at least a solid confession. Let's go and see what our Mr Blacque has to say for himself, eh?'

On the way, as Hall drove, West told him about Sylvia's past. 'You'd never heard any rumours?' he asked him.

Hall shook his head. 'There was speculation about who Finbarr's father was, of course, but she never said.' He frowned. 'It happened before Easter, you said?'

Edel, crammed in the back between Andrews and Jarvis, leaned forward to answer. 'She said she was daydreaming about the upcoming Easter parties. I checked. Easter that year was early. It was in March.'

West glanced at Eamonn. 'Does that mean something?'

'No, it's just good to have a time frame, don't you think?' When West nodded, he continued with a smile. 'Finbarr looks so like her that the last gossip I heard said he'd probably been cloned.'

They were in luck; the gates to Toormore House were open. They drove up and parked outside the front door. Their knock was answered within a few seconds. Linda raised her eyes when she saw who it was, but she refrained from uttering any sarcastic remarks and stood back to allow them in.

'We'd like a word with Mr Blacque,' West said without elaborating.

With a shrug that said it was no concern of hers, she opened the door to the lounge they'd used before and left.

It was fifteen minutes before the door opened and Julius Blacque appeared. He was dressed in clothes more fitting to his gallery than a weekend in a country house. The dark suit was obviously expensive, the crisp, white shirt double-cuffed and sporting square emerald cufflinks that nobody for a moment thought were fake. Adding flamboyancy to ostentation, he wore a wildly patterned tie in vivid shades of purple and green. A spiv, West thought, the vulgar term springing into his mind, forcing him to look away for a second.

Julius Blacque nodded all round, took a sip from the glass he was holding, and sat. He put the glass on the small table beside the chair and dropped his hands in his lap, all evidence that he was relaxed and totally in control. 'You wished to see me, I believe,' he said. And if he hadn't managed to convey sufficient boredom by tone of voice, a yawn, barely stifled, was added for effect.

West wasn't fooled. It was a good act, but Blacque's eyes were too sharp and his hands had gone involuntarily from relaxed and open to white-knuckle gripped. 'We had an officer taking samples from the area in and around the passageway yesterday, Mr Blacque,' he said, and saw the man's lips tighten. 'We've had some preliminary results.'

Only Edel blinked at this blatant lie. A quick glance at the others told her it was as big an act as the one Blacque was attempting. Bigger. But it was succeeding. Before her eyes, she saw Blacque change, the posturing replaced with a hunted look.

He gave a reptilian lick to his lower lip, and then grunted a half-laugh. 'And?' he said, attempting carelessness.

'I think you know what we've found, Mr Blacque. It was easy to get a match, you know. One of my team visited your gallery. You have a nice set-up there, and your assistant was most helpful.'

A range of emotions crossed Blacque's face, from angry through defiant and then, oddly, to relief. 'It got out of hand,' he said quietly. 'All I wanted to do was clear some of my debts.'

West stopped him with a raised hand. 'I think before we go any further, we should read you your rights. Garda Hall, as this is your beat, will you do the honours?'

They all sat motionless as Hall read the dissolving Blacque his rights. His pomposity deflated, he suddenly looked foolish rather than flamboyant. 'What now?' he asked.

'You'll be taken to Westport. You can contact your solicitor there, and he'll be able to advise you.'

Blacque nodded. 'In the world I mix in,' he said, 'there's always drugs of some sort or another, you know. I joined in, to be one of the crowd and to make the contacts I needed. The art world is fickle, you can be agent of the month one moment and then, like bell-bottomed trousers, you're out of fashion. So, I'd take the odd pill.' He pursed his lips. 'The odd pill,' he repeated softly. 'Of course, you gentlemen will know better than most, that it's often the way with drugs. You think you can control it until suddenly it controls you.

'Once I started on the cocaine, things went quickly downhill. My judgement was seriously affected.' He sighed and rubbed a hand over his face. 'At a gallery showing early last year, I made the stupid mistake of offering Finbarr a couple of pills. Sylvia found out and threatened to report me. I begged her not to and she relented, but since then she's given me none of her work to sell.'

'That's why you're broke?'

Blacque showed no surprise that they knew his financial position. He nodded. 'That's why I'm here. Well, one of the reasons.' He tried a weak smile that died a quick death.

'When did the dealing start?' West asked.

'Dealing,' Blacque repeated, as if he'd just become aware of how serious an accusation it was. He shook his head. 'I was always generous with my pills; at gallery openings, they'd be available, free of course, for friends and acquaintances. Pills are cheap, after all.' He lifted a shaking hand to his face and rubbed his eyes. 'But cocaine isn't, and by this stage, I needed it. My supplier was understanding when I told him cash flow was a bit difficult, and he gave me some on tab.'

West and Andrews exchanged a knowing glance. The story was an old one, they knew what was coming.

Blacque caught the look and frowned. 'Yes, I know,' he said, 'I was reeled in like a fish. Within a few weeks, I was in debt for thousands, and they had me. They knew of this place and my connection to Sylvia, of course. They wanted to drop drugs at the marina, I was to pick them up and take them to the mainland when I returned.'

'But you had a better idea,' Andrews suggested.

Blacque shrugged. 'Sylvia had invited me to see her studio when she first moved here. One of the builders was still here, finishing off bits and pieces, I happened to get chatting to him and he mentioned a passageway he'd discovered when exploring. He reported it to his boss, but he'd already had run-ins with the Heritage people and archaeologists about building the house and didn't want any more difficulties. He told him to put a hatch on it and forget about it.

'It sounded fascinating, so I took a torch and went down to see for myself.'

Several raised eyebrows greeted this remark. It was difficult to imagine the pristine, elegantly suited man descending the passageway.

Blacque appeared not to notice. 'It was amazing, but I closed the hatch and forgot about it until a few months ago.'

'When your friends wanted you to do some drug running for them?'

'Yes. I brought the rope and pulley system over with me and took it down the first day I was here. It would have worked according to plan, except Breathnach died. With you lot swarming all over the place, I didn't think it was the best time to be carrying drugs anywhere. I went back to the quay the next day and contacted the supplier. Luckily, he agreed to defer the delivery until the situation was resolved.'

'But Edel and I stumbled on the passageway and you were afraid your little game was up?'

Blacque looked down, clenching his hands in his lap. 'I had no choice. If I don't do what they say, I'm finished. The bank is ready to foreclose on my loans, and Sylvia has refused to allow me to continue as her agent.' There was a hint of pleading in his voice when he repeated, 'I had no choice.'

'There's always a choice, Mr Blacque,' West said, 'you just made the wrong one and now, on top of everything else, you'll face a charge of attempted murder.' There was silence for a moment and then, with a shake of his head, West asked, 'Why did you kill Eoin Breathnach?' It was the last piece of the jigsaw, once it was slotted into place, it would be over.

Blacque reared back in surprise. 'Now listen here,' he said, raising his hand and jabbing his index finger in West's direction. 'I didn't kill him. You're not pinning that on me.'

30

'Do you believe him?' Jarvis asked when Blacque was gone.

Hall, taking the man into custody, had gone with him to pack his bag. He and Jarvis would bring him to the station in Westport where he would be charged with attempted murder. The attempted drug-running charge would be more difficult to make stick. West planned to hand that over to the drug squad. Bob Phelan might be able to mount a sting of sorts. The drug squad had their ways. He'd leave it to them as long as they didn't attempt to negotiate away the attempted murder charge – that wasn't an option.

He looked at Jarvis who was patiently waiting for an answer. 'Yes, I do. The drug running was an easy means to an end for him; he thought it would solve his money worries. A one-off and everything would go back to normal. He's a fool; they'd never have let him off the hook, but I think locking us in the passageway was a spur-of-the-moment thing. Breathnach's murder, on the other hand, was planned. Personal. Nothing to do with money.'

'So, we're no closer to solving the original crime than we

were at the start?' Edel said, glancing at West, Andrews and Jarvis in turn, bemused.

'It does look like that, I'm afraid,' West said.

'Won't you get into trouble for lying to Mr Blacque?' she asked, curious.

The three gardaí smiled. 'What lies did I tell?' West asked.

Puzzled, Edel hesitated. What lies had he told? 'You told him you'd found forensic evidence around the passageway and matched it to evidence you'd taken from his gallery.'

'I told him we'd found forensic evidence, I never claimed it was his. I told him his assistant had been very helpful, but I didn't say we'd taken any samples from there. He made the assumption. But,' West said, 'I'll ask Sylvia if we can take that glass' – he nodded to the glass Blacque had carried in with him – 'we'll get DNA from that. Just in case he changes his mind about being co-operative.'

'Gosh, you're a sneaky lot,' Edel said, looking at them all with amazement.

'A career criminal wouldn't have fallen for it,' West said, 'but Blacque is just a foolish man, a victim of his own stupidity.'

There wasn't room for all of them in the car. Andrews, who wanted to make a few phone calls at the quay, volunteered to go with Hall and Jarvis and come back for West and Edel.

'Let's walk,' Edel said, pointing to the window. The heavy clouds had dispersed leaving a few fluffy puffs of white in a blue sky.

'Good idea,' West agreed.

'Well, don't go down any more rabbit holes,' Andrews said with a smile and left.

Edel was still silently staring out the window. West moved to sit beside her and put an arm around her shoulders, pulling her close. 'You doing okay?' he asked, kissing her lightly on the top of her head.

'He didn't even say he was sorry.' She turned to look up at him with tear-filled eyes. 'He wanted to get his life back on track so much that he was willing to end both of ours. What kind of a man is he?'

West, who had met many of the same sort, just shook his head. 'The self-obsessed selfish sort. He'll be locked away and will lose everything he cares about; the gallery, his self-esteem, his reputation. Everything.'

Edel thought of Blacque in prison. 'He'll be less flamboyant there, won't he?' Pulling away from him, she stood. 'Let's go,' she said. 'Would you mind if we walked to the passageway? I'd like to see it.' She smiled. 'Call it closure, if you must.'

'We can call it whatever you like. Let's get out of here anyway.'

The day had brightened, but it was still cold and both were glad they'd borrowed warmer coats from the guesthouse. They strode out briskly, following the garden wall until they found an exit to the surrounding land. The passageway entrance was a mere ten minutes' walk away and they covered the distance in silence.

The hatch had been closed, a padlock ensuring it stayed that way. 'Hall had a local carpenter put it on,' West said. 'It won't be used for drug smuggling now.'

Edel shivered and turned away. 'Closed,' she said with a smile and then, hand in hand, they took the path back to the road. They'd just joined it when they saw Finbarr Breathnach coming from the house. He was the last person either wanted to see, but it would have been churlish, if not impossible, to have ignored him.

'Well, well,' he greeted them, with a huge smile. 'I heard the scandal. Imagine, the great Julius Blacque arrested for attempted murder. How the would-be mighty have fallen.'

'You didn't like him?' West guessed, falling into step beside him.

'Lord, no,' Finbarr said. 'I'm not sure anyone did, really. Sylvia tried; he'd helped her enormously when she was just starting. She would have stayed with him too, if he hadn't...' He broke off and shrugged.

'Tried to give you drugs?' West finished for him.

Finbarr grunted. 'Is there nothing you don't know?'

West looked at him. 'We still don't know who killed Eoin. But we won't stop trying to find out.'

'So I should hope,' Finbarr said, and waved a hand down a track. 'This is where we part company, I'm afraid.'

West peered down the grassy pathway but it curved out of sight. 'What's down there?' he asked, unable to resist.

Finbarr laughed out loud. 'Are you trying to prove there are some things you don't know? This is the way to our marina.' He looked at the garda, with a puzzled expression. 'Seriously, you didn't know?'

West shook his head.

'It's just a five-minute walk. We call it a marina' – Finbarr shrugged – 'but it's a jetty where we tie our boat up. The maximum it can berth is two, and the steps down to it are very steep.' With that, he gave a casual wave and headed down the track, vanishing round the bend as West and Edel stood and watched.

'I wondered what Julius meant when he mentioned the marina,' Edel said, 'I thought he meant the quay.'

West nodded. So had he. He frowned. There was something... he couldn't quite put his finger on it. He shrugged. It would come to him eventually.

They continued on the road to the quay, arm in arm, chatting about nothing in particular. The Grand Canyon came into the conversation again. 'Let's look into going next year,' West said, giving her arm a squeeze. 'At least there, I won't get involved in a police investigation.'

They met Andrews in the pub, a pint in one hand, mobile phone in the other. A fire crackling in the grate drew the new arrivals, both holding out their hands and moving zombie-like towards it. 'I'll get you a drink,' West said, rubbing his hands together, 'what would you like?'

Edel shivered. 'I think an Irish coffee would go down a treat.'

'Good idea.' He ordered one for each of them, and another pint for Andrews, carrying them over to the table while Edel stood warming herself by the fire.

Andrews hung up and frowned. Seeing the fresh pint, he nodded his thanks. 'You're not going to like what I've got to tell you.'

West groaned. 'Get it over with,' he advised Andrews, 'then I can enjoy my Irish coffee in peace.'

Andrews took a deep breath. 'That was the forensic lab. The stake we sent; the possible murder weapon? It was contaminated. They can't process it.'

West closed his eyes and let out a long hissing breath between his teeth. 'I saw Hall put the damn thing into a proper evidence bag. He sealed it. What the hell went wrong?'

'According to the laboratory admin who checked in the evidence, the bag was torn. It was with a number of other evidence bags which were intact but the stake could have been contaminated by particles from the outside of them. They've had to register it contaminated, and therefore will not be processing it as any evidence could be disputed.' Andrews took a long drink from his pint. 'That's what they said, anyway.'

Edel joined them, sat and picked up her coffee with a smile

of thanks. 'You don't look too happy, what's Peter been saying to you?'

He told her.

Edel, her top lip white with cream from her coffee, shrugged. 'You have no idea who killed him anyway, so there's nobody to compare evidence with, is there?'

West and Andrews both raised eyes to the ceiling. 'Firstly,' West explained, 'it doesn't look good when we mess up crucial evidence. Secondly, we may have no idea, just yet, but we will. Maybe not today, or even this year. The important thing about DNA evidence is it can be compared years from now. Not being able to prove the stake was the murder weapon is a big blow.'

Edel wisely kept an answering remark to herself and concentrated on enjoying her coffee. The fire had warmed her; the whiskey was finishing the job. As the alcohol hit her, she relaxed and let her mind wander, ignoring the two gardaí who were talking shop. Going back over what Sylvia had told her, she'd certainly view her work in a different light from now on, looking for the darkness in them. The painting of the lighthouse was beautiful, lighter; sometimes she'd managed to hide what had happened to her. Edel remembered something else Sylvia had told her. A lull in the conversation between the two men seemed the perfect place to pop it in. 'Sylvia said something else to me,' she announced, drawing their eyes to her. 'She said that she and Breathnach never slept together, that he considered her way too old for his taste. She was only fourteen when she was raped. Obviously, he had a thing for young girls. Maybe she wasn't the only one?'

Both men looked at her, and then at one another. Maybe she wasn't. Now that Blacque was out of the picture, they had to look elsewhere for a motive. West ran a hand over his face tiredly. 'It's something we'll have to look into.'

Andrews picked up his phone again. 'I'll give Seamus a ring; see if he can correlate reported rapes of underage girls with dates Breathnach was known to be in their area. If we can get a list of names, we'll see if any of them ring a bell. Of course, there will be those like Sylvia that went unreported.'

After telling Seamus what they wanted, Andrews' face turned sombre as he listened to what the other man said.

'Hang on a sec, Seamus, let me tell Mike.' He held the phone in his hand, picked up his pint and drained it. 'Seamus has a contact in the foreign office. It appears that for the last few years, Breathnach's been unable to visit his hotel in Cambodia. He was thrown out and asked not to return. He escaped prison by paying a very substantial bribe to the right person. His crime: sex with underage girls.'

'He's a paedophile?' Edel said, shaking her head in disbelief. She shouldn't be surprised after what Sylvia had said and wondered if she knew. If she did, and had done nothing about it, didn't that make her an accessory of some sort?

Andrews told Seamus to work on correlating reported rapes of underage girls with Breathnach's presence in Ireland. It was a vague, probably thankless job but it had to be done.

'So, what?' Edel asked, looking puzzled. 'You think he raped another girl and she or a relative decided to get revenge? Why wait until now?'

West ran a hand through his hair. He was sick of this case. Morrison would not be impressed. This was, after all, their third attempt to find a motive for Breathnach's murder. It was beginning to feel a lot like throwing a dart at a board of motives and seeing which one stuck. And there was something niggling him but he just couldn't work out what it was.

He had a quick word with Bob Phelan who was pleased they

had Blacque in custody but agreed with West that bringing a case against him for importing drugs was probably a no-go.

'All he has to say is that he would never have gone through with it,' Phelan said. 'On the plus side, they won't risk using Clare Island for a while; your adventure down the rabbit hole has brought too much attention to it. Keep in touch,' he said and hung up.

The rabbit hole. It was the second time the passageway had been described as such. West guessed he'd hear it many a time more before something else happened to entertain people.

There was nothing else to do. Deciding to head back to the lighthouse, West gave Tadgh a ring. 'He'll be here in fifteen minutes,' he said, hanging up. 'I'll just give Morrison a call while we're waiting, get it over with.'

Inspector Morrison reacted very much as he had predicted but, in light of West's recent experience, obviously felt unable to say much. 'It seems a bit tenuous, Sergeant West,' he said finally.

'It's just another line of enquiry, sir,' West said, and then decided to be blunt. 'It could go absolutely nowhere. But we have to follow them; you know what it's like.'

Morrison did. 'Keep me posted,' he said, and hung up.

'Let's wait outside,' West said to Edel and Andrews as he pocketed his phone.

Tadgh was earlier than expected and pulled up just as they stepped out. Just as well, West decided, feeling the cold bite. Back in the lighthouse, he and Andrews sat in front of the lounge fire puzzling over the case, while Edel headed to her room for a shower.

They'd not come up with any bright ideas when West's mobile chirped. It was Jarvis, ringing to say Blacque had been processed. 'It's too late to get back now,' he told them. 'I'll check into somewhere here in Westport for the night and be back in the morning.'

Hanging up, West said, 'Jarvis is staying there for the night.' He grinned, remembering his phone call with Morrison. 'Actually, I half expected Mother to demand you both return.'

Andrews yawned. 'I think he's pally with his Galway counterpart. It's quiet back in Foxrock anyway, we'll not be missed.'

West said nothing. He knew Andrews was lying; it was never that quiet. But he appreciated his company and his assistance, the case was turning into a right bugger. 'That building work in Westport must have lasted a few months,' he said, thinking back to what Edel had told them. 'Maybe Sylvia wasn't the only victim there.'

'There may have been more, but if they haven't been reported, there's no hope of finding out who they were.'

West took out his phone again. 'Sam, tomorrow, go into the local station and see if you can find any information on reported rapes, twenty-five years ago when Breathnach was in the area. We're wondering if Sylvia wasn't his only victim. If there are no reports, speak to one of the older officers, see if there's any gossip from that time. Okay?'

Hanging up, he redialled Hall's number. 'Eamonn, everything went well, I gather. We've had a bit of a hiccup with the stake we sent to forensics, the evidence bag was open, contaminated. Will you have a word with your colleagues there in Westport; tell them it was a mess. I don't want to go in all heavy-footed, but I can't let it slide.'

'No problem,' Hall said, 'I'll have a word with the garda who took it to Dublin, ask him for an explanation.'

'Fine,' West said, putting it out of his head. 'I've asked Jarvis to do a bit of digging there too, we're wondering if Sylvia maybe wasn't the only victim.'

'I could have done that,' Hall said, his voice sounding slightly affronted.

'No, sometimes people are freer with strangers,' West said

firmly. 'We'll see you back here tomorrow, we want to go and speak to Sylvia again.'

Both men finished their pints. 'I'm going to have a quick shower before dinner,' West said, standing. 'See you at seven?'

∼

He opened the bedroom door just as Edel came from the bathroom wrapped in a robe, her hair in wet tangles around her shoulders. 'I was hoping I would be in time to join you,' he said, putting his hands around her waist and pulling her towards him for a kiss.

'Perhaps you shouldn't have had the pint then,' Edel said, tasting the beer on his lips and giving him a smile. 'Too late now.'

West pulled her tighter. 'It's never too late,' he said, untying her robe and moving his warm hands over her damp breasts, squeezing gently. When she moaned, he pushed her onto the bed, pulling back only to strip quickly before joining her, moving the robe away to run his hands and mouth over her, making her moan even louder. 'God, you are so beautiful,' he whispered, and slowly entered her, feeling her orgasm before losing himself in his own and collapsing on her.

They lay for a few minutes in silence, neither of them moving. 'Am I hurting you?' West asked, levering himself up to look down on her.

Reaching up, she kissed him. 'No, but we'd better get moving. I don't want to see a knowing smile on Peter's face if we're late.'

West got up, pulling her to her feet. 'You need another shower,' he said, taking her with him into the bathroom.

A quick shower and she left him to it, returning to the bedroom to dry her hair and dress. Seven on the dot, they walked into the lounge where Andrews was chatting to two new arrivals. Seeing West and Edel arrive, he made his excuses and came and joined them.

'Journalists,' he said softly.

West gritted his teeth and nodded. They'd been lucky so far, but it was only a matter of time. 'They know who we are, I assume,' he said.

'Oh, I think we can safely bet on that, Mike.'

With all the guests sitting around one table, a forced conviviality that West normally enjoyed, there was no escape. Tonight, they'd have to guard their tongues.

Daisy called them for dinner and did quick first-name introductions as they seated themselves. The first few minutes were lost in a discussion of the six-course meal they were about to enjoy. West and Edel spoke of the meals they'd already had, using superlatives that had the two journalists, Ralph and Tony smiling.

'If it's half as good as you're saying, we're in for a treat,' said Ralph.

Conversation remained light while they all ordered. Once the food arrived it settled into a series of appreciative comments. It was followed by chat that revolved around food and wine, the two journalists telling tales of restaurants, good and bad, they'd been to with their job. 'We don't normally get to stay anywhere as gorgeous as here,' Tony said.

'Nor do we,' West said blandly. 'We're heading to the Grand Canyon next year, have either of you been there?' It was a good question; both men had and were quite happy to tell them of their experiences, suggesting routes, hotels and places to avoid.

It wasn't until coffee was poured that Ralph sat back, cup in hand and asked, 'It must have been quite a scary business being locked down that passage.'

At least he hadn't called it a rabbit hole, West thought and nodded. 'It was a bit,' he admitted, catching Edel's eye across the table.

Tony's eyes flicked from one to the other. 'I don't suppose you'd fancy doing an interview, would you?'

'The garda press office handles all requests for interviews, surely you must know that,' Andrews piped in.

'How about you, Edel,' he said, undeterred, 'you're under no restrictions.'

Edel merely smiled. Sometimes, even if it did go against the grain, playing dumb was the easiest thing to do.

'This is an expensive place to be staying, isn't it? Garda expenses must be good,' Ralph said snidely.

West had had enough. If it was going to descend into innuendo, he'd stop it now. 'We are here on holiday, at our own expense. Garda Andrews is staying at my request, and also at my expense. Unlike you, our stay here won't be submitted as expenses. Now, if you will excuse us, we're going to get some fresh air.'

In the hallway outside, they bumped into Daisy, her face creased in worry lines. 'I am so sorry,' she said, reaching out a hand to pat West's arm. 'I didn't know who they were until too late.'

'We can handle it,' West said, putting his hand over hers. 'Please, don't upset yourself over it.'

Daisy smiled gratefully and headed into the dining room. Putting on their coats, they heard her firm voice. 'There's been a mix-up, I'm afraid,' she told the two journalists, 'you're welcome to stay tonight, but after that, the rooms are unavailable.'

They heard the men remonstrating with her as they closed the door and faced the cold Atlantic breeze. 'She's well able for the likes of them,' Andrews said, turning up the collar of his coat.

It was too cold to walk far from the house. West, remembering that the lantern room was unoccupied, went back to get the key and led Edel and Andrews up to the viewing platform, a glint in his eye when he noticed Edel's blush.

Andrews was suitably impressed. They walked around the platform, admiring the distant lights on Achill and the clusters of lights on the mainland. Out at sea, the darkness was dense, and for a second Edel was reminded of Sylvia's triptych before she looked up and sighed with pleasure. Once again, the sky was cloudless, its darkness pierced by a million tiny pinpricks of light. 'Magical,' she whispered.

West put an arm around her shoulder. Yes, he thought, it was certainly that.

31

When they met for breakfast at nine the next morning, it was to find that the two journalists had already gone.

'I told them breakfast was served between seven and eight,' Daisy told them as they sat around the kitchen table. 'They had it at seven thirty. They've already left, so they won't be annoying you this morning.'

'That was so kind of you,' Edel said, touched by the woman's consideration.

Daisy smiled. 'You came here for a relaxing holiday. It hasn't really turned out that way, but there's no way we're going to add to your problems. We're well rid of them.'

'They won't cause you problems, will they?' West asked, thinking of poor reviews and bad press.

'Bless you, no, they won't. If they write a poor review, it will be offset by the hundreds of good ones we get. But, do you know, I don't think they'll bother.'

With that she headed back to her range and proceeded to deliver up three huge cooked breakfasts.

'What time did Hall say he'd get here?' Andrews asked, pouring himself another coffee.

'He didn't,' West said, holding his cup out. 'He'll probably be over shortly. He lives near Roonagh Pier, so it's just a twenty-minute boat ride. Then a ten-minute drive.' They'd finished their breakfast, and were ready to leave, but there was still no sign of Hall.

West's phone chirruped. He answered, expecting to hear Hall's voice. Instead, it was Jarvis.

'I'm heading to speak to Sergeant Brady in Westport,' he explained. 'Afterwards, I'll get a lift to Roonagh Pier somehow and get the late ferry to the island.'

'Have you heard from Hall?' West asked him.

'No, I haven't seen him since we left Blacque at the station yesterday,' Jarvis said. 'He was heading back to Roonagh afterwards. To be honest, I didn't find him the chattiest of blokes. I don't think he said one word on the journey.'

'Okay,' West said, 'keep in touch.' Shutting his mobile, he frowned. The same niggle that had annoyed him yesterday was back. He was missing something but he was damned if he knew what it was.

He tried Hall's number. 'Straight to voicemail,' he said, putting his mobile down.

'Why don't you leave him a message, and ask him to berth at Toormore's marina? We could ask Tadgh to drive us to Toormore House, and he could meet us there,' Edel suggested.

To her surprise, West's frown deepened and he said nothing for a few seconds. He closed his eyes briefly, and when he opened them, they were bleak. 'That's what's been niggling me,' he said. He looked at Andrews. 'Hall and I discussed the possibility of it being someone from the mainland. I asked him how long it would take to walk from the quay to Toormore House.'

'He said it would take an hour,' Edel said, remembering the conversation.

West nodded, his expression grim. 'But he never told us it

was possible to berth a small boat only ten minutes away, did he? And he must know about it. I bet he uses it, if he needs to visit the house or anyone on that part of the island.'

Andrews looked puzzled. 'What're you saying, Mike?'

West ran an impatient hand through his hair. 'Why didn't he mention it? He's an efficient garda; he'd have known it was important. Even if he hadn't thought to tell us then, he's had plenty of opportunity since.

'Add it to the mess-up over the possible murder weapon being contaminated and it makes me wonder about him.' Rubbing his face with both hands, he said, 'I suppose what I'm saying is, we'd better take a good look at Eamonn Hall.'

'We don't know that he was to blame for the evidence mess-up, after all, he didn't take it to Dublin, he just handed it over. The marina,' Andrews agreed, 'well, that's a different matter. That was a serious piece of information to leave out of the mix.'

He met West's eyes. Only something important would have made Hall conceal such a crucial piece of information; he was hiding something.

'I suppose it wouldn't do any harm to ask a few questions,' Andrews said. 'But we'd better be very, very careful here.'

Edel looked from one to the other. 'You're kidding, aren't you?' she asked doubtfully. 'You can't seriously think that Eamonn killed Eoin Breathnach. Why would he? He barely knew the man.'

'You don't have to know someone to want to kill them. Hall's from Westport. I think we'd better look into his family.'

Seeing where his thoughts were going, Andrews nodded. 'Jarvis is meeting Sergeant Brady, he's been there for years, if anyone knows anything, he will.'

Reluctant to go to Toormore House to interview Sylvia with this new idea running through their heads, they sat in the lounge and drank coffee, the pots supplied on a regular basis by a smiling Daisy. Plates of scones appeared mid-morning, accompanied by home-made jam and butter. They all looked, intending not to eat but the smell was tantalising and, as always, one after the other they gave in.

West had just taken his final bite when his phone rang. It was Jarvis and he sounded worried. 'I'll put you on speaker, Sam. Okay, go ahead.'

'Is Garda Hall there?'

'No, just Andrews, Edel and me. What've you found out?'

The sigh came loud through the speaker. 'It's not good. Sergeant Brady was very informative. There was only one reported rape, in May of that year. It was brutal and the girl was hospitalised.' His voice cracked. 'She needed surgery and afterwards… well, it seems she never spoke again. She committed suicide five years later, and shortly afterwards her mother took a dive off the Cliffs of Moher.'

'Did you get her name?' West asked, dreading the answer, suspecting it before Jarvis said the words.

'Sinead Hall. Eamonn's older sister. There were only the two of them Sergeant Brady said, and they were very close. Hall was really cut-up about the rape, and then her suicide, but he never spoke about it. Brady assumed he'd come to terms with it.'

'They never found who was responsible for her rape, did they?'

'Nope,' Jarvis said, 'she wasn't able to tell them anything. DNA evidence was collected, of course, and it should still be available. They eventually put it down to a transient; the case wasn't closed but it was certainly shelved.'

'Okay,' West said, 'get back here, Sam.' He put his phone down looking worried. 'We need to find Hall. He must have found out that Breathnach raped Sylvia and guessed he was responsible for his sister's rape too.'

'But who would have told him?' Andrews asked. He looked at Edel. 'Did she mention telling anybody else?'

Edel frowned. 'No, in fact, I was under the impression she'd never told anyone apart from Breathnach.'

'Why now?' West put in. 'Breathnach has lived around these parts for the last twenty-five years.'

Edel's eyes opened wide, and she grabbed West's arm. 'I bet Finbarr knows. Sylvia wouldn't have told him, but you've met him, he's sly as a fox and I bet he found out. It would explain his attitude to his father.' Her grip on his arm tightened. 'Do you remember a comment Finbarr made, the second time you spoke to him and you asked who would have wanted to kill his father. He said, *tell them, Eamonn* or something like that. Eamonn brushed it off, but maybe that's what Finbarr was referring to.'

West and Andrews, looking grim, agreed. It was a definite possibility.

Edel gasped. 'Oh God,' she cried, startling both men. 'Easter. Sylvia was raped before Easter, in March. His sister was raped in May. If Sylvia had reported Breathnach and he'd been stopped, his sister would still be alive.'

Everything had fallen into place. 'And that's why he's missing,' West said, getting to his feet. 'It's his last play; the final revenge for his sister. He's going to try and kill Sylvia. We've got to get to Toormore.'

They found Daisy in the kitchen peeling potatoes; she looked up and wiped her hands on her apron.

'We need to get to Toormore House. It's urgent.' West's tone of voice said it all. Daisy didn't hesitate; she reached up, took her car keys from a hook and handed them to him. 'It's parked around the back,' she said.

The car was a battered, and very old, Ford Fiesta. West looked at the key ring for the fob to open the door and realised it didn't have one. With a shake of his head, he inserted the key in the lock and then reached through the car to open all the other doors.

He drove quickly and, on the way, theorised about what happened. 'Hall left his boat at the marina and killed Breathnach. Then he returned to his boat and sailed to the quay where he bumped into us. What a perfect alibi we gave him, eh? It was just his bad luck that his sergeant fell and broke his leg and we became so involved in the case. He probably hoped his tale of a dramatic accident would have been believed and that would have been that.'

The gate was closed, but they didn't bother trying to get someone to open it, parking the car they ran to the house. West pressed the doorbell several times, paused for a second, and pressed it again. The housekeeper opened it with a face like thunder. 'What in heaven's name do you think you're at?' she spat at them. 'One ring is–'

What one ring was, she never got to tell them, West interrupting her bluntly. 'Where's Sylvia? She may be in danger.'

'Hardly,' Linda said, unimpressed, 'she's with Garda Hall.'

32

'Where are they?' West asked. 'In the studio?'

Finally grasping the fact that something was wrong, Linda frowned. 'No. At least, not now. They were there for a while, but when I looked in to see if they wanted a drink, the room was empty. Their coats are missing. They must have gone for a walk.'

The cliff path.

They turned, and with West leading the way, ran around the side of the house. The curve of the path made it impossible to see far ahead. They kept running and after a few minutes rounded a bend to see Hall walking slowly towards them, his head down.

Their feet were loud on the stony path and hearing them Hall looked up. Immediately he started to run toward them, shouting, 'Help, come quickly, there's been an accident.'

'Where is she?' West asked, gripping him by the arm.

'Oh God, it was terrible,' Hall said, covering his eyes with his hands. 'We were walking along the path chatting. Sylvia wanted to show me the scene she planned to paint next and moved closer to the cliff edge. I warned her to be careful, but she wouldn't listen and without warning the path gave way and she fell.'

'Show us where,' West said, his voice hard. Tightening his grip on Hall's arm, he turned him back.

'It's not far,' Hall said. He shook his head and snuffled. 'What a tragedy.'

West caught Andrew's eye. They had no proof it wasn't more than that. Gut instinct didn't count. He couldn't believe such a brilliantly talented woman would die in such a senseless way. Sylvia was a victim, just like Hall's sister. And he'd killed her.

'It was here,' Hall said, pointing to a spot where the path had indeed given way. But West's keen eye saw moss on the stones; this had happened a considerable time ago.

Andrews moved closer to the side to peer over. The cliff was steep; there was no gentle gradient to cushion her fall, and far below, wild Atlantic waves lashed the cliff base. She wouldn't have had a chance. He was turning away, his face grim, when he heard a cry. In disbelief, he peered over the cliff again, stepping closer despite Edel's warning to take care. 'She's there,' he shouted back to them, 'my God, she's standing on a narrow ledge.'

Andrews stepped back and dropped to the ground. He shuffled towards the edge on his belly, leaning his head over to call to the woman below. He had to shout to be heard over the noise of the wind and waves. 'Sylvia, we can see you. Don't move. Don't look up. Are you hurt?'

The answer was faint. 'No.'

'Okay,' Andrews said, 'we're going to get help. Just hang on, don't move.'

West was in a dilemma. He needed to get to somewhere where there was a phone signal, but he couldn't leave Hall. He was capable of anything. 'Stay with Peter,' he called to Edel who nodded, and then pushing Hall ahead of him, he ran back to the car.

'Get in,' he said to Hall, opening the passenger door and pushing him in before running around and jumping into the driver's seat. Keeping his phone in his hand, he flicked a glance at it every few minutes as he drove at speed along the road to the quay. If she fell... it didn't bear thinking about.

'You're under arrest, by the way,' he said to Hall, and read him his rights. 'You understand your rights as I have told them to you?'

'Yes,' Hall said, in a weary voice devoid of emotion.

'Why?' West asked, taking a turn too fast, hitting the soft edging and almost going off the road, swerving back with a grunt.

Hall waited a moment before saying softly, 'Breathnach raped my sister, destroyed her life, my parents' lives. He deserved to die.'

It was difficult to argue the case, except for one thing. 'You're a member of the Garda Síochána and have sworn to uphold the law. You could have had him in prison, for a long time. That would have been justice.'

Hall laughed, the sound bitter and twisted. 'He forced her to perform oral sex on him, can you imagine that? She was fourteen. Not content with that, he sodomised her, perforating her rectum. She had problems the rest of her short life because of that. After, when he had no more use for her, when she lay semiconscious on the dirty floor of an abandoned building, he left her there like discarded trash.

'You think a few miserable years in a cushy prison would have been justice for that?'

West checked his phone, still no service. 'Why Sylvia?'

'She knew who he was; she could have stopped him, and

saved Sinead. But she did nothing and then,' he laughed again, this time in disbelief, 'she married the bastard.'

West, checking the phone, saw what he was looking for. A signal. He pulled over, dialled the emergency number and asked for the coastguard. Quickly and precisely, he gave them the details. 'One of my colleagues is speaking to her. She seems quite calm and claims not to be hurt. The ledge she's on is narrow, there's no manoeuvrability.'

Hanging up, West did a U-turn and sped back to the house. Pulling Hall from the car, he dragged him to the front door and hammered on the doorbell. Linda answered, her usual expression of long-suffering replaced with a worried look. 'Is she okay?'

'Is Jim here?' West asked, ignoring her question, pushing Hall before him.

Linda nodded.

'Get him,' West said, and when she didn't move, raised his voice slightly. 'Now.'

Only seconds later, Jim arrived. He looked askance when he saw Hall being gripped tightly. 'What the hell is going on?'

'I need you to watch him for me,' West said. 'He's under arrest for the murder of Eoin Breathnach, and the attempted murder of Sylvia. I need to get back. She's on a ledge on the cliff; there's a coastguard helicopter on the way.'

Jim hesitated, just a moment, disbelief replaced by acceptance, and nodded. 'I'll lock him in the pantry.'

West left him to do just that and sped back to the clifftop.

Andrews was still lying on his belly looking down at Sylvia. He'd continued talking, knowing she probably couldn't hear what he was saying, but also knowing the sound of his voice told her she wasn't alone.

Edel, standing back, looked pale. West put an arm around her shoulders and drew her close. 'The coastguard is sending a helicopter from Galway. They should be here in a few minutes,' he told them both.

Andrews relayed the information to Sylvia, shouting, determined she would hear this piece of news at least. 'They'll have you off there before you know it,' he said.

Five minutes later, they heard the distant thwop-thwop of a helicopter, the sound growing reassuringly louder. As it approached, Edel and West stood on the cliffside waving, their action acknowledged by a flash of light.

The crew were skilled at maritime rescue. Battling the strong Atlantic wind, they lowered a winchman. It was a quick, efficient rescue and seconds later the three onlookers cheered to see Sylvia being hauled up into the safety of the helicopter.

West waited while Andrews backed away from the edge and rolled over before reaching down with a hand to pull him to his feet. 'A close thing,' he said, holding his hand tightly.

'Too damn close.' Andrews brushed dirt and gravel from his chest. 'Where's Hall?'

'Jim Higgins has him locked in the pantry. I read him his rights, so he's officially under arrest for murder and attempted murder.'

They turned to head back to the house.

'We were right?' Edel said. 'He confessed?'

He put an arm around her, hearing the shock in her voice. 'It's not always a good thing to be right, you've discovered. But yes, we were. His sister's rape was even more brutal and sustained than Sylvia's. It tore the whole family apart.'

They were almost at the house when they saw Finbarr, his face grey with shock, racing toward them, Roger Tilsdale puffing several feet behind.

'She's all right?' Finbarr said, grabbing West's arms.

Surprised at the strength of the young man's grip, West hastened to reassure him. 'She wasn't hurt, Finbarr. A few scrapes and bruises. That's all. The coastguard will take her to hospital to be checked over, but I'd imagine they'll release her within a few hours. She was incredibly brave.'

Finbarr didn't release his grip, in fact West felt the fingers digging deeper. 'Jim says it was Eamonn. That he pushed her over. Why would he do that?'

Reaching up, West removed the hands and turned him toward the house. 'Let's get back inside. We'll sit down and talk.'

'Shocking, it's all shocking,' Roger Tilsdale said, still puffing. He put an arm around Finbarr's shoulder as they made their way back to the house.

The front door was open when they arrived, Jim standing in the doorway watching for them. 'I saw the helicopter,' he said, 'she all right?'

Seeing West nod, he breathed a sigh of relief and directed them toward the lounge. 'We've lit the fire. Linda is making tea. Sit.'

They all did, finding space and sitting silently. Penny Tilsdale, her eyes wide with disbelief, had been roped in to help in the kitchen. She carried in a tray of cups and saucers, depositing them noisily on the coffee table, apologising unnecessarily for the noise and then disappearing mouse-like. Moments later, she returned with a heavy teapot and milk jug.

She stood with them, finding nowhere to put them and looking like she wanted to cry. Taking pity on her, Edel stood and helped, lifting cups for Penny to fill, adding milk and handing them around.

West, watching her with a measure of amusement, thought it was a brave person who was going to refuse to take it. He certainly took his, drinking the over-milked brew while he waited for someone to say something.

It was Finbarr who started. He held the cup and saucer in his hand as if not too sure what to do with it and looked at West, his face unusually serious. 'Eamonn killed Eoin, and tried to kill my mother, is that right?'

'Before we go into that,' West said, putting his cup and saucer on the floor, 'can I ask you something?'

Puzzled, Finbarr nodded.

'Were you aware that Breathnach was your biological father?'

Tilsdale gasped. 'What? That's preposterous.'

Finbarr merely shrugged. 'Their relationship puzzled me, so I did some digging a few years ago. Sylvia has drawers full of papers, newspaper cuttings, gallery programmes. You know the sort of stuff. I went through it all, and discovered she'd had an unhealthy interest in him, way before they were married.' He continued with a catch in his voice. 'The oldest photo was one celebrating the completion of the housing development in Westport, months before I was born. Breathnach's face had been circled; his name underlined. It didn't take long to find out how old he'd been at the time; how old she had been.' He sighed loudly, but without his usual dramatic flair. 'I remembered the way she couldn't bear to have anyone touch her, even me. Add to that, the look of intense dislike I'd see on her face when his name was mentioned, and how she never made any secret of the fact that she'd married him for his money. Even to his face. And the way he never retaliated.' He looked around at their faces. 'It wasn't too hard to put it together.'

'You never told her you knew,' Edel said.

Finbarr laughed softly. 'Do you know why?' He didn't wait for an answer. 'Because I didn't want her to confirm my suspicions. Truth is an overrated quality, if it forces you to face up to something best kept hidden.'

'But you did tell someone,' West said.

Finbarr looked at him, surprised. 'No, I...' he started to say, his eyes widening as he remembered. 'Oh God, I told Eamonn.

A few months ago. He was criticising me for hanging around, doing nothing. He was in uniform, looking all smug and entitled, and he bloody well looked down on me.' The cup rattled in the saucer he still held. Tilsdale, reaching over, took it from him. 'I wanted to wipe that smug look from his face, so I told him. And it worked, he looked shocked.'

West listened quietly. Shocked, of course Hall was. After all the years, he had discovered the identity of the man who had destroyed his sister.

Finbarr, looking puzzled, said, 'I don't understand. He killed Eoin because he'd raped Sylvia?'

'Not exactly,' West said with a sigh. 'Didn't you know about his sister?'

Frowning, Finbarr ran his hand through his lank dark hair. 'She was much older than Eamonn. I heard she committed suicide. He never spoke of her.'

'She was raped and never got over it.' West met his gaze. 'They never found who did it.'

'It was Eoin?'

'We don't have any proof, yet, but the circumstances are similar. We'll have the DNA checked. But it's a pretty safe bet that he was responsible, yes.'

Finbarr shook his head sadly. 'I thought about killing him, you know, when I found out. But I saw how much Sylvia tortured him, and figured she was doing a pretty good job of making him pay. Anyway' – he gave a slight smile – 'surprisingly enough, I'm not really the violent type.' He thought for a moment. 'Why did Eamonn try to kill Sylvia? She never did him any harm.'

West looked to Edel and gave a slight nod. He knew she felt guilty for telling Hall when Sylvia's rape occurred. He'd let her tell her own tale.

'Your mother told me that the rape happened on her way

home from school just before they broke for Easter.' Edel sighed. 'When I told Eamonn about it, he queried the date. I said Easter, and that it had been in March that year. The problem is, Finbarr, his sister was raped in May. Hall knew that if your mother had reported Breathnach, his sister would never have gone through that terrible ordeal and might still be alive.'

Roger Tilsdale reached across and put a reassuring hand on Finbarr's arm. 'She was just a child, they both were.'

'There's no blame attached, Mr Tilsdale,' West agreed. 'They were both victims of an evil man.'

'What will happen to Eamonn?'

'He'll go through the legal system. He's admitted the murder and the attempted murder. We'll take him to Westport; he'll be processed there.'

The door opened. Linda, her face pale, said, 'There are two reporters outside. They've heard about Sylvia; they want to know if someone will come and talk to them. They're not taking no for an answer from me.'

Tilsdale stood. 'Leave them to me. I'll get rid of them,' he said, patting Finbarr on the hand and leaving the room with Linda.

'He's been very kind,' Finbarr said, 'much more than I've been to him.' He looked at West. 'What happens now?'

'We're taking Hall to Westport to be charged.' He took in Finbarr's glum expression and for the first time, felt a twinge of sympathy. 'If you like,' he suggested, 'I can have a car meet you at Roonagh Pier to take you to the hospital.'

Finbarr nodded. 'That would be good, thank you.'

Roger Tilsdale came back muttering about journalists. He was told the state of play and, nodding, said he'd go with Finbarr. 'Those damn journalists already know where she is, they said they were heading that way.'

'We can cross on our boat,' Finbarr said, 'they'll be stuck waiting for the ferry.'

'I'll make sure they're delayed a bit more,' West said firmly. He'd give Westport a ring when they had a phone signal, get them to stop the two journalists. Ralph and Tony needed to learn a lesson.

Jim Higgins came with them to the marina, keeping a firm grip on Hall who was quiet and subdued. Nobody spoke to him, and Tilsdale kept Finbarr at a careful distance.

The steps down to the marina were, as Finbarr had explained, steep and tortuous, opening at the bottom to a short pier. The boat berthed there was just big enough for the six people sailing across. Bidding a farewell to Jim, Finbarr cast off and within minutes they were heading for Roonagh Pier. They were halfway there before they got a phone signal. Andrews rang the station in Westport and organised transport while West filled a stunned Morrison in on the identity of their murderer.

'How long will it take the gardaí to get from Westport to Roonagh,' West asked Finbarr after he'd hung up.

'About forty minutes,' he answered. 'It's a pretty windy road.'

Disembarking on the mainland, they had to wait thirty minutes in an uncomfortable silence before three garda squad cars and one unmarked car arrived.

The gardaí all knew Hall, of course, and their faces were stony as they looked at him, still in his uniform, disgracing it. Without a word, two of them manhandled him into the back of one of the vehicles.

Finbarr and Tilsdale were directed to the unmarked car.

'They'll look after you,' West said as they got in. 'Somebody will visit your mother, when she's feeling up to it, to get her statement.' He shut the door and the car sped off.

'What do you want to do, sir?' one of the Westport gardaí asked respectfully.

'Can any of you handle the boat?' West asked, pointing to the Breathnach boat.

The four gardaí looked at each other, as if he were asking a trick question. Realising he wasn't, the same garda answered with a grin, 'We all can, sir. It's necessary in these parts.'

That decided it. He and Edel could spend another night at the Clare Island Lighthouse. He looked at Andrews who nodded and smiled. 'Off you go,' he said, 'I can handle Westport and get that confession written up before he thinks better of it.'

West gripped his arm. 'I'll join you tomorrow.'

Edel gave Andrews a peck on the cheek. 'I'll babysit for you anytime,' she promised.

~

An hour later, they were back for their last night at the guesthouse. 'I might be able to swing another couple of nights,' he said to Edel as they stood in their room watching the stars come out.

'You've promised to join Peter in Westport tomorrow. With Eamonn being from these parts, he's going to need your support. We'll have other holidays, don't worry.'

Other holidays. 'This hasn't ruined everything for us?'

Edel smiled. 'Put it this way, if we've come out at the end of this week still interested in seeing one another, how amazing will it be when we actually do have a relaxing holiday?'

West couldn't think of any response to that, so he kissed her.

33

West pulled up into the car park outside her apartment. 'I'll be back for you in an hour,' he said, 'I just need to check in at the station, make sure everything is okay.' He'd been away longer than he'd planned, certainly longer than the station had expected. He'd call in, show his face and leave them to it. Edel needed to collect some fresh clothes, it was the perfect opportunity.

Edel waved as he drove away, went into her apartment, and dropped her suitcase onto her bed. Checking her watch, she decided she had plenty of time for a cup of tea, herbal, since she had no milk, and she sipped the hot aromatic drink looking out over the sea. She'd spent so little time here, but she didn't regret buying it. Not for a second. It had been a necessary step – and it had worked. Now she'd move back in with West, but it would be different.

Anyway, she thought, looking around the spacious, beautifully furnished apartment, this would rent easily. It had been a good investment and she needed the income; the road of the writer was not paved in gold.

Finishing the tea, she washed the cup, left it to drain and went to deal with her suitcase. She took another holdall from the cupboard and tossed all her dirty laundry into it. Going through wardrobe and drawers, she filled the suitcase with a selection of clothes.

It took longer than she'd expected, some items of clothing bringing memories with them, some good, some not-so. Being brutal, she threw the not-so clothes into a black plastic bag. Charity, she decided. Life was just too short and too valuable. And one thing she had learned from events on Clare Island, she was never going to compromise again.

Checking her watch, she was surprised to see the time. He was thirty minutes late. Obviously, things weren't as straightforward at the station as he'd expected. Making herself another cup of tea, she switched on the television, channel-hopped until she found an episode of *Frasier* and settled back to enjoy it.

They were playing episodes back-to-back. Edel chuckled through the first and second, but by the time the third came on, her watch now telling her that West was an hour and a half late, she'd stopped smiling.

When the phone rang an hour later, she answered, the words sitting on the end of her tongue falling away unused when she heard his voice saying her name. Something was terribly wrong.

'Mike, what is it?'

'Edel,' he said again, and this time she could hear the thickness in the word.

Gripping the phone tightly, her head spinning with all the things it could be, she tried again. 'Mike, tell me?'

A deep sigh, and then his sombre voice. 'Denise Blundell,' he said, 'she stabbed Ken again. This afternoon. He's dead, Edel.'

Edel had muted the television when the phone rang; she stared at the screen, the same people, same situations, but without sound not so funny anymore. She listened to West as he explained that it might be better if she stayed in the apartment for the moment. 'I made the wrong decision,' he told her, 'there may be consequences.'

He hung up before Edel could think of anything to say, before she could remind him that there were always consequences. Hadn't the last week proven that?

She sat for a moment, watching the silent flickering screen, thinking of Breathnach and what he'd done. Then, as her thoughts often did, they drifted to her late husband, Simon. 'Consequences,' she said aloud and reaching for the remote, switched off the television.

She stood, grabbed a warm coat and her bags.

West had to come home sometime. When he did, she'd be waiting.

ACKNOWLEDGEMENTS

Grateful thanks to the team at Bloodhound Books, and in particular Betsy Reavley who has been so encouraging, Tara Lyons for her patience, Heather Fitt for getting my books out there and Ian Skewis for making them better.

A huge thank you to all the readers, reviewers and bloggers who read, review and share – it makes it all worthwhile.

Ongoing thanks to my brother-in-law, retired Detective Garda Gerry Doyle, for answering my questions so patiently – any errors are mine alone.

Thanks also to my writing buddies who offer unconditional support especially the writers, Jenny O'Brien and Leslie Bratspis.

And, of course, thanks as always to my wonderful family and friends.

I love to hear from readers – you can contact me here:
https://www.facebook.com/valeriekeoghnovels
Twitter @ValerieKeogh1
Instagram valeriekeogh2

Printed in Great Britain
by Amazon